The Clopton

The Clopton Hercules

DUNCAN SPROTT

faber and faber
LONDON · BOSTON

This is Ercles' vein, a tyrant's vein.

A Midsummer Night's Dream

First published in 1991
by Faber and Faber Limited
3 Queen Square London WC1N 3AU
This paperback edition first published in 1992

Phototypeset by Goodfellow and Egan Ltd Cambridge
Printed in Great Britain by
Cox & Wyman Ltd, Reading, Berkshire

Duncan Sprott is hereby identified as author of this work
in accordance with Section 77 of the Copyright, Designs
and Patents Act 1988

A CIP record for this book is available from the
British Library

ISBN 0–571–16422–6

ONE

The summer of 1846 was so hot that the Avon steamed and Stratford stank of drains and suffered a troublesome plague of flies. The river ran lower than anyone could remember it having run before, all the fish died and the prospect of drought loomed, for there had been no rain since April.

The streams of visitors from America who used to come and peer through the windows of what was said to be Shakespeare's Birthplace, and who beat a path to the door of the Misses Reasons' Museum of bogus Shakespearean relics, dwindled away into nothing more than a trickle, and when all roads leading to Stratford-upon-Avon melted in the intense heat the streams of visitors dried up altogether.

All through the stifling months of May and June, when there was not the slightest breath of wind and the leaves hung dead on all the trees, grey-haired, hawk-nosed Dr Pritchard tapped daily at his barometer, muttered uneasily about typhoid and cholera and went about the dusty streets telling his patients, 'Don't drink the river water without boiling it,' only to be laughed at and told by everyone, 'The river has boiled already!'

In July the temperature hit 95 degrees in the shade, the water-pumps ran dry and the man who drove the water-cart was out of a job, so that Stratford's thirty-two public houses did a roaring trade, for there was nothing left to drink but beer.

When the needle factory shut down following an outbreak of heat exhaustion and women started to faint away in the sun, all trade ground to a halt and Dr Pritchard began to go about under a giant umbrella, jumping the cracks in the ground, advising people not to venture out of doors when the sun was at its zenith, and recommending the benefits of taking a siesta in the Italian manner.

That was all very well for the gentry, who could afford to be idle, but Stratford's labourers and shopkeepers, with a living to earn and wives and children to support, just had to keep on working in the heat and put up with the discomfort of their shirts sticking to their backs all day, brush the sweat out of their pricking eyes and grin and bear it.

3

But the temperature kept on going up and up and it was not long before midsummer madness took over. The most diligent workmen began to abandon all pretence of work and crowded the bathing-place in the river morning, noon and night. Undeterred by the smell of fish and the drowning of several youths who could not swim, they threw off clothes and caution in order to sit and splash in what was left of the soft-flowing Avon in a desperate attempt to cool down.

Scandal spread, of course, and the genteel ladies of Stratford-upon-Avon stepped out expressly to see what was going on. Dark sweat stains spread under their arms and their fans fluttered hopelessly, unable to keep either heat or perspiration at bay, but they goggled and twittered under their pink parasols all the same, made the fullest use of their lorgnettes and telescopes, and remained perching uncertainly on the river bank for some time. They pretended not to look, and averted their eyes, but looked again and again at the scores of agricultural labourers and apprentices and shopkeepers' assistants, and walked home composing pained letters of complaint to the editor of the *Warwick Advertiser* about the declining standard of decency in the town: How it was a disgrace to the Birthplace, Home and Grave of the Immortal Bard; how it was a shocking example to the young; how it was a horrid deviation from the rules governing genteel society; how it was a hazard to health, and so on, and so forth.

But the ladies were back again the next day in spite of their outrage, to have another look, and as the days went by the crowd of female spectators grew and grew.

And it was not only the genteel ladies who were very interested in the public exhibition of Stratford's manhood for their delight, for the town's numerous prostitutes quite abandoned their usual haunt – the churchyard, which afforded a shady and secluded spot for them to ply for trade – and flocked in their droves to the bathing-place instead, where business was better, and where they hung about all day, painting and re-painting their faces against the ravages of perspiration, and waving and calling to the bathers, displaying all the charms they could without actually going so far as to take off their clothes.

One particularly hot afternoon a severe, iron-whiskered

Primitive Methodist preacher in shovel hat and black clothes appeared by the river, Bible in hand, in order to preach an extempore sermon on The Evils of Indecent Exposure. He exhorted the shameless revellers in the water to put their trousers on and return to Christ; to forswear their foolish ways; to remember the scourge of the cholera, and to have some feeling for the offended sensibilities of the female inhabitants of Stratford-upon-Avon.

But the female inhabitants did not appear to be offended at all and the bathers just laughed or jeered or took no notice, and after three hours of ranting and raving the preacher's throat dried up and he walked off, shaking his fists in the air and dripping with sweat, croaking about the Day of Judgment, and was locked up by stout, red-faced Constable Reason for disturbing the Queen's Peace.

As for the bathers, Reason reasoned that he could hardly arrest the entire male population of Stratford-upon-Avon, for his police cells were already full of poachers, and his own sons liked to disport themselves in the river as well – and so, when duty did not call, did Joseph Reason himself, who would fold his blue uniform neatly on the bank and plunge into the water, to the applause of the female spectators of the less genteel kind, and roll and splash and blow out spurts of air like some monster of the deep long denied access to its natural element.

Moreover Dr Pritchard said it was positively beneficial for the people to cool down, and indeed, that it was highly important that they should cool down. The Mayor and Aldermen and Burgesses of Stratford all agreed, for they too, in the heat of the evening, liked to go discreetly down to the river to bathe as well. The Beadle and the Police agreed to turn a blind eye, and thus an unofficial seal of approval was put on the bathing, and it went on unchecked as all authority joined in.

In time the spectacle of all the youth of Stratford cooling down and all of Stratford's labouring men and all the Mayor and Corporation cavorting in the waves or reposing on the banks of the Avon without their clothes on came to seem nothing very unusual at all, as if all Christian manners had been suspended for the duration of the heatwave.

In fact, on Sunday mornings, to the great concern of all the clergy, there were more people sitting in the river keeping cool than there were sitting steaming in the pews in church praying for rain and for deliverance from the prevailing pestilence of the cholera.

By mid-July there were few working men who had not been tempted to take the plunge apart from Joseph Callaway of Oak Farm, who was keen for people to do what was right, and who reported the deviant behaviour of all his neighbours to the magistrates without effect, and who carried on sweating into his thick corduroy with his face the colour of beetroot, and took down the names of the most familiar faces in the water whenever he happened to pass by the river.

And then the scandal of polite Stratford increased when the first of the painted ladies, who had been hovering on the brink for weeks, ran squealing down the river bank and launched herself with ecstatic screams upon the water, and all the other ladies of easy virtue followed suit, and sat half in and half out of the water, half in and half out of their dresses, floating about and splashing about for the rest of the summer, and screaming with raucous laughter at their bathing companions of the opposite sex.

In the afternoons Mr Warde, the handsome young giant of Clopton House, in the prime of his life and the thirty-third year of his age, used to drive out with his children in an attempt to whip up some cool air, and his gleaming, dustless carriage that had been liberally doused with Burnett's Disinfecting Fluid would stop by the river so that Mr Warde could take a look at the famous Avon swans as they picked their way about on the bank, or paddled about in the water, caked in mud and filth.

Mr Warde would step down from the carriage, stretch his long limbs, mop at his fashionable side-whiskers, shake the sweat from his golden hair, and shade his perfectly blue eyes against the blazing sun as he looked, while his four pale-faced, golden-haired children pressed their perfect noses to the plate-glass carriage windows that were steamed up with their hot breath, and giggled at the scene in the water and chattered like parrots in some overheated tropical jungle.

The bathers, not a few of them in Mr Warde's employ, would nod awkwardly in his direction, not quite sure of the niceties of behaviour prescribed for greeting the Squire when in a state of undress, and bowed and tugged at their forelocks and curtseyed in the water.

Some beckoned to Mr Warde to come in and join them, and called out 'Come here, come here' and splashed the water towards him and roared with laughter. But the river was hardly a place where a gentleman of Mr Warde's station in society could even show his face, let alone less familiar portions of his anatomy. Mr Warde felt bound to maintain his impeccable image of gentility at all times. He had to keep his clothes on and he could not cool down. He just grinned his famous grin, looked longingly at the inviting water, shook his great head slowly and climbed back into the carriage, which had been specially built to accommodate his enormous person, but creaked and sank on its springs none the less, and ordered James Duck, the coachman, to drive on.

And the carriage ground its way home to Clopton House, the rambling old mansion which Mr Warde had completely modernized, having whipped up nothing but a cloud of dust a mile long and a lingering smell of disinfectant.

At Clopton the air was like treacle but father and children could sit in private for hours on end unobserved, soaking in tubs of cold water that was never quite cold enough, until their perfect skins began to shrivel up like rotten apples and an alarmed Mrs Warde decreed that they must soak no more, and said she was sure tomorrow would be cooler.

But the heat went on and on and tomorrow was not cooler, but even hotter, and Mr Warde had to simmer away inside his thick black frock-coat of the very finest cut, and stay buttoned up inside his striped waistcoat and Ford's Eureka Shirt that was guaranteed to remain tucked in however much a gentleman threw himself about, without the benefit of a cooling tub of water at all.

Mr Warde boiled away under his impeccably starched wing-collar and silk cravat, and the sweat trickled down his neck and down the legs of his pale Anaxyridian Trousers that buttoned straight up the front in the very latest fashion and prickled and scratched and drove him almost to distraction, but which he refused to give up wearing because they had been specially made to fit his extraordinary measurements at double the normal price.

7

Mr Warde continued to be perfectly charming to everyone he met in spite of the unbearable temperatures, and while less important men were losing their tempers all over Stratford and reduced to fisticuffs at the slightest provocation, Mr Warde kept calm, serene and smiling, and the sweat trickled on down his handsome face that was untroubled by the cares of the world, untouched by age and unmarked by worry of any kind.

But as the heat kept on growing and the temperatures pushed into the upper nineties, even Mr Warde's composure began to slip. He scarcely knew what to do with himself, and his discomfort was made worse by the fact that he did not have anything to do, and had nothing to occupy his endless spare time.

For Mr Warde was fortunate enough to be able to sit at home all day enjoying a life of ease and luxury, and he had never done a day's work in his life. Though, in fact, he did not sit about all day doing nothing: he had to keep moving, even if it was round in circles, for he could not sit still for five minutes.

And so it was that every morning Mr Warde would don his tall stove-pipe hat and his warmest clothes and stride out into the blistering heat to do nothing at all, and pass the time between meals by slashing with his gold-topped walking-stick at the dusty nettles that grew everywhere on his extensive estates. He padded back and forth like a caged animal, a towering figure, sometimes with a gun, sometimes with his dogs, sometimes with his friends, but more often alone, walking and walking, with nothing better to do than watch other people working. Or he would sit on a tree-stump or stand in the shade of an oak tree, jingling his money as if he did not know what to do with it; as if it were burning holes in his pockets.

Wherever he went Mr Warde was watched by the hungry eyes of scores of handsome young women who had been employed for the summer months by his neighbour at Lower Clopton Farm, Fisher Tomes Esq, to pull the weeds out of the corn, and who worked all day in the sun with their light cotton frocks in all the colours of the rainbow tucked up to reveal bare brown legs, and their sleeves rolled up to reveal strong brown arms.

They watched Mr Warde for several good reasons, not least of which was the fact that he was made of money. For they had seen him down in the town spending money like water, oozing money from every pore, and they knew that he got through more money in a morning than any one of them could hope to earn in twelve months. They had seen him throwing handfuls of sovereigns to the children in the streets. They had heard tell of him emptying his pockets into the hands of grateful widows, giving his money away whenever he got the chance, so that everywhere he went he was universally respected and universally looked up to, and not only because of his enormous height.

And what was more astonishing to the field-women was the fact that not only did Mr Warde give his money away but that he also left it lying about on the ground. And this was no idle rumour, for Eliza Johnson swore she had picked up pounds and pounds of money in the plantations on Mr Warde's estate and there was no one else who could have left it there but him: it was as if he had been out sowing the money that seemed to grow on his trees, or had been throwing it away, as if he could not think what better to do with it, he had so much.

The women would murmur 'He's a fine upstanding man and no mistake' or 'He's a wonderful gentleman to be sure' whenever Mr Warde appeared, and they found it difficult to take their eyes off him. He was a dream come true, and the answer to most of their problems, for he provided employ winter and summer, indoors and outdoors; he did not object to the women picking up sticks on his land; he was only too pleased to help anyone in need, and however grand the company he was with, however humble the passer-by he met, he was not too proud to stop and pass the time of day, or ask after husband or wife or baby, and to make polite conversation about the astonishing weather.

The field-women made sure they kept more than half an eye on Mr Warde, and made doubly sure that they searched the places where he stood watching them at work, as if they thought he would leave a trail of money; as if they thought a trail of gold would spring up from his very footprints.

When Mr Warde returned to Clopton House in the evenings Mathieu the French valet would wring a pint of sweat out of Mr Warde's sodden Anaxyridian Trousers and hang them up to dry. Mathieu knew that Mr Warde went out with his pockets

9

full of sovereigns and Mathieu did not fail to search the pockets every evening, but he was always disappointed, for when Mr Warde came home his pockets were always empty.

Every evening Mr Warde would wash, don fresh clothes and join his amiable, charming, stunningly beautiful wife and resume his place as head of the family in time to give his charming children elephant rides up the grand staircase to bed, whooping and trumpeting and stamping his feet and counting the stairs as he climbed, so that Ada, George, Emily and Charlotte Warde squealed and shrieked with delight and Mr Warde revelled in playing the part of the perfect papa.

Every evening, having handed the children back to their nurse, Mr Warde would raid the extensive cellars that contained upwards of 3,000 bottles of fine old wines and vintage port dating from the years of the French Revolution, and every evening he would drink deep and make merry with a dozen or more dinner guests, all of them rich and handsome and distinguished, while his children peered down through the banisters at the comings and goings below, wide-eyed and wide awake, too excited to go to sleep or do anything their nurse told them.

Every evening after dinner Mrs Warde and the ladies, all of them weighed down with gold and diamonds and emeralds, would withdraw to a gilded drawing-room to talk about Mr Warde and about ladies' things; and Mr Warde and the gentlemen would withdraw to a billiard-room thick with cigar smoke, to drink deeper and make merrier round an immense mahogany billiard-table, and the click of billiard-balls, and the clink of brandy-glasses, and the pop of corks and the roars of hearty laughter continued late into the night.

When the party drew to a close Fuller the butler and Mathieu the valet would show the visitors to their carriages or their bedrooms, count up the empty bottles, pull Mr Warde insensible from beneath the immense billiard-table, or from wherever he happened to have collapsed, and prepare to perform the nightly ritual of dragging his dead weight up the grand staircase to his room, pausing to rest where the staircase turned, puffing with the burden, and blowing out the lamps as they went.

They stripped the body with the efficiency of tomb-robbers, helped themselves to anything portable in the way of loose change, gold studs, the finest Havana cigars, Turkish delight, none of which Mr Warde ever missed, tucked Mr Warde's handsome and substantial body into his handsome and substantial bedstead with gold bed-knobs, and blew out his candles.

And Mr Warde would sleep the sleep of the innocent for upwards of ten hours until Wild, the housemaid, came in to light his fire in the morning.

Day after day Mrs Warde put on the bravest of her pale doll's faces, bathed her wrists in lavender water, lamented her lack of health and vigour, and sat fanning herself at her bedroom window. She watched Mr Warde walking purposefully out along the new tarmacadam carriage-drive that shimmered in the heat, grew stickier as the day went on, melted on everyone's shoes and in the end made it impossible to use the carriage at all, and she wondered why her husband would never tell her where he was going, or what he was doing, or when he would be coming back.

All he ever said was, 'I am going out my dearest, I shall see you this evening.'

So that Mrs Warde was left alone to fret about her illnesses, and worry about Dr Pritchard's strict orders that she was to pass her time in rest and quietness, to spend her mornings in bed, her afternoons on the sofa, and her evenings in doing nothing, absolutely nothing, more strenuous than playing the harp or the pianoforte.

She worried that she was not allowed to dance, and she worried that when they graced the Warwick Race Ball with their presence in the autumn she would have to put up with the sight of her husband dancing with other women all evening, and would not be able to dance with him herself.

But she had quite enough on her mind already without worrying about what her husband was or was not doing all day. It was enough that he was in good health.

'I love him as he is,' she told her friends, and she had long since given up asking him to tell her about his daily affairs.

So Mrs Warde sat quietly on her gilded *chaise longue* with her clothes sticking to her day after day through all the long hot summer, with only her lady's maid, Harriet Meller, for company, and passed the long days in sewing, reading to her children, writing letters to her family, in taking her patent medicine on the hour every hour, and in waiting impatiently for Mr Warde to come home. Clopton ran like clockwork under Mrs Warde's efficient management but the time hung heavy on her hands and she found the heat almost unbearable. She seemed to see less and less of Mr Warde during the day, and fatigue obliged her to retire to her room earlier and earlier each night.

When Mr and Mrs Warde did meet they were frequently too exhausted by the weather even to speak to each other.

One evening early in August Mr Warde came in looking more worn out and hotter than ever before, and said, 'I am going to wash.' He stood at the handsome marble-topped wash-hand stand soaking his hands in tepid water.

Mrs Warde, in the next room, suddenly heard a noise like an animal roaring, dropped everything and ran to see what had happened and was in time to see that the sleeves of her husband's shirt had fallen down into the water and that he was frenziedly ripping the cuffs off with a violence she had never seen before.

'Why, Charles,' she exclaimed, 'whatever is the matter?'

'It's this heat,' he said, 'this heat is the Devil. I cannot stand the heat any longer.'

Mrs Warde did not know what to say, but she took a towel and dried his hands and kissed his face, and spent the rest of the evening sitting beside him with a pair of gold-plated bellows, pumping away furiously, and directing the air at his face, up the back of his shirt, down his neck and down the front of his trousers, as he stood frowning with arms and legs spreadeagled, trying to get the maximum breeze. But it was a useless exercise for the air from the bellows was as hot as the air anywhere else and the ridiculousness of the operation made Mrs Warde giggle. After two hours her arms gave out and she abandoned the experiment and went off to bed early, hotter than ever, unable to open her windows because the owls and bats and half the insects in Warwickshire kept flying in.

Night after night Mrs Warde lay alone behind locked doors in a separate room and in a different wing of the great house from her husband, perspiring profusely, wide awake in spite of the softest feather-bed that money could buy, unable to stop the day's worries from flooding back through her mind, and unable to stop the stories she had read in her newspaper from racing through her brain, so that her nights were filled with Frightful Murder and Suicide, Fatal Accident and Dreadful Shipwreck, with Mr Warde featuring in every bloody scene.

She felt that her perfect existence was too good to be true, that Mr Warde had been too lucky, that wealth had come to them too quickly and too easily, that they were being hurtled to the brink of a sheer cliff and that everything she cherished was about to be propelled into the abyss.

But however many times she told herself it was absurd, and however many times Dr Pritchard told her not to worry her pretty head about it, she could not get the idea out of her head, she could not stop worrying, and she could not get any sleep at all.

And so Meller was up and down stairs all night, banging about, and could not get any sleep either, for just as she dropped off Mrs Warde would ring the bell for yet another glass of cold water, yet another cold compress, yet another dose of Collis Browne's Chlorodyne. In the end Meller dragged her iron bed down to her mistress's bedroom and trained herself to reach out automatically every fifteen minutes without waking up, in order to bathe Mrs Warde's red-hot forehead as she lay gasping for breath in the dark.

Mr Warde was fond of saying that Meller's face was ugly enough to stop all the clocks and that she was as blind as a bat, and it was true that poor highly-strung Meller could hardly see beyond the end of her nose, so that as she ran too fast along Clopton's endless passages she bumped into doors and dropped trays full of glass and china, and the house often resounded with the crash and tinkle of her progress, and her wild hysterical laughter.

Mr Warde kept saying, 'The cost of replacing the china is more than Meller's annual wages – Meller must go.' But Mrs Warde would not have a word said against her and whenever Mr Warde raised the subject of her dismissal Mrs Warde declared, 'Meller is worth her weight in gold. I will not hear of her being sent away.'

Although Meller's eyes were bad there was nothing wrong with her ears, which were finely tuned to pick up the faintest whiff of scandal, so that she had achieved notoriety as a walking encyclopaedia of Stratford gossip and would frequently be seen standing on street corners in the town with her chin wagging away, exchanging the latest horror stories with a wide circle of acquaintances and informants.

During this summer more than ever before Meller wondered at what she heard, for the gossip had begun to be about Mr Warde, and try though she did to listen to not a word of it, she could not help but hear what was said, and she could not help remembering what was said, and filing it away in the back of her mind, for the women were saying the most extraordinary things about him that were on the one hand too dreadful to be true, but on the other hand too good to be missed.

Meller did not believe a word of it and tried to think of pleasanter things, but more often than not Mrs Warde and her ailing health filled her thoughts, and she spent a considerable part of each day trying to come up with new topics of conversation for her mistress in order to keep Mr Warde off the subject of the Railway, for Mrs Warde had in an unguarded moment let slip a disturbing remark which now kept Meller awake at night more than the infernal heat, and the very thought of it made her eye-glasses steam up and obliged her to brush the sweat from her incipient moustache with the back of her hand, for Mrs Warde had said, 'If my husband so much as mentions the subject of the Railway or Railway Shares, or Railway Timetables *once more* I shall have to go back to my mother.'

Clopton continued airless and stifling and time seemed to stand still. Stratford was permanently shrouded in mist as if it was melting away in the heat and had ceased to exist altogether. When harvest came at last the stunted corn was cut down, loaded up and stacked away, and every man, woman and child on the estate laboured until well past midnight for two weeks for no extra remuneration in order to get the work done before the weather broke.

In the extreme dryness the fields around Clopton caught fire, and long lines of labourers came running with brooms and spades to beat out the flames. Clopton was wreathed in smoke and the fields round about took on a drabness as the gleaning women moved in, as if some terrible battle had been fought and they were picking over the dead in search of valuables.

The young women in threadbare shawls, stout boots with the toes out and cast-off dresses that had been fashionable twenty years before, talked of nothing but Mr Warde and paused from time to time in their stretching and bending to rest their aching backs and gaze after him, for he was out walking again in the distance, calling to someone, his words too far off to make sense.

They continued to call Mr Warde 'Sir' or 'Squire' as they had always done. They continued to curtsey when Mr Warde went by, as he had instructed them to, and they were ever hopeful that he would stop and speak to them in his deep rich purring voice like honey; ever hopeful that he would ask them to run some errand so that they could earn some extra cash; ever hopeful that some of his magic would rub off on them, and that they would be turned to gold and released for ever from the bondage of work, and from grinding poverty, and from the threat of the Stratford Union Workhouse.

Those women who did return to Stratford with sovereigns clutched in their palms counted their lucky stars and passed as rich and famous for several days, but they were few in number and there were always more whose days did not become red-letter days as a result of a chance meeting with Mr Warde. They kept their thoughts to themselves, treasured up their observations for a rainy day, and went on their way bent double under their loads of sticks like ancient women, old before their time, nursing their envy of Mr Warde's good luck and good fortune.

In late August the rainy day arrived with a vengeance and a violent hailstorm dashed the remaining crops to the ground and reduced the charred fields to a sea of mud. Great balls of ice fell and terrified the country people, who spent the greater part of the night on their knees in prayer, thinking that the Day of Judgment, with all its promised horrors, was upon them.

Every window at Clopton was smashed, as if inside the house there had been a violent explosion, and there followed three hours of torrential rain which restored Stratford's water supply but drenched Mr Warde, who was out in his landau returning from the Railway Station at Coventry.

Mr Warde was not alarmed by the damage. He called in an

army of glaziers, flashed his money and had his new windows in place and the mess cleared up within twenty-four hours.

'There's nothing money can't do,' he said. 'If Clopton House was knocked down I could have it put up again by the end of the week.'

He carried on walking for hours on end, or drove out in his landau at a spanking pace through the avenue of horse-chestnuts which lined the carriage-drive through Clopton Park and which were turning the colour of flames. His deer browsed under every tree. His labourers in smock-frocks pulled at their forelocks as he swept by, spattering them with mud, and Mr Warde held on to his tall hat and lounged back in his seat and smiled and waved merrily as he went.

Mr Warde had every reason to smile and be pleased with himself, for he had everything money could buy and his life was perfect. He was a Justice of the Peace, a Deputy-Lieutenant of the County of Warwick, and in this year High Sheriff of Warwickshire as well, a roaring success, and gathering honours so thick and fast that his acquaintances were wont to remark that there was almost nothing left for Mr Warde of Clopton House to achieve, and that he would have to stand for Parliament.

For Mr Warde was universally admired by town and county alike and was the kind of man everyone was bound to vote for. He was unfailingly polite and charming. He was the life and soul of every party for miles around. Everyone said the Wardes were a charming family, a perfect family, and that Mr Warde was the perfect gentleman.

Or so it seemed. For Rumour told quite a different tale, and the fact was that Mr Warde's numerous acquaintances were beginning to be divided up into those who swore that everything about Mr Warde was true, honest, pure, lovely and of good report, and those who thought exactly the opposite, and said darkly that what most people saw and heard and knew of Mr Warde was only half the story.

Down in Stratford-upon-Avon, on the river bank and in the churchyard, the tongues were wagging as they had never wagged before, in eager anticipation of spectacular and astonishing revelations about Mr Warde of Clopton House. Some said that Mr Warde had lost all his money, every penny of it, and that it would only be a matter of time before he appeared in the bankruptcy court. Others said that for people with the right kind of information there was money to be made, and plenty of it, for Mr Warde was still a man with everything to lose.

Hearing the rumours Mr Bury the solicitor decided to strike while the iron was still hot and sent in his bill for £3,351 13s 10d while he thought there was still some chance of Mr Warde being able to pay it.

Mr Warde carried on as usual. He drove out in the carriage and he drove back in the carriage and seemed to have nothing better to do than to ride grandly around the narrow lanes dreaming of his glorious future and wave and call 'Good afternoon' to everyone he met. Or almost everyone.

When Mr Warde passed Ann Davis with mud on her boots, walking in the road, her rough red face lit up in a big gap-toothed smile when she saw who it was, and she waved wildly. But Mr Warde's face was set solid as rock and he kept looking straight ahead as if he did not see her.

When Mr Warde passed Mrs Grimes walking along, taking her few vegetables to market, it was Mr Warde's face that broke into a smile and he stood up in his seat and called 'Mrs Grimes, Mrs Grimes' out of the carriage window and waved with both arms as he went by, and kept on waving as she was left behind, getting smaller and smaller, but Mrs Grimes stared stony-faced ahead of her, pretending that Mr Warde did not exist.

When Mr Warde passed Mr and Mrs Southam, out in their donkey-cart delivering milk from their parched and bony cows, both the Southams looked dead ahead of them, pretending that Mr Warde was invisible, in spite of the fact that his carriage forced them right off the road into the hedge. But Mr Warde did not stop, or look back, or avert his gaze from the moon, which had appeared conveniently early and had suddenly caught his attention.

When Mr Warde met Joseph Grimes, out delivering coal in a very broad waggon, the carriage was unable to sweep by at all, for Grimes stopped on purpose in the middle of the road when he saw it was Mr Warde, and refused to let him pass, pretending that his horse would not go, so that Mr Warde was obliged to tell Duck to make use of his whip and to be quick about it.

17

But when Mr Warde saw William Brown, one of his thirty gardeners, he nodded and grinned most affably, and tossed a sovereign into the air, which Brown caught in his hat. And Brown bowed and scraped and waved his stick in gratitude, and said 'Thank you, sir' over and over again until Mr Warde had disappeared into the distance.

Everyone Mr Warde passed was thinking much the same thing whether they acknowledged his existence or not:

'There goes Mr Warde. What has he been up to?'

'Where's he off to now?'

'Who the Devil does he think he is?'

'It won't be long before he comes to a sticky end.'

'Pride goeth before a fall.'

As if they knew a thing or two about Mr Warde that Mr Warde seemed not to know about himself.

Mr Warde did not appear to know that his past was catching up with him and that his very own Day of Judgment was fast approaching. He did not seem to know that the charm in his apparently charmed life was fast running out and that the bottom was about to fall out of his perfect world.

TWO

In the year 1813 Mrs Charlotte Warde, wife of the Reverend Thomas Warde, curate of the God-forsaken village of Cubbington in the County of Warwick, had stretched and strained and screamed for three days and produced, to everyone's surprise, the largest baby anyone had ever seen.

And no one was more surprised than Mrs Warde herself, who had hoped and prayed for a child for so long that she had almost given up hope and was almost resigned to the prospect of a long and barren middle age.

For eleven years the Curate had lain with his wife as prescribed in his Bible, innocent of the need for any physical contact beyond his nightly peck on his wife's cheek in order to beget a son.

And as the eleven years went by Mrs Warde spent longer and longer on her knees beside her bed beseeching the Almighty to send her a child, any child, she did not mind what it was like, so that the vast fortune which her two bachelor brothers were sitting on would have an heir, assign and residuary legatee, and would not go to some very poor relations living in Birmingham.

But the harder Mrs Warde prayed the less likely the miracle seemed, and the grey hairs appeared on her head and the lines were graven deep in her face before the Cubbington doctor casually enquired into the detailed geography of the Curate's sleeping arrangements and the Cubbington midwife belatedly hissed a few facts into Mrs Warde's good ear.

Husband and wife made up for lost time, prepared for bed earlier and earlier each night, said their prayers faster and faster, and got up later and later, until the day came when Mr Warde was late for his own Sunday Morning Service and was seen by an impatient congregation running across the tombstones hastily doing up his trousers.

When Mrs Warde fainted away with a long moan in the middle of Mattins and made her Book of Common Prayer fly with fluttering pages high up into the chancel arch, no one suspected the truth, and to the last Mrs Warde herself refused to believe that her grossly distended stomach was the result of anything but over-eating, or that her labour pains were anything but indigestion until, on 4 October 1813, a day which happened to be sacred to Hercules, a giant baby was pulled howling into the world and it was clear that the miracle had indeed occurred.

On 13 October 1813, ignoring all his parishioners' superstitious mutterings about the unlucky date, the Reverend Thomas Warde carried his son to church and baptized him with the name of Charles Thomas Warde.

The two wealthy uncles showered their nephew with silver spoons and drank champagne until Christmas, but Mrs Warde complained of being bitten to death and sent for a wet-nurse.

'Another child will kill me,' she announced, and she began to move her personal possessions into a room apart from her husband, refused ever again to share his bed, locked herself in every night and spent the rest of her life reclining on a blue satin sofa recovering from the shock of motherhood.

The Reverend Thomas Warde channelled all his new-found energy into an attempt to complete Dugdale's *History of Warwickshire* and spent the rest of his days scouring the county in order to collect the epitaphs of extinct families, fighting his way into overgrown castles with his measuring rods, and making meticulous drawings of derelict mansions and decaying churches.

Meanwhile Charles Thomas Warde grew and grew, and kept on growing, and when he was old enough to hold on he travelled with his father, bouncing about in the back of the trap as they galloped from one magnificent ruin to the next, with the green lanes retreating before him, and while the father was absorbed in his indefatigable search into the beauties of perishable antiquities, the son would wander off unnoticed, idling away his time, rambling in woods, doing damage where he could, banging on strangers' doors and running away again, and practising his cheeky tongue on unsuspecting servant girls.

As he grew larger, bursting out of his clothes, he went off in search of bigger and bigger trouble, running wild and wreaking havoc wherever he went, so that the tales that winged their way home to his parents grew more and more alarming, for he was said to have thrown rocks at the stage-coaches and to have shot at passers-by with a fowling-piece and was fast becoming the sort of boy who did exactly the opposite of what he was told.

But what he lacked in good behaviour Charles Thomas Warde made up for with charm. His smile dissolved every enraged heart, his cherubic looks turned away all wrath, and he was forgiven for and got away with escapades and offences for which other boys were soundly beaten. 'Butter', people said, 'will not melt in Charles Warde's mouth. He is a lovely boy.'

The day came, however, when the ageing parents ran out of excuses for Charles's wayward behaviour and they began to spread their hands helplessly as if they did not know what to do with him.

Mrs Warde gave up pretending after a while and said quite openly, 'The Reverend Mr Warde cannot control his own son,' and thus turned the mild-mannered clergyman from preaching a gospel of peace and goodwill to preaching a furious crusade of violence against his son. But on the first occasion when he reached for his stick he succeeded only in dislocating his own shoulder, was unable to drive the trap and lost valuable time on his *History*. When Mr Warde was panting for breath, purple in the face and it seemed that he could beat no more, Charles stood up, grinning, and said, 'Papa, you must *swing your arm*,' and he walked away whistling, as if the beating had not hurt him in the slightest.

The result of Charles's remark was that one morning in the year 1826 father and son set off together with a sizeable trunk on top of a stage-coach going in the direction of Wales, on an excursion whose purpose was not immediately revealed lest the son should take it into his head to run away.

When they reached the town of Shrewsbury father and son dismounted and made their way towards Shrewsbury School, where Charles Warde was introduced to the headmaster, Dr Samuel Butler, a Warwickshire man who was later Bishop of Lichfield, and who undertook to turn his new charge into a gentlemen, or as nearly a gentleman as was possible, and who promised to beat the boy as hard and as often as he could.

The Reverend Thomas Warde made his way home with a lighter heart to Leamington and set about delegating the duties of his new parish of Weston-under-Wetherly to a curate so that he could live a life of ease and luxury, with nothing to worry about but the *History of Warwickshire*.

Meanwhile Charles Warde's introduction to Latin and Greek

began in earnest, for Shrewsbury was famous for turning out dozens of brilliant classical scholars year after year, and Charles Warde would perhaps have been turned into a brilliant classical scholar himself had not Shrewsbury been equally famous for brutality and violence, and had he not devoted himself naturally and rapidly towards the latter branch of learning. For Charles Warde was able to continue his former career without much difficulty: bird's-nesting, duelling with sticks and swords, frightening old women, terrorizing the neighbourhood, joining in the Shrewsbury Boar Hunt – in which a domestic pig was harried with sticks and cudgels across the countryside and killed in order to supplement the boys' meagre diet – breaking all the rules in the company of a wide circle of new accomplices and partners in crime.

A year after delivering his son to school the Reverend Thomas Warde put about a story that his son's departure from Shrewsbury was owing to ill health, for he was a sickly child, but this was so evidently not the truth that the Vicar's fellow clergymen laughed aloud when they heard it. The fact was that not long after his arrival at school Charles Warde was invited to leave, and his education had to be continued at home under the eagle eye of his newly determined father, who was obliged to summon the assistance of the nearest able-bodied young curate in order to administer the beatings which he deemed necessary to keep his son in some semblance of order.

In the year 1831 the exasperated parents packed the strapping youth off to Belgium in the company of Jevon Perry, whom they judged quite wrongly to be the most level-headed of his friends. Having provided Charles with enough money to last at least six months and having dispensed with the extravagance of a tutor, they prayed that a change of scene would bring about a miraculous change of character, and that the sowing of some wild oats abroad might prevent the looming scandal of wild oats sown at home in the corner of some Warwickshire field.

By the time Charles Warde returned from gaming in Brussels, drinking the waters at Spa (after which, he said, he never felt the same) and picking up souvenirs on the field of Waterloo, he had somehow acquired enough learning or enough influence to be admitted to Sidney Sussex College, Cambridge, and this advance in the career of a scholar not renowned for his academic prowess was directly traceable to the death of his very wealthy Uncle, George Lloyd Esq., of Welcombe House, Stratford-upon-Avon, sometime High Sheriff of Warwickshire, whose Will provided an allowance for his nephew at the University, and named him heir to the Lloyd estates and fortune, which he would inherit on the decease of his other Uncle, John Lloyd Esq., of the same place.

Armed with financial rather than intellectual clout, Charles Thomas Warde migrated, after a minor scandal with a female domestic servant, to Downing College, as a Fellow Commoner, a member of a much flattered and much privileged class of undergraduates, the sons of rich gentlemen, who ate better than their inferiors, were allowed to take wine with their meals, wore gold and silver lace and formed the fastest set in Cambridge – riding to hounds, duelling with pistols at dawn, neglecting their studies late into the night and not giving a damn about anything.

It did not matter to Charles Warde that Fellow Commoner was synonymous with *Empty Bottle* (for they were not considered over full of learning and left a trail of wine bottles wherever they went); it did not bother him that he was wasting his uncle's money and his own time and setting a bad example to his fellow men. Taking a degree was a matter of no importance to him, for he knew perfectly well that he would never have to worry about earning his own living. For the moment he was happy to lead the wild life at Cambridge, indulging in a higher class of prank, vandalism and debauchery than he had yet been able to aspire to or afford: sleeping all day, drinking all night, sniping at the hats of passers-by, and shooting the corks off champagne-bottles in crowded rooms to tumultuous applause.

Cambridge, however, was enough to lay a veneer of respectability over the roughness remaining from the Warwickshire days when no one could do anything with him. It was at Cambridge that he picked up the genteel manners and genteel habits of the civilized world, and he quickly became one of the lights around whom the moths of Cambridge society (and later of Warwickshire) fluttered endlessly.

He had become a gentle giant, upwards of six feet tall, and he could do no wrong. He knew how to turn on the charm; he knew how to get his own way and how to get out of trouble. He could talk himself through any door and out of any difficulty. He had become, in spite of his parents' darkest fears, the perfect gentleman.

More than anything else Charles Warde had reason to be grateful to Cambridge for introducing him to Miss Lawes. He fell in love at first sight. He followed her to her lodgings in Trumpington Street, kept up a nightly vigil under her window and refused to go away until she told him her name. He followed her to Bath, discovered her address in Hertfordshire and bombarded her with letters every day, telling her that her lips were like cherries, her skin like pearls, her hair like spun gold, all of which was true, for Miss Lawes was renowned for her beauty. She was the perfect match.

At first, though, Miss Lawes did not want to have anything to do with the enormous young man who sat in the rhododendrons in his stovepipe hat waiting to catch a glimpse of her and getting mud all over his pale trousers, and she would scream at him in exasperation to go away and leave her alone.

'He must be mad,' she said to her mother, 'I want nothing to do with him.'

But he kept on sending her mountains of red flowers and kept on showering her with exquisite gifts in gilt boxes, none of which she could bring herself to throw away. One day, without thinking about it, she found herself pasting his letters into her album and drying the latest offering of scarlet flowers. After a month she found that when she looked out and Mr Warde was not sitting there grinning up at her she felt a twinge of disappointment, and on the days when the postman brought no letters she could do nothing but sulk and slam doors.

At first her mother was against the match, and thought that Mr Warde behaved rather strangely at times, but when she was told how great were Mr Warde's expectations, and found out exactly how wealthy he was going to be, she changed her tune overnight and invited him into the house. His great shadow fell across the threshold, he sensed victory, and Marianne Lawes began to smile at last and fall in love by gradual degrees.

Mrs Lawes suddenly became most insistent, for her late husband's country seat, Rothamsted Park, near Harpenden in

Hertfordshire, was vast and rambling, leaked like a sieve and soaked up cash like a sponge.

'I could do with some money,' said Mrs Lawes. 'Marianne, I don't care who you marry as long as you marry money. Mr Warde is a lovely man. If I were twenty years younger I should marry him myself. I don't know what you are waiting for.'

And so Marianne Lawes was married, in a sumptuous dress of ivory satin threaded with gold, in October 1834, shortly after Charles Warde's twenty-first birthday, when he came into a sizeable sum of money. The ceremony took place at Harpenden Parish Church, with the blessing of the whole population of the town, who turned out in force to wish the Harpenden Beauty well, and to throw rice and orange-blossom at her.

In the congregation, wondering whether the match was such a wise thing after all, were Mrs Lawes, the bride's mother; John Bennet Lawes, the bride's brother, a budding agriculturist, who had dragged himself away from his chemical apparatus in order to be present; the groom's aged parents, who sat worrying that no one had mentioned anything to them about a dowry; the groom's solicitor, who sat thinking about charging a fee for his attendance; and a handful of servants, among them plain Harriet Meller, lady's maid of a fortnight's experience, who sported a brand-new lace-trimmed bonnet and was armed with the most detailed instructions for the new Mrs Warde once she was beyond the reach and control of her mother, and who blinked and blinked and wiped the mist from her eye-glasses, but could not see as far as the altar.

No sooner was Marianne Lawes married than her mother began to have fresh doubts, for Mr Warde suddenly announced that he would leave straight after the ceremony without stopping for the wedding breakfast on which Mrs Lawes had spent a considerable sum.

Mrs Lawes was flabbergasted. 'What sort of man is he,' she declared, 'that he cannot wait for his own wedding breakfast?'

But Mr Warde said, 'I am sorry, we have to catch the tide for the Isle of Wight,' and with Meller in tow, who was so excited that she could not stop talking and had to be told to be quiet, the Wardes set off in great haste for Westover, a wedding-cake of a mansion on the south of the island, where they lived happily enough, with their peace disturbed only by the wild screams of the peacocks that strutted in the ornamental grounds.

Mr and Mrs Warde strolled about arm in arm, enjoyed the panoramic view of the English Channel, went for long walks on the deserted shore and visited in the smartest society the Isle of Wight could offer. Untroubled by the need to earn his living, Mr Warde had nothing to do but wait patiently for Uncle John Lloyd to pass away so that he could move into his substantial country-house and get his hands on an apparently inexhaustible fortune.

Within a year Mrs Warde was delivered of a large baby, but the Isle of Wight midwife, in spite of pummelling the blue infant for upwards of one hour, was unable to persuade it to breathe.

The distraught parents visited countless London doctors, who all scratched their heads and prescribed mild winters and bottle after bottle of repulsive medicine recommended by the Royal Family and All the Crowned Heads of Europe.

The Wardes did as they were told, wintered in Paris, visited in the highest society and mooned about the Jardin des Plantes looking at the monkeys until it was time for Mrs Warde to take her next dose of medicine.

In the following year she was brought to bed of a second child, but all the doctor's efforts to make it cry were unsuccessful, and all the reports from Stratford-upon-Avon said that Uncle John Lloyd was very well thank you, very much alive and looking forward to his hundredth birthday.

The Wardes wintered a second time in Paris and spent whole days tramping the cobbled streets in search of a physician, surgeon, quack or fortune-teller who could give Mrs Warde something to solve her problems, but all the experts spoke so fast that Mrs Warde's French could not keep up, and she was afraid to admit to her husband that she could not understand what it was that the Monsieurs wanted her to do.

Back on the Isle of Wight the Wardes kicked their heels and counted shipwrecks, and Mrs Warde dutifully drank her medicine every day, until a tremendous gale washed twenty-five corpses up on the shore near Westover, bloated and sodden, with their faces eaten away. Mrs Warde's stomach turned over a third time, and a third miniature tombstone was erected in the windswept churchyard overlooking the sea.

One night shortly afterwards Mrs Warde's sang-froid fell quite to pieces and she screamed at Mr Warde, 'I do not want any children anyway!'

That night the *Clarendon* went down in sight of Westover with eleven passengers and seventeen crew on board, all but three of whom were lost. In the morning Mr and Mrs Warde went down to the beach to inspect the damage and found a family of drowned children still in their nightclothes, which haunted Mrs Warde's dreams for a month, until she woke Charles in the middle of the night and begged him in tears, 'Take me away from this terrible island, take me away.'

But Uncle John Lloyd showed a marked reluctance to depart this life and Mr Warde, who had been running through his funds with alarming rapidity, said he had paid the rent for five years in advance.

'No,' he said, 'we cannot afford to live anywhere else.' And they were the richer by only a couple of puncheons of rum, a stranded turtle and a few damp coconuts.

In the year 1837 Queen Victoria came to the throne and the Wardes' fortunes took a turn for the better.

The news arrived at last that John Gamaliel Lloyd Esq. had given up the ghost and Charles Warde set off in high spirits for Stratford to attend the funeral and the reading of the Will. He fidgeted through the burial-service and stayed close to the family solicitor at the graveside, who told him that he would receive a very considerable sum of money, and the two rambling mansions, Clopton House and Welcombe House, where John Lloyd had fired cannon at the horizon on festive occasions and amassed a vast collection of badly stuffed tropical birds, all the same shade of moth-eaten scarlet.

Mr and Mrs Warde made a bee-line for Welcombe House and had moved all their possessions within a month, but after a week of unpacking and pulling cobwebs out of his hair, Mr Warde had had more than enough of Welcombe House, where everything reminded him of his uncles, and where the smell of decay from the bird collection was overpowering, and where there was no challenge for a gentleman with twenty-four long hours a day to fill.

One afternoon Mr Warde decided to walk over and take a fresh look at Clopton.

It was a house with a dark history and an evil reputation.

There were four ghosts, all reputed to walk, and an indelible bloodstain marked the spot where a murdered priest had been dragged across an attic floor and hurled into the moat that once surrounded the house.

The Gunpowder Plotters had rented the place in the early 1600s.

It was overgrown with brambles. It was draughty and in bad repair. Dry rot sprouted from every floor. But it was a more imposing residence, standing in open parkland with superb views. More important than anything, it had not the ridiculous name of Welcombe.

Clopton presented Mr Warde with the challenge that he needed. It would give him something to do. He decided on the spot that Clopton was where they must live, and he began planning its restoration at once.

The next morning Mr Warde went down to Stratford-upon-Avon armed with fistfuls of banknotes, which he pressed into the hands of Mr John Lattimer the builder and was thus able to jump to the head of a long queue of minor works. By the afternoon of the same day Clopton was swarming with workmen and echoed to the sound of frenzied banging and sawing. The jungle surrounding the house was razed to the ground. Carts went up and down with materials; bonfires blazed with builder's rubbish and a pall of acrid smoke hung over the house for weeks.

On the day Queen Victoria was crowned a procession of 1,000 carefully washed children wound its way through the streets of Stratford-upon-Avon in brilliant sunshine, singing 'God Save the Queen', and 2,000 Stratfordians were treated to a monster feast at which 9,000 knives, forks and spoons danced their way through 3,000 pounds of meat, 600 loaves of bread, 300 plum puddings and 2,000 eggs, all washed down with 7,500 pints of beer.

Not wishing to miss his first chance to become Stratford's principal benefactor, Mr Warde sent the liberal subscription of £10 to the Coronation Fund and made sure the fact was reported in the newspaper.

But giving with one hand he took away with the other, for when his labourers came to ask for the day off in order to attend the festivities Mr Warde said no.

'No,' he said, 'my house has got to be finished, and you must keep working.'

Down in Stratford the whole populace danced and rejoiced and ran races in honour of Queen Victoria. Mr Warde was there, beaming and distributing largesse, and was himself awarded first prize in the grinning competition, for his extraordinary grin outgrinned all the other grinners, and he wore his garland of evergreens for the rest of the week. In the evening fireworks and illuminated fire balloons lit up the sky, but up at Clopton the work went on, and the heavy hammer blows that had resounded throughout Coronation Day continued late into the night by the light of flaming torches.

Before long Mr Warde was celebrating in his own right, for Mrs Warde at last presented him with a healthy child, which was rushed off to church at her insistence to be christened before it was too late, and named Ada Lloyd Warde after nobody in particular.

'I suppose,' said Mr Warde, 'a daughter is better than nothing.'

Work on Clopton House proceeded. Sixty or a hundred men laboured for six months, ripping out old staircases and putting in new ones. Ancient oak floors were replaced by deal and old English fireplaces were ousted by Italian marble. Waggon-loads of what Mr Warde called lumber – wainscot, old carving, old Tudor benches, a worm-eaten four-poster bed presented to the Clopton family by Henry VII – things of the past, the perishable antiquities of which his father was so fond but which Charles Warde could not stand – were carted away or went up in flames.

Superb and costly modern furniture stood about on the lawns waiting to be taken inside. The grim Clopton portraits that had hung on the walls for two or three hundred years were pulled down and thrust into a back gallery on the floor. 'I did not know what I could better do with them,' said Mr Warde, 'they are wretched affairs and I am not at all related to the family.'

And he hoisted into position sparkling new paintings of a far higher quality than anything the Cloptons had ever known, and commissioned new portraits of all the Wardes for the grand staircase, where the sun would glint in their gilded frames.

When Mr Warde's works were complete and the house was ready to move into he made a final tour of inspection with Mrs Warde and Mr Lattimer, nodding and approving of all the improvements, and slapping Mr Lattimer repeatedly on the back so that he was black and blue.

There was a brand-new conservatory made of glass, with rows of orange-trees in terracotta tubs, forming a most picturesque entrance to the house.

There was a noble library with half a mile of unread books in leather bindings, all stamped with Mr Warde's crest in gold.

A noble dining-room seated up to twenty-six diners at a twenty-six foot dining-table.

A brand-new billiard-room was crammed with antlers, stags' heads and game birds, all shot by C.T. Warde Esq. and all properly stuffed by the best taxidermist in Paris, and the largest billiard-table that Messrs Burroughes & Watts had ever constructed.

Two elegant white and gold drawing-rooms decorated at great expense in the style of Louis XIV were stuffed full of gilt pier-glasses, gilt chairs and sofas, a grand pianoforte, a gilded chamber organ, lion-skin rugs and crystal chandeliers with hundreds of lights.

The sixteen substantial bedrooms all had fine views of Clopton Park and the lands that belonged to Mr Warde, which stretched almost as far as the eye could see, to Stratford and the Meon Hills beyond, blue and misty on the horizon.

The kitchens were full of sparkling copper pans, fine china and scrubbed kitchen-maids, all toiling without seeking for rest. There was a brand-new range of servants' offices: a housekeeper's room with a merry fire; a butler's pantry full of brandy; a spotless dairy full of spotless cows; a wash-house full of Mr Warde's pristine white Eureka Shirts; a brewery full of beer and elder wine; handsome stables full of handsome horses; coach-houses full of the latest shining vehicles. There were hay-lofts full of hay, a harness room full of whips and gleaming leather, a courtyard and a stable yard with spotless cobbles.

In the ornamental gardens an army of thirty gardeners

already laboured without very much reward and the two walled kitchen gardens of an acre each were already full of prize vegetables, all growing to gigantic proportions under the expert supervision of the green-fingered Mr Bevington.

There were dog-kennels, piggeries, cow-sheds, glasshouses full of rare and exotic plants and specimens, and a vine heavy with black grapes: nothing had been omitted, nothing had been forgotten. The fine old family mansion was restored to life, with every modern convenience for the modern family, and everything was perfect.

Mr Warde celebrated by opening bottle after bottle of vintage champagne. He presented every workman with a gold sovereign, thanked each one of them very warmly and condescended to shake every one of them by the hand. In fact he shook hands with such a formidable grip and for so long that they all wondered if he was ever going to let go.

After the workmen had gone Mr Warde gave his wife a smacking kiss, picked her up, carried her squealing over the threshold and squeezed her so tightly that she had to ask him to stop.

'Well, my dearest,' he said, 'the house is finished. What shall we do now?' And they both realized that there was nothing left to do, nothing else left to plan and, once again, nothing to occupy Mr Warde's time.

At this stage of his life Mr Warde's crime of crimes was said to be the utter destruction of Clopton's ancient character, and the complete Italianization of Stratford-upon-Avon's finest ancient mansion, a house where Shakespeare must have visited, and where, according to some, *The Taming of the Shrew* must have taken place.

Mr Warde's decision to hide Clopton's old deep-red bricks under a coat of plaster brought forth the most adverse comments, but the yellow paint with which he chose to cover the house was almost the last straw. It made his neighbours talk of bad eggs but Mr Warde thought of it as the colour of MONEY, and although he had not yet been to Italy he said it reminded him of the Villa Borghese.

'I don't care what anyone thinks,' he said. 'It is my house and I shall do what I like with it. I shall do just what I like.'

*

33

A week after the builders and decorators departed the Lord-Lieutenant of Warwickshire called unexpectedly at Clopton House and announced that he had been given Mr Warde's name as a fitting and proper person to perform the duties and fill the office of a Magistrate for the County of Warwick.

Mr Warde's smile spread out towards his ears. He was perfectly charming and terribly polite. He showed the Lord-Lieutenant the gilt plasterwork in his public rooms, asked the Lord-Lieutenant's opinion of paintings by Panini and Pompeo Batoni, consulted him about the proper feed for the racehorses he was grooming for the Leamington Stakes, plied the Lord-Lieutenant with glass after glass of sherry wine and talked away nineteen to the dozen about his outings with the Warwickshire Hounds.

The Lord-Lieutenant was most impressed with the house and most charmed by Mr and Mrs Warde. He was particularly taken with the orange-trees in the entrance hall, and when he returned home the Lord-Lieutenant sat down at once and wrote a letter to the Lord Chancellor recommending Mr Warde's name for admission to the office of Justice of the Peace.

The appointment was, as usual, for life, and the only qualification property worth £100 a year, which caused Mr Warde no trouble at all for Clopton was worth more than twenty times as much.

Mr Warde took his duties most seriously and investigated the procedure for calling out the militia and the Stratford Yeomanry Cavalry and the circumstances under which the Police Force might be called.

He stood on a dining-chair in front of his wife and rehearsed the reading of the Riot Act, trying hard to keep a straight face.

He practised looking serious as he swore in Harriet Meller as a Special Constable so that he would be ready should any emergency arise.

He spent weeks poring over the Justice's Manual, memorized all the indictable offences and learned the recommended punishments for minor breaches of the peace: for drunkenness in public places, for vagrancy, for trespass, for thefts under the Game Laws, and for minor assaults, so that when the great day came and he was able to take his seat on the Grand Jury at Warwick Assizes he was able to join in as if he understood what

34

was going on, and was able to participate in the sentencing of the most abject criminals to the severest possible fines, or to the maximum period of transportation to Australia, or to the longest terms of imprisonment in Warwick Gaol, and to play his full part as a Pillar of the Community.

In February 1840 Stratford celebrated Queen Victoria's marriage to Prince Albert with bands marching through the streets, cannon firing salutes, church bells pealing, and the thousand children enjoyed their second monster feast in three years.

Shortly afterwards Clopton was awash with champagne and beer once more for the birth of George Lloyd Warde, heir to the Clopton and Welcombe estates, and the proud father seemed to be throwing his money everywhere, almost beside himself with delight.

In the summer Mr and Mrs Warde were accorded the great honour of being presented by the Earl and Countess of Warwick, who had become their closest friends, to Her Majesty the Queen and His Royal Highness the Prince Albert at Buckingham Palace, and for many months afterwards they were unable to begin a sentence without prefixing it with 'As the Queen said to me . . .' even if she had not, or 'As I said to His Royal Highness . . .' in spite of the fact that their audience had lasted only a few minutes and they had only been invited because Mr Warde asked Lord Warwick if he could arrange it.

In the autumn, full of their new importance and anxious to do the right thing, the Wardes set off for Italy on a Very Grand Tour.

The party comprised the doting parents and their two infant children, a nurse and a courier, two liveried footmen, the lady's maid, two new carriages, a shining new coach and a brand-new chariot, four coachmen, children's beds, three tin baths, all the sheets, towels, pillows, tea, arrowroot and disinfecting fluid they would require, and a substantial brassbound medicine chest brim full with Mrs Warde's bottles, as supplied to Her Majesty Queen Victoria.

The procession crawled through Calais, Paris, Lyons, over the Alps in a blizzard, to Turin, stopping at suitably grand hotels where ostlers and flunkeys ran round in circles to accommodate Mr and Mrs Wardes' every whim, and where Mr Warde flashed his money as unostentatiously as he possibly could.

At Rome Mr Warde inspected the Colosseum, descended into the Catacombs on the Appian Way, poked about in the ruins of the Forum and purchased bogus antiquities from shady dealers.

At Naples the Wardes moved into a vast villa with a panoramic view of the Bay, and settled down for nine months, living in considerable style and working through Mrs Warde's address book, which was full of Principessas and Contessas. They trailed round Pompeii and Herculaneum in the blazing sun, fought off clouds of flies, were driven 'to the brink of madness' by the ceaseless noise of the cicada, and toiled as far up Vesuvius as Mrs Warde could be persuaded to go.

At every town and village they stopped to hunt for choice pieces of furniture, fine paintings, antique busts of Roman emperors, and all manner of exotic junk which they did not really want, until the carriage procession resembled a travelling auction-house, people mistook them for aristocratic refugees, and Mrs Warde had to say, 'We must buy *nothing else* or we shall never be able to carry everything home.'

Even so, the servants were obliged to travel outside for the long return journey, sheltered from the extremes of heat and cold only by Mrs Warde's seven silk parasols, and they all had to walk up all the hills, and help push the carriages over the Alps.

When they arrived exhausted at Clopton one afternoon in the spring of 1841 Mrs Warde was again pregnant and the household servants (whom Mr Warde had dismissed from his service for the duration of the tour and only now re-employed) lined themselves up with fixed smiles outside the house to welcome the Wardes home: butler, cook, five housemaids, two pages, a string of grooms, stable-lads and kitchen boys, thirty gardeners, and all the farm labourers.

Mr Warde shook everyone by the hand and went straight to bed, leaving his wife to supervise the unloading and unpacking, which took her most of the night.

The following summer Mr Warde the Horticulturist's gargantuan vegetables caused great excitement at the Warwickshire Horticultural Society Exhibition, for they were the largest vegetables the county had ever seen.

In the autumn Mr Warde the Gentleman of the Turf was, with

the Earl of Chesterfield, joint Steward of Warwick Races, and could hardly contain his excitement as his own horse, Regalia, led all the way in the Leamington Stakes, and he could hardly contain his disappointment when Regalia was beaten in the last furlong.

Afterwards at the Race Dinner Mr Warde's health was drunk with three times three cheers by the whole company and he was congratulated and slapped on the back by the many personages of the highest distinction who were present.

Shortly before Christmas Mr Warde the Liberal Proprietor and his friends dispatched on the Clopton estate some 500 pheasants, 200 hares, six partridges, twelve woodcock and 65 rabbits in the course of three days' shooting, so that the game larder dripped blood for days, and the Wardes feasted for weeks and every caller at the back door left carrying a bloody parcel.

In the inclement weather of the New Year Mr Warde the Philanthropist presented sufficient money to the Mayor of Stratford for twenty-three gallons of excellent tomato soup to be served out twice a week to the necessitous poor of the town, so that Mr Warde's name was on everyone's lips, and everyone said how kind and generous he was.

Early in 1842 Mrs Warde was safely delivered of her third strapping infant, who was named Charlotte Purefoy Lloyd Warde after her grandmother and in defiance of another Charlotte, Charlotte Clopton, who was reputed to have been buried alive in Stratford Church, and whose ghost, according to Meller and indoor servants of a nervous disposition, still walked the upstairs passages at Clopton every night.

In the summer Mr Warde was elected President of Stratford-upon-Avon Horticultural Society, awarded himself seven First Prizes – for Pineapples, Black Grapes, Balsams, White Celery, Greenhouse Plants, and for the Best Pineapple – and was obliged to present the prizes to himself, which he did, with a great grin on his face, to the thunderous applause of all the green-fingered gentlemen of the neighbourhood. And such was the esteem in which Mr Warde was held that nobody minded and nobody complained.

Early in the year 1844 Emily Frances Lloyd Warde was born and thanks to prayer and old wives' tales, and to her hundreds of bottles of patent medicine, Mrs Warde's health seemed to be fully restored.

In the spring Mr Warde the Amateur Architect completed the construction of Clopton Tower, a folly which he described as 'the grandest cottage and the smallest castle in the kingdom', and where the Wardes would all go to take tea and observe the landscape from the topmost turret through Mr Warde's new telescope. But by the time summer came Mr Warde was growing tired of Clopton and tired even of his new folly, and he went out one day and bought the largest house in Bedfordshire, where he would be able to employ his abilities as Architect, Landscape Gardener, Horticulturist, Sportsman, Pillar of the Community and Employer and Benefactor of the poor and needy on a far grander scale and in a far grander style, and where he would be able to increase dramatically the scale of his entertaining.

In 1845 Mr Warde the Rising Star was appointed a Deputy-Lieutenant of Warwickshire and a Member of the Committee of the Warwickshire & London Railway Company, and as a result of the latter appointment he enjoyed travelling Free, Gratis & For Nothing backwards and forwards to London as often as he liked, flashing his free pass whenever he got the opportunity.

By 1846 Mrs Warde's family would be complete, with the birth of Henry Charles Lloyd Warde, for Dr Pritchard advised her not to have any more children, and told Mr Warde that another child would undoubtedly endanger his wife's life.

Mrs Warde was very pleased, sighed with relief, and poured the last of her disgusting medicine down the drain. Mr Warde just shrugged his enormous shoulders, frowned, and tried to think no more of the dynasty he had been planning, which had required at least ten more children.

'Fifteen children would be a nice round number,' he had said. 'Though one might aim for twenty. I think twenty-five children would be a little excessive.'

Mrs Warde had screamed with laughter at the very thought of it.

In the year 1845 Mr Warde's meteoric rise into respectability and affluence looked set to reach a new and exalted level when it was rumoured about that he would be the next High Sheriff of Warwickshire.

Mr Warde's head began to swell. He ordered the requisite landau in anticipation and sent details of his coat of arms, with the crest of a wolf's head, to be painted on the doors on both sides, and with instructions for as much gold-leaf as possible. But it turned out that Mr Warde's name was passed over, and he promptly cancelled the order for the landau, which was already half built.

The following year Mr Warde was successful and he sent new and more elaborate orders for the landau, and when it was delivered he made sure he was seen in public, riding in it as often as he could, driving through the streets of Warwick drawn by four splendid grey horses and attended by postilions in elegant livery, the whole (as the newspaper noted) 'combining splendour with a neatness that is exceedingly pleasing to the eye, and courting the gaze of the multitude by gorgeous display.'

Mr Warde swore the usual oaths of office as High Sheriff, diligently attended the Quarter Sessions, inspected the County Gaol according to custom, and expressed his sincere admiration for the extreme cleanliness and neatness of the whole establishment, adding with a great roar of laughter, 'I should not mind spending a night or two here myself.'

The High Sheriff and his Javelin Men duly conducted the learned Judge through Warwick to open the Summer Assizes; they duly attended Divine Service at St Mary's Church, in sight of the gallows, and heard the High Sheriff's Chaplain (who was also his cousin) preach an excellent and improving and interminable sermon on the text *If one man sin against another, the Lord shall judge him; but if a man sin against the Lord, who shall intreat for him?*

In Court the Grand Jury, comprising all Mr Warde's landowning neighbours, the Justices of the Peace of the County, all of whom were his personal friends, was duly sworn; the Proclamation against Vice, Profaneness and Immorality was read, and the business of the Assize began.

Amongst others Richard Tomes was found guilty of stealing fifty-one brass fittings; John Buggins was found guilty of stealing four penny pieces, a halfpenny, a file and part of a paddle; and William Waring was found guilty of stealing 350 pounds of bacon.

All three were sentenced to Transportation to Australia for seven years.

A fourteen-year-old boy was found guilty of stealing a silver spoon from his master and was sentenced to fourteen days' gaol with hard labour.

And George Wheeldon Esq., charged with common assault, was acquitted.

Mr Warde could not help grinning behind his hand, but quickly brought himself under control.

In the same year Mr Warde was fortunate enough to witness the hanging of James Crowley, member of a family 'whom Providence hath been pleased to afflict with Insanity' for the wilful murder of William Tilsley. A crowd of 2,000 spectators jammed the streets of Warwick, some having walked up to twenty miles in order to enjoy the show. But the people cheered so loudly that Crowley, who was going to address them, could not be heard, and he was launched into eternity amid great applause without being able to protest his innocence, and without his last words being recorded.

Mr Warde could not help winking at him when he caught his eye.

One evening in February 1847 Mr and Mrs Warde were sitting reading on either side of a roaring fire in the gilt drawing-room at Clopton House. Their four golden-haired children slept peacefully in their beds. The new baby was in the capable hands of his nurse. There was no sound but the roaring of the fire, and turning of pages, and the steady tick of the magnificent ebony and ormolu timepiece made in Manchester, the city upon which the Lloyd fortunes had been built.

Mrs Warde no longer remarked upon or even noticed the dull thud of ghostly footsteps on the floor above, or the closing of doors in rooms which she knew to be empty. She was quite used to the 'ghosts' and had trained herself to put her trust in the Church of England and the Book of Common Prayer, and to ignore superstition.

From time to time husband and wife looked up. They smiled warm smiles at each other and carried on reading.

At eight o'clock the magnificent timepiece chimed its magnificent Cambridge chime of eight bells and Harriet Meller burst through the drawing-room door as if all the Clopton ghosts were after her at once, and ran to whisper something in her mistress's ear.

Mrs Warde snapped her book shut, got up immediately out of her white and gold armchair and ran to the door in a rustle of expensive silk.

Mr Warde, deep in Railway Tunnels, Railway Cuttings and Railway Finance, carried on reading and did not look up.

Fifteen minutes later Mrs Warde returned, went slowly up to her husband's chair and grasped his arm quite convulsively.

Mr Warde looked up at her and smiled. He noticed how pale Marianne was, sprang out of his chair and sat her down in it, and said, 'What on earth is the matter?'

Mrs Warde stifled a sob and said, 'Charles, they want to take me away from you.'

Fifty alarm-bells went off inside Mr Warde's head.

'Who do?' he asked. 'What on earth do you mean?'

'My mother,' she replied, and she took from her sleeve the note that Meller had given her, and begged Charles to read it.

It was in her sister Emily's handwriting, and it said that she was sitting in the Shakespeare Hotel down in Stratford-upon-Avon at that very moment, waiting to take Marianne away from Clopton for ever, and that she was waiting for an answer.

Mrs Warde, though, would have none of it. 'I'm not going,' she wailed, and the tears began to roll down her cheeks. 'Nothing, nothing will induce me to leave my poor husband,' she said.

And they embraced each other and felt their hearts beat in unison, and no more was said about the incident, or the letter, or Emily's visit to Stratford at all.

Two months later, on Tuesday 26 April 1847, Mr Warde set off with his wife in the newest carriage and in their customary grand style for the Railway Station at Coventry, some eighteen miles away, in order to see Mrs Warde off on the train for London, where she intended to visit her brother and spend a few days with her mother at Rothamsted.

She wrote affectionately to Mr Warde every day, addressing him as 'My dear Charles' or 'My dearest Husband' and at the end of the week, on Sunday morning 1 May, Mr Warde set off by train to London himself, in order to have the delight and pleasure of travelling free on the Warwickshire & London Railway, and in order to have the delight and pleasure of accompanying his wife home again.

In the late afternoon Mr Warde called at Hatchett's Hotel, where he knew his wife and her mother would be staying. He asked the manager of the hotel for Mrs Warde.

But the manager said he was sorry, there were to be no callers.

A hundred alarm-bells went off inside Mr Warde's head.

'Is she unwell?' he asked, as he sprang for the staircase.

'She is quite well, sir,' said the manager, as he barred the way, 'but she has left strict instructions. There are to be no visitors, and Mr Warde in particular is not to be admitted under any circumstances.'

Mr Warde tried to push his way past the manager, but four burly policemen appeared from nowhere, seized Mr Warde and propelled him into the street before he had time to retaliate or think what was happening.

The alarm-bells in Mr Warde's head would not stop jangling.

He did not know what to do. He could not think what had happened. He could do nothing but return to the Grosvenor Hotel in Park Street, where he always stayed when in London, and where his wife, he knew, would be able to find him. He sat down in his hotel room to wait and see what would happen next, wondering what he could have done to upset Marianne, but his conscience was clear, and he could think of nothing at all that he had done wrong.

Early that evening a Dr Alexander John Sutherland was shown to Mr Warde's room and presented his card, which revealed that he was a Doctor of Medicine and that he lived at Number One Parliament Street, Westminster.

He was a young man, no older than Mr Warde, who noticed that the Doctor was simply dressed, wore no watch-chain, carried no impedimenta such as bag, hat, gloves, coat or cape: nothing at all, but was empty-handed. He was head and shoulders shorter than Mr Warde and his hands hung by his sides, as if ready to come to his defence.

'I have come to see you at your friends' request,' said the Doctor. 'I understand you have been poorly.'

Mr Warde shrugged his huge shoulders. 'There's nothing wrong with me,' he said, 'I feel perfectly all right.'

'Oh, and I've brought you a letter from your wife,' said Dr Sutherland, and produced an envelope from an inside pocket and turned it over in his hands.

Mr Warde snatched the letter at once, without waiting for the Doctor to give it to him, and he ripped it open with a savagery that made the Doctor raise an eyebrow.

Tears immediately began to pour from Mr Warde's eyes, and he shook all over, and shook his head from side to side as he read. He was speechless for some time, and read the letter over and over again as if unable to believe what it said, crumpling it up into a ball, and then smoothing it out in order to read it again.

'What does it say?' asked Dr Sutherland at last, who knew very well what was in the letter.

'I will read it to you,' said Mr Warde. 'It says – there are no terms of endearment – it just says – To Charles Warde.

> This is the last letter you will ever receive from me. I know everything. A life of the most devoted affection has been returned with the most abandoned profligacy; even to the last I wished to remain with you, but a letter from one to whom you promised marriage has opened my eyes to the dreadful manner in which you have deceived me, and to the fact that my life is no longer safe in your hands. Nothing, after all I have heard, will induce me to see you more. I need not add reproaches. If you have one spark of good feeling left, or indeed, any feeling at all, your conscience will do so sufficiently.
>
> Your much-abused and insulted wife
>
> Marianne Warde

THREE

Mr Warde's perfect life collapsed like a house of cards and he was forced to face the fact that things had been going wrong for a long time. He could not pretend any longer. It was true: what most people saw and knew of his affairs was only the tip of the iceberg.

The blame for it all he laid squarely at the feet of his brother-in-law, John Bennet Lawes, the brilliant young agriculturist, who was happiest when experimenting with new forms of manure and liked to boast that one day he would make his fortune out of muck.

Mr Warde traced the beginning of all his troubles back to the morning in 1844 when John Bennet Lawes turned up at Clopton bubbling over with the news that the Marquess of Bute had put his house up for sale.

Mr Warde's face lit up and his grin stretched out towards his ears, for he had long coveted Luton Hoo, though he never dreamed it would ever come on to the market and never dreamed that he would ever be able to afford to buy it. But as soon as John Bennet Lawes opened his mouth all Clopton's shortcomings were magnified a hundred times, and Mr Warde's house seemed at once very small and mean in comparison.

For Luton Hoo was a giant of a house, an elegant and noble mansion on a very grand scale indeed, with a pedimented portico of massive classical columns like the entrance to the Parthenon, and noble apartments of herculean size by Robert Adam. It stood in 3,500 acres of lush green parkland laid out in the eighteenth century by Capability Brown, and only now coming to maturity. There were delightful pleasure grounds, vast lawns, and extensive parterres that reminded Mr Warde of Versailles. Mature woodland teemed with pheasant and partridge and promised excellent shooting. A fifty-acre lake teemed with trout and carp and all kinds of exotic and ornamental waterfowl. There would be private fishing, private boating, private duck shooting, private swimming: complete privacy and complete luxury. Clopton had nothing to match it.

Luton Hoo was a very stately place indeed and Mr Warde was

tempted to drive over with his brother-in-law at once in order to take a fresh look at it.

Mrs Warde did nothing to dissuade Charles from setting off, never really imagining that he would give up Clopton, on which he had spent so much time, so much energy and so much money, but John Bennet Lawes actively encouraged him to look into the possibility of making the purchase.

He talked Mr Warde into consulting his solicitors and accountants, and he kept on saying, 'Warde, you are really a very wealthy man – you know very well you could afford to buy Luton several times over.'

So that on the day of the sale Mr Warde and Mr Lawes found themselves gravitating in the direction of the Auction Rooms in a buoyant mood, after a largely liquid lunch.

The time for the sale drew near and they found themselves loitering in a crowd of well-heeled gentlemen outside the door.

When the bidding began Mr Warde found himself sitting in the front row of seats under a small cloud of cigar smoke, and waving his cigar in the air with some regularity, egged on by his brother-in-law.

In no time at all Mr Warde found he was the proud owner of Lord Bute's stately mansion and he was very pleased with himself. He whooped and sang and opened bottles of champagne all the way back to Warwickshire, and got very drunk indeed.

When he sobered up he justified the purchase, which took him somewhat by surprise in the cold light of morning, by saying to himself, 'It makes sense to have one substantial mansion rather than two medium-sized chicken-houses more than half a mile apart, neither of which is big enough for the kind of entertaining a gentleman of my station in society should be doing. Luton is, after all, a place where the Queen and Prince might be accommodated in a very fitting manner.'

In bed at night Mr Warde dreamed of the unsurpassed splendour of his new residence, and he dreamed of the day when Royalty would come riding up his stately carriage-drive to dine and sleep under his roof, and he dreamed of the title he would take, and of his introduction to the House of Lords.

When Mrs Warde found out what Charles had done she thought differently. 'I was greatly surprised,' she said, 'that you went off and bought a new house without consulting me.' And she tossed her head in annoyance.

'It was meant as a surprise, my dearest,' said Mr Warde. 'You were meant to be surprised. It was meant to be a birthday present. I thought you would be delighted. You are delighted really, aren't you?'

But Mrs Warde was bitterly disappointed. She liked living at Clopton. It was the perfect modern family house and she had got used to the things that went bump in the night, and she could not conceal her disappointment.

Charles Warde pressed on with his plans regardless. 'There are one or two repairs to be done,' he said, 'but I'm sure you will like it when it's finished. I am sorry. There's no turning back now: the contract is all agreed with His Lordship.'

Mr Warde had already secured the very expensive services of Mr Sydney Smirke the Architect to draw up the plans, and was determined to spend as much money as he could. There would be gold-leaf in every room; gold-encrusted ceilings; gilded Corinthian columns, and a vast golden ballroom with enormous new portraits of all the Warde family in new gilt frames. The whole would produce an effect of the utmost nobility.

If Luton Hoo had been ready to move into all might have been well, but Lord Bute was only selling his vast house because of a disastrous fire that had made necessary a complete restoration if not a complete rebuilding, neither of which the Noble Lord could afford. He had moved away elsewhere and abandoned the house to ivy and creeper and tramps and stinging-nettles.

But Mr Warde was a man who did not know what a shortage of money was, and he proposed to move his family at once into a most convenient and comfortable snuff-box at the rear of Luton Hoo while his army of superior workmen moved in to restore the mansion to its former splendour, as a monument to the greater glory of Charles Thomas Warde Esq. He had already planned another Very Grand Tour so that Marianne would be spared the worst of the chaos.

But he mentioned none of this to Mrs Warde, who had not visited Luton for years and was under the impression that all that was needed was a coat of paint.

49

When Mr Warde took his wife to see Luton for herself the tears rolled down her cheeks, for it was blackened by smoke, open to the sky and there was little left but the façade. Rats ran in and out of such rooms as survived. A bat flew into her hair. A small tree grew in the entrance hall. Every corner had been used as a tramps' lavatory.

'It will be the very pinnacle of perfection,' said Mr Warde, 'can't you imagine it?'

Marianne could imagine it only too well. She could think of nothing but the dust and the noise and the banging and the disorder that she would have to put up with all over again. She knew very well that the smell of charred wood that lingered in the ruins would take years to get rid of, and she dreaded the thought of the heat and enervation of a further Italian journey. She complained so bitterly that Mr Warde settled for spending the summer at Brighton instead.

'It is the most frightful house,' Mrs Warde said. 'I would really rather remain at Clopton, where I have been very happy.'

But Mr Warde did not listen. He was undeterred by the prospect of interminable building works and he could not understand his wife's objections. He was spurred on by the thought of a new challenge and by the prospect of something to occupy his limitless spare time, and he spent hours sitting at his architect's-table doodling, and screwing up endless giant sheets of paper with loggias and obelisks and rustic temples scribbled all over them.

It was true that all Luton's faults could be put right – at a cost – but most devastating of all was Mrs Warde's discovery that Charles had undertaken to pay the most astonishing sum of money for the ruins, far in excess of their value.

'How much did it cost?' she enquired at the end of the visit.

'One Hundred and Sixty,' said Mr Warde, 'Thousand,' and blew a smoke-ring.

'Pounds?' gasped Mrs Warde.

'No,' he said, 'Guineas.'

Marianne thought Charles must be out of his mind, and she kept on telling him so most of the way home, until he snapped at her to be quiet, and they drove on towards Stratford in stony silence, listening to the coachman's whip and the clatter of hooves, with Marianne biting her lip and wondering and wondering what on earth was going to happen next.

Mr Warde could easily afford to pay One Hundred and Sixty Thousand Guineas of course, though to raise the money he would have to mortgage Clopton and sell Welcombe outright, but these things he was perfectly happy and willing to do.

'I never did like Welcombe,' he said, 'I'll be glad to get rid of it.'

Thus in due course Welcombe was sold and Mr Warde invested the proceeds of the sale, a very considerable sum, in Railway Shares, for the Railway was his great passion, until the contract for Luton Hoo could be completed.

Here Mr Warde's troubles began in earnest. He was a country gentleman possessed of an affluent fortune and accustomed to spending the greater part of his time in country pursuits, with nothing to do but sit back and let his money grow and grow on its own. There was nothing at all to interfere with his freedom and nothing to limit his life of luxury.

When a gentleman mentioned the word *Railway* Mr Warde's eyes would sparkle and he could talk for hours about Gradients and Viaducts and Signalling, but when *The City* was the subject of discussion Mr Warde would more often than not roll his eyes, or snort, or yawn pointedly, and wander off in search of a billiard-table.

'I am no businessman,' he said, 'I don't mind admitting it: The City bores me to death. I am a Sportsman.'

In the year 1845 securities had reached an extreme high, but Mr Warde neglected to ask for anyone's advice, preferring to trust his own judgment and avoid the sharks in Lombard Street. When the time came to invest the Welcombe money he put all his eggs boldly into the same basket and felt very pleased that at last someone was taking positive action to advance the noble cause of the Warwickshire & London Railway.

Mr Warde thus became one of the largest shareholders in the company and he rode home waving the share certificates in great excitement all the way.

And then he did nothing. Time after time he allowed the letters to pile up on his desk unopened, saying, 'It's too hot for business, business can wait' or 'The Railway Shares can look after themselves: the Railway is as safe as houses.' And he neglected to keep up with financial affairs. For weeks on end he failed to look at his copy of *The Times*, which regularly ended up mopping up the floods of water on the kitchen floor or in the scullery before he thought about opening it.

The financial pages of the newspaper were everywhere but on Mr Warde's desk, and Mr Warde was everywhere but behind his desk in his noble library keeping up with what was going on in the outside world. He carried on walking about the estate, his mind on other things.

One morning, just before the Wardes set off for Brighton, the news arrived that Mr Warde's Railway Shares had plummeted in value, were almost worthless, and that most of his considerable sum of money was gone for ever.

Mr Warde ranted and raved and tore his hair behind the closed doors of the library all morning, and sounded like a wild beast.

When Fuller and Mathieu finally plucked up the courage to look round the door to see if Mr Warde was still in one piece they saw documents in shreds all over the floor, debris everywhere, and Mr Warde sitting, too late, at his desk, with his head in his hands, weeping. The portraits were crooked on the walls. The busts of Roman emperors were smashed to smithereens. A scene of total chaos was revealed.

Mrs Warde did not know what to do at all, and was too upset by Charles's outburst to go anywhere near him.

Mr Warde was by no means the only investor to find that his fortunes had been suddenly damaged by the Railway Crash, but his Railway Mania took an unusual turn: his mind was affected to a certain degree and he was plunged into a situation of great embarrassment. Not only had he agreed to pay much more for Luton Hoo than he should have done, but now he could hardly afford to buy it at all, let alone carry out his ambitious programme of works, which had already begun even though the sale was not yet complete.

Mr Warde's castles in the air came crashing down. He had told all smart Warwickshire about his new project. Everyone from the Earl of Warwick to the women working in the fields knew about Mr Warde's new palace at Luton, and everyone regarded him as the coming man. He was left looking very foolish indeed, and all Mrs Warde's efforts to calm him down and cheer him up had not the slightest effect.

More than once Mr Warde sat at his desk into the early hours of the morning trying to compose a letter to Lord Bute which began with 'My Lord Marquess . . . I regret . . .' but never got much further without being screwed up and hurled onto the rich oriental carpet.

Mr Warde did not know what to do. He did not want anyone to know what had happened. Mrs Warde was at a complete loss. She was expecting another child and her health had begun to deteriorate. She could only hope that the change of air and the holiday at Brighton would bring about a change in Charles's temper.

But she found herself writing to her mother from Brighton, 'His manner is daily more and more violent . . . Charles has begun to snarl at me.'

To her sister Emily she confided, 'Charles blames all his misfortunes upon our family.'

Under the strain of it all Mrs Warde called in the doctor and sent to London for a crate of her old medicine.

The collapse of the Luton purchase was enough to affect Mr Warde's nerves and damage his finances severely, but it was by no means his only problem, for there was an altogether different matter preying upon his mind and influencing his behaviour and making him very angry indeed: his mother-in-law.

Mr Warde had married Miss Lawes thinking that she was possessed of no fortune at all, and it had not mattered to him at the time, for he was rich, or was going to be, and he had no scruples about telling all his numerous friends and acquaintances exactly how much he was worth.

He quite understood that Miss Lawes was marrying him without the substantial sum of money he might normally have expected to receive as a dowry.

He quite understood that the Lawes family had fallen upon hard times and that the Lawes fortune, once the envy of all Hertfordshire, had been severely damaged by the late Mr Lawes' lavish entertainment of the Prince Regent and all his circle when they hunted and fished and shot at Rothamsted, stayed for weeks on end and seemed not to want to go away. Mr

Warde knew all about that, for Mrs Lawes and her daughters, even twenty years afterwards, could talk of almost nothing else and would let no one forget that they had moved in the very highest society.

In 1834 Mr Warde had been quite happy to have none of Mrs Lawes' money at all. He knew she had no money to give. He was most charming about it. 'It is a matter of no importance to me,' he said, 'I have plenty of money already. I don't need any more.'

So that Mrs Lawes was heard to exclaim, 'How lucky my daughter is' and 'What a lovely man Mr Warde is after all' and for some time Mr Warde could do no wrong and everything he did and said was wonderful.

The events of 1845 made Mr Warde change his tune. In the autumn of that year, shortly after the bottom fell out of the shares in the Warwickshire & London Railway Company and all the other Railway Companies in the country, Mrs Lawes' other daughter, Emily Catherine Lawes, announced her betrothal to an impecunious Welshman, Lewis Mathias Esq., of Lamphey Court in the County of Pembroke, and the information somehow reached Mr Warde that far from not having two halfpennies to rub together his mother-in-law was sitting pretty on a Trust Fund containing the handsome sum of £6,000 and that she had a power of distribution *in favour of her two daughters*.

Mr Warde flew into a temper on hearing the news and said it was a slight on him and his wife. It was bad enough that they had lied to him about the existence of the fund, but there was worse than that, for the information also leaked out that two-thirds of the money – some £4,000 – had been earmarked for the sole use of Emily Catherine Lawes on the occasion of her marriage.

Mr Warde's rage was terrible to behold. He furiously scribbled letter after letter to Mrs Lawes demanding to know why the devil she had not mentioned the fund's existence to him back in 1834.

He told her, 'The impression on my mind is that the concealment of the fund is not an accidental thing, and that I have been treated in a way I ought not to have been treated at all.'

Mrs Lawes wrote not a word to Mr Warde in reply. She sent no message and offered him no explanation whatever. She pretended that she had never received his irate and abusive letters, and had thrown them all on to the fire.

Mrs Warde pretended to know nothing about the existence of the fund and could find no plausible explanation to offer her husband.

After three weeks of unbroken bad temper Mr Warde climbed into his shining carriage, stormed all the way down to Rotham-sted in the snow, and drove the horses faster up the pot-holed carriage-drive than he should have done, in order to demand an explanation.

He stood in the middle of Mrs Lawes' best threadbare carpet and shouted at Mrs Lawes in an ungentlemanly manner that his circumstances had changed and that he could do with some of her money to pay for his wife's dresses.

'The impression on my mind,' he snarled, 'will be removed immediately if you appoint the residue of the fund in favour of my wife.'

But Mrs Lawes screamed, 'I will do no such thing, and I will not be bullied in my own house,' and she rang for all her menservants, who came running with shotguns and saw Mr Warde off the premises without any ceremony.

Mr Warde raged all the way back to Clopton and told Mrs Warde over dinner what had happened, when Mrs Warde said for the first time what she thought about the matter herself, and took the part of her mother and brother and defended their conduct.

'Charles,' she said, 'you know very well that you still have so much money that you hardly know what to do with it. Emily is marrying a man who has next to nothing. Although Mr Mathias has good expectations he is worth only £600 a year. Emily needs the money far more than I do.'

Then, to Marianne's horror, the top blew off the volcano of Mr Warde's temper, and he subjected his wife's family to a searing attack, abusing its run-down estates, vilifying its reputation, pouring scorn on all its pretensions to gentility, and lashing the name of Lawes with the sharp side of his tongue for more than an hour, scarcely drawing breath and repeatedly banging his fists on the dining-table so that all the glass and china jumped and all the silver rattled.

Mrs Warde did not dare to move a muscle. She heard for the first time in her life a quantity of words which she realized from the vehemence of Charles's delivery must be terms of abuse. She bore the avalanche of insult for as long as she could, but when he shouted at her, 'I never want to see any member of your family again,' she ran weeping from the room, locked herself in her bedroom and in spite of Meller's repeated and insistent knocking refused to come out or speak to anybody until the next morning.

Mr Warde began to twitch his way down the carriage-drive every morning, with his arms waving like windmills, and he slashed ever more violently at the nettles with his gold-topped walking-stick. He began to eat less and to drink more, and he took to carrying a flask of the very best Cognac Brandy in the pocket of his Anaxyridian Trousers wherever he went.

When Mrs Warde left Clopton on 26 April 1847 it was with every intention of returning home on the Railway with her husband at the end of the week, in spite of their disagreement about the Trust Fund, in spite of his outbursts over Luton Hoo, in spite of everything, for she still entertained the deepest affection for him.

But when she arrived at Rothamsted her life was turned immediately upside down. Instead of the usual warm welcome from her mother and sister she was met by cold, solemn faces and restrained formal greetings.

Mrs Lawes sat Marianne down in the draughty drawing-room and said, 'Prepare for a shock, my dear, or rather, a series of shocks.'

'Marianne, my dear,' began Mrs Mathias, for Mrs Mathias she now was, although Mr Warde had refused to attend her wedding and Mrs Lawes had refused to invite him, 'Charles has been unfaithful to you.'

Marianne was thunderstruck. She opened her mouth to ask a dozen questions, but closed it without saying anything.

'Unfaithful,' hissed Mrs Mathias, 'not with one woman, but with many many women, all of them kept at your door.'

Marianne goggled at them in amazement.

'He has squandered hundreds of pounds, frittering away his inheritance on abandoned women, stinting you in everything in order to provide for his hosts of illegitimate children.'

'So that is it,' said Mrs Warde, 'that explains all the women in the fields. That explains where all the money has gone.'

'And now,' said Mrs Lawes, 'he has gone so far as to promise marriage to a woman from Brighton. He has gone too far and something has to be done.'

Hot tears poured down Marianne's cheeks. 'But I don't believe it,' she wailed. 'You have muddled him up with another. You have made a terrible mistake. You must have made it all up. Why are you telling me all these lies? How can you sit there and say such things about my husband? Charles is a perfect gentleman. He would not do such things. I cannot believe it. I will not believe it.'

But Mrs Lawes and Mrs Mathias told her the whole sordid story and filled in all the horrid details and described in whispers the dreadful things that had taken place in the plantations not half a mile from her house.

Marianne Warde shook her head in disbelief. 'It is impossible,' she said.

'No matter what you think,' said her mother, 'no matter what you say, you will not be going back to your husband. We will not allow it. You will not be going home at all. You will never be going back. Your marriage is finished, and you may as well forget that Charles Warde ever existed. He has brought disgrace upon his family and he has brought disgrace upon yours, and the whole town of Stratford-upon-Avon knows about it and is talking about him.'

'Marianne,' said Mrs Mathias gravely, 'you must believe us. You have married a monster. It is not safe for you to return to him.'

And Marianne had no choice but to comply with her mother's orders, and she was locked up for the rest of the week in a bedroom where the servants would not be able to hear her screams and sobs, and she was fed on nothing but beef tea and dry toast.

Mrs Warde's whole world turned on its head. She could not understand what had happened or how it had happened. She was afraid for the five children she had left at home with only a nurse for their protection, and she was afraid for the future. 'What will become of me?' she thought. 'What will become of my children? Whatever will Charles do without us all?'

When sleep finally came to her in the early hours of the morning Mrs Warde dreamed lurid dreams in which Charles featured, sitting at the mahogany telescope dining-table, knife and fork in hand, with the blood running down his chin on to a vast white table-napkin tucked into the collar of his Ford's Eureka Shirt, as he ate his way through his five children one by one, grinning horribly all over his handsome face.

Every morning Mrs Lawes and Mrs Mathias submitted to Marianne's detailed questioning, bathed her ruined complexion with cold water and handed her dry handkerchief after dry handkerchief to mop up the tears. They patiently repeated the story of Charles Warde's misdemeanours to her several times a day, and they seemed to have all the answers.

'Charles has been deceiving you for years,' said her mother, 'and not a soul of respectability will ever notice him more.'

'How do you know all this,' Marianne asked, 'when I myself never dreamed it was going on and suspected nothing at all?'

'Our spies have been watching your husband for months,' said Mrs Mathias, 'following him to see what he got up to in the copses on his estate and watching his every move.'

'And Harriet Meller,' added Mrs Lawes, 'has kept us fully informed by letter.'

'Without dear Meller,' said Mrs Mathias, 'we should have known nothing. It is Meller we have to thank for all our information. It is Meller who has saved your life. We all owe Meller a great debt.'

But Marianne thought, 'So, it is *Meller* I have to thank for the loss of my husband. It is my *maid* I have to thank for the breakdown of my marriage.'

Mrs Lawes and Mrs Mathias had no doubts at all. 'There cannot be the slightest doubt that Meller is right,' said her mother. 'It is nothing but the truth. You've got to believe it.'

'But Meller is the most frightful gossip,' said Mrs Warde, 'how can you possibly believe a word she says? It is nothing but a pack of lies.'

At the end of the week Mrs Lawes, Mrs Mathias and a still protesting and still tearful Mrs Warde made their way to London on the Railway to consult the family solicitor about a

Deed of Separation, and about arrangements for a settlement that would make Mrs Warde financially independent of her husband, and about a Divorce, and about how best to break the news to Mr Warde that his wife had left him for ever.

Marianne could not understand why it had to be done at all. 'Even if it is true,' she said, 'I would be happy to go back to him provided he promises to reform his ways. I love him still. I should be quite happy to forgive him. Is not *to forgive* what Christian people are supposed to do?'

'Don't talk such nonsense,' snapped her mother, 'you are not going to forgive him and you are not going back to him. I forbid it. If you are going to spend the rest of your life alone you are going to need some money, for I am sure *I* am not going to support you and your five children.'

And Mrs Lawes dictated a letter to Mr Warde and made Marianne sign it and address it 'To Charles Warde' informing him of the step she was taking. And then she called in Dr Sutherland, with a view to his taking the letter to Mr Warde, and with a view to his taking a professional look at Marianne as well.

Mrs Lawes whispered in the Doctor's ear, 'Has not my daughter brought all this upon herself?'

While Mr Warde was trying to gain access to his wife's hotel room faithful Meller was being rushed back to Clopton in Rothamsted's ancient carriage with a posse of muscular labourers, low of brow and heavy of hand, who in due course lowered Mrs Warde's five children on ropes out of their nursery window at dead of night and carried them off to safety under the protection of their Uncle John Lawes.

Five pale faces peered bewildered out of the carriage window into the darkness, not knowing what was going on. One by one the children pulled at Meller's sleeves and asked her, 'Meller, where is our papa?' and 'Meller, when shall we see our papa?' but Meller could not bring herself to mention the name of Mr Warde and she could not bring herself to tell the children that they would never see him again.

When they asked Mrs Warde the same thing and demanded more and more desperately, 'What has happened to our papa?' thinking that some dreadful accident must have befallen him,

Mrs Warde's lips twitched and she fought back the tears, but she would not reply, and pretended she had not heard the question.

In his room at the Grosvenor Hotel a tearful Mr Warde admitted to Dr Sutherland that he had been unfaithful to his wife, and he asked the Doctor what he should do.

Dr Sutherland pulled at his side-whiskers and said, 'I would advise you to keep yourself tranquil, and to write immediately to your wife, acknowledging your sins and begging her to forgive you.'

Mr Warde began the letter at once, with the tears still pouring down his face, soaking the front of his shirt, and he went on weeping, unable to control himself, as he wrote his reply, kneeling on one knee at an octagonal table in the middle of the room, so that the paper was covered with blots and smudges, and with crossings out, because he could hardly see what he was doing.

He wept and sobbed and exclaimed all the time he was writing, and when he had finished he stood up, went over to the mantelpiece, gave the letter to the Doctor to read, and stood with his head resting on the mantelshelf and said, 'I don't mean to deny that I've had other women besides my wife since my marriage – as everyone else has. It's nothing unusual.' And he went on telling the Doctor all his troubles for more than an hour, with the tears dripping on to the hearth-rug, and Dr Sutherland found it difficult to get a word in edgeways and could not get away.

The Doctor rather regretted getting mixed up in Mr Warde's affairs in the first place. He had been approached first by Mr Warde's solicitors, Mr Butt and Mr Bury, who had called on him early that morning when he was still in bed, and they had stayed so long and talked so much that they had prevented him from going to church.

Mr Butt said, 'Mr Warde has been going on in such an extraordinary manner that his family wish to have your professional opinion respecting the state of his mind.'

Mr Bury said, 'Mr Warde has been carrying on an open system of lust, and the animal passions seem to have quite got the upper hand of him.'

In the end, to get rid of the solicitors, Dr Sutherland agreed to go along to the Grosvenor Hotel to interview the patient and to deliver Mrs Warde's letter, and he set off that evening, leaving Mrs Warde with her mother and sister at a house in Portugal Street, all of them red-eyed and biting their nails, thinking that Mr Warde would be violent, and all of them afraid to go anywhere near him.

Dr Sutherland had no such fears, for he had plenty of experience of this kind of interview. The card he presented to Mr Warde made quite clear that his medical practice was confined almost exclusively to cases of mental derangement and he stationed his three burly assistants, experts in the handling of lunatics without lucid intervals, outside Mr Warde's door in the usual manner, with the largest strait waistcoat in the metropolis, ready to confine the patient if necessary and carry him off to Dr Sutherland's Private Asylum in the black padded carriage with reinforced windows that waited in the street below.

Mr Warde admitted in his smudged letter to his wife that he had been wicked and dishonourable to her, but he solemnly denied promising marriage to anyone but her.

He confessed his many sins but made his excuses as well. 'My faults were solely the outsprings of heated bodily temperature owing to the extraordinary hot weather, and were the result of heedlessness and thoughtlessness and of sheer impulse, but not of Vice: they were the result of bodily strength and inclinations which all healthy flesh and blood is liable to. Any man can tell you that such things are perfectly possible in the same breath as devoted love and attachment to one person.'

Near the end of the letter he wrote, 'My soul abhorred such thoughts only a few years since, and will do so again with your help, but my bane has been idleness.'

He begged Marianne to take into account all the trials he had to put up with, all the annoyances and irritations. 'If we had been left alone,' he wrote, 'if this unwise purchase of Luton Hoo had not been forced upon me, none of this would have happened; this terrible blow would never have been, my honour would have been untarnished and we should still be together.'

He begged Marianne for a meeting so that he could ask her forgiveness on his knees.

He begged her not to cast him away to utter and complete ruin, saying, 'Without your forgiveness my life will be a complete blank and the world a desert. How without you can I avoid running headlong into crimes that at present are unknown to me?'

He begged her to come back to him.

He begged her not to abandon her children, not knowing that she had already taken them away.

He promised to be virtuous and righteous.

He promised to lead a very different life.

He promised to reform his ways.

But Marianne sent his letter back to him with a curt note refusing to have anything to do with him, and she refused to see him ever again.

Three days later John Bennet Lawes wrote to Charles Warde approving of the step his sister had taken in leaving Clopton for good.

'The result of your conduct,' he wrote, 'has been to deprive you of every friend you had in the world, and if you keep the management of your affairs in your own hands you will shortly become a beggar. Nothing but an entire change of life and perfect rest to your mind can save you from insanity.'

John Bennet Lawes could not forget the 3,500 acres of arable land at Luton Hoo just waiting to be turned into model fields in the largest experiment for artificial manure in the kingdom, and he offered to take over the entire management of Mr Warde's financial affairs and said he would be pleased to do so on condition that Marianne was made independent.

But Lawes also issued a stern warning: 'If you refuse to co-operate we shall be forced to reveal your guilty secret to an astonished world.'

There was, of course, no question of any meeting taking place between husband and wife.

'My sister is not so weak,' wrote Lawes, 'as to suppose that the promise you now make so easily will bind you for even a week, or that the life of profligacy you have been leading for so long is suddenly going to change overnight. Your first attempt to see my sister will make you my enemy.' And John Bennet Lawes ordered new and stronger gates for Rothamsted Park, gave instructions for spikes and broken glass to be stuck into the top of the eight-foot-high wall that surrounded the estate, and bought his lodge-keeper and all his gamekeepers the most expensive new shotguns he could afford.

Unable to persuade Mrs Warde to meet him, Mr Warde had to conduct his campaign to get his wife back by letter. Endless laconic communiqués passed between Clopton and Rothamsted until Mrs Warde (or her mother and her solicitors) drew up a Deed of Separation and told Mr Warde he would have to sign it, for there was no hope or possibility that his wife would ever go back to him now, and no hope or possibility of her forgiving him after what had happened, and that the only thing to be done was for him to hand over a large portion of his property at once in order to make Marianne self-sufficient.

The Deed stated that Mrs Warde should be entitled to live separate and apart from her husband; that Mr Warde should not send or cause to be sent to her any letter or message of any kind; that Mr Warde should not attempt to remove or entice the children from Mrs Warde's care, custody and control; that he should not interfere with the children's education; that he should at all times permit them to reside with their mother, and that he was never to see or try to see them again.

Mrs Warde's letters stated her conviction that Charles Warde was a man steeped in profligacy, reeking with the most abominable sins, a cruel man, a hardened man, an individual who was not to be trusted in the company of his own children, or even to breathe the same air that they breathed.

Mrs Warde's Deed proposed that Mr Warde should brand himself under his own hand and seal, voluntarily and willingly, with the indelible stamp of degradation and infamy that he was unfit to live under the same roof or even enter the same room that his children were in, or for one moment to be in their society.

Mrs Warde would have no other Deed but this Deed.

Mr Warde flatly refused to sign it. He tore the document into shreds and sent the pieces back to Rothamsted by return of post with a letter that said, 'I am prepared to undergo almost any trial you care to mention as proof of my good intentions. I will gladly move out of Clopton and let you live there, for I know that you love the place. I refuse only to put my name to this terrible Deed, which banishes me from society and labels me for the rest of my life as an unnatural parent, unfit to enjoy the company of my own children. I absolutely refuse to part with them.'

Mrs Warde's words and intentions were not her own, however, for her mother was still looking over her shoulder and telling her what to write. It was Mrs Lawes who opened Mr Warde's letters every morning and chose what to read to Marianne and decided what it was best for her not to hear.

Marianne Warde, still on an invalid's diet, was too weak and too confused to think or argue, and in any case the shock of the upheaval in her life had made her lose her voice.

Underneath all the confusion Marianne's love for her husband was still as strong as it had been when she was eighteen years old, when she first decided that she loved Charles Warde. But her mother had sown the seeds of doubt in Marianne's mind, and the doubts were beginning to grow.

Some days Mrs Warde would croak, 'I still love Charles to distraction. I want to go back to him. He is my husband. I should like to go and see him today, now.'

But her mother said, 'Don't talk such nonsense. You are not going to see that man. You are never going to see him again.'

On other days Marianne said, 'I have tried by all means in my power to please Charles. In return for all my love and all my devotion I have received only neglect and abuse and insult. I have received from him every sort of ill-treatment a man could possibly offer his wife except for personal violence.'

She could not forget a story from Paris which she had read in her newspaper: how the Duchess of Praslin, an excellent and amiable woman, devoted to her husband, had been murdered in cold blood by that husband so that he might pursue uninterrupted an amour with his children's governess.

Marianne saw in her drugged sleep every night the image of Charles Warde creeping about in the dark with the silver carving-knife and fork, brutally stabbing her as she slept in her bed. She saw the pillows soaked in blood and she saw Charles driving off in his landau with his arms round the woman from Brighton. And night after night Marianne would wake up screaming in a pool of perspiration, with her pillow chewed and wet with tears, and her mouth full of feathers.

As the days slipped by and nothing was done to bring about the reconciliation that everyone except the Lawes family thought would be a possible thing and certainly a desirable thing, Marianne Warde grew hardened in her resolve to have nothing more to do with her husband.

At last she said to her mother, 'You were right. I cannot go back to him after what he has done. I know that Charles will be violent.' And she broke down and told her mother everything that Charles had done, and stopped pretending that her marriage had up till April 1847 been a perfect marriage, and she wept for another week without stopping.

She wrote to one of Charles's friends, Captain Edward Walhouse, who had cast himself in the thankless role of peacemaker and had spent hours talking to both Mr and Mrs Warde to no effect, 'If you could give me the whole County of Warwick I would not now go back to him.'

And so it was that in the month of November 1847 the case of Warde *v.* Warde was brought before the Vice-Chancellor in the Court of Chancery in London and a bitter battle began, as Mr and Mrs Warde fought tooth and nail for the custody of the children of their marriage.

Mr Warde supported his natural right as the father to have the custody of the children which nature and the Law had given him.

Mrs Warde supported her right to the custody of the children, alleging that Mr Warde was a most unfit person to look after them because of his violent manner, his habitual profligacy, his irreligious habits, and because of his constant use of profane and violent language.

FOUR

Shortly before Christmas a distinguished-looking lady dressed in the best of everything money could buy was escorted to her carriage at Euston Station by a procession of porters carrying expensive-looking parcels.

The lady travelled First Class in the front of the train; her maid travelled Third in the rear.

The lady's carriage was full of respectable-looking gentlemen in black clothes who were going home after a long day toiling in the City, and their newspapers rolled back to admit her. She sat in a corner seat with her back to the engine and her parcels crammed on to the luggage-rack opposite her, where she could keep an eye on them.

As the train steamed slowly out of London the lady's attention was held by the view of the suburbs, but as the light faded her gaze was drawn inwards, to her brightly coloured parcels, which were dislodged from time to time by the motion of the train and fell upon the heads of the gentlemen of business below.

The gentlemen smiled behind their papers, reading of scandal and adultery and profligacy; they smiled at the thought of this spectacularly beautiful lady going home for Christmas in the country with presents for her children, to a world where litigation, affidavits, chancery suits, residuary legatees and bitter legal wrangles did not exist.

Mrs Warde's gaze kept returning to her parcels, presents not to but from her children, purchased and wrapped in secret with the connivance of their governess, and Mrs Warde's troubles, so long suppressed, welled up from deep inside her. Floods of tears coursed down her tired face and she was unable to stop them, unable to conceal them, and she made no attempt to mop them up.

She sobbed and groaned and wailed and bit the backs of her gloved hands but she could not stop herself. There was no escape for the starched gentlemen in their tall hats. Hide behind their newspapers though they might, smile upon her sympathetically though they did, no amount of English stiff upper lip could close their hearts against Mrs Warde's grief and agony.

The Harpenden train ignored their prayers for it to go faster. Mrs Warde ignored their prayers for her to alight at the next station, at any station, and they had to put up with the frustration of not knowing what was the matter with her, for she could not bring herself to answer their solicitous questions and she shook her head when they asked if there was anything they could do to help.

The tears rained down and all she could think was: I have lost my husband. I have lost my children. They have taken my children away. All my little ones. My babies. I have lost everything. And her mind raged hopelessly back and forth over the court case that she had lost so easily, and she cursed herself for having been so stupid as to let her mother hire the cheapest counsel she could find.

When the train arrived at Harpenden Meller found her mistress in such a state that she had to commandeer the waiting-room and run down the road to fetch the doctor, for by this time Mrs Warde was hysterical, beside herself with grief, so that the station-master and all the railway porters, who knew very well who Mrs Warde was, and what had happened, for it had been fully reported in all the newspapers, stared after her shaking their heads, thinking that she must have lost her mind.

Mrs Warde could not remember a time since her marriage when her life had been free of some trouble or other but the beginning of the trouble in her marriage she traced back to the year 1845, when the whole family had spent the summer at Brighton. It was a place which should have held happy memories, for it was at Brighton, in the Royal Pavilion, that the Prince Regent had dandled her as a child on his knee and fed her chocolates and indulged and spoiled her as if she were a Princess of the Blood Royal herself.

Now all those memories were overshadowed and ruined by Charles's extraordinary behaviour and the magic of Brighton was gone for ever. All she could remember was Charles in a foul temper, Charles growing more and more irritable as the summer went on, and Charles growling angrily at her across the breakfast table every morning, until it was so bad that she had to travel all the way up to London in order to ask her solicitor whether she was entitled to some protection from her husband's violent conduct.

She wrote to her sister, 'I cannot understand why Charles's attitude towards me has changed. I have always loved him. I still love him. Is it my fault that he bought Luton Hoo? Is it my fault that he has lost all his money on the Railway? I have tried to please him in every way I can. Now I can do nothing right. I do not understand him any more. I am at my wits' end.'

At first Mr and Mrs Warde stayed for some weeks at the Albion Hotel, Brighton's grandest establishment and a very suitable place for a gentleman of Mr Warde's fortune and station in society, with pages bowing and scraping in every corridor. But Mrs Warde found her suite of sumptuous scarlet and gold rooms oppressive and feared that they were far more expensive than they could really afford if, as Charles now said so often, they were paupers.

She tried to talk him into giving up the hotel and looking for something less expensive, but he would not hear of it.

'I am the next High Sheriff of Warwickshire,' he snapped. 'I simply cannot be seen to stay anywhere cheaper than the Albion. I cannot let it be known that we are ruined. *Cheap* is a word I am not meant to know.'

But Marianne was determined to save money and as soon as Charles was absent from Brighton on a mysterious and unexplained excursion to London she went out and rented a small house in Broad Street for the remainder of the holiday.

It was in a backwater, not far from the sea but hundreds of yards from anything that could be called fashionable, but it was cheap, and Mrs Warde lost no time in moving children, servants and all their voluminous luggage on the same day, so that when Charles Warde returned to the Albion Hotel late at night and burst into his room he found his bed occupied by strangers, who sat up in the dark and demanded to know what the devil he was doing.

Mr Warde's mouth hung open. He could not understand what had happened. His key fitted the lock. The room was the same room. He demanded to know what the devil they were doing in his bed. He shouted and stamped his foot and yelled at the top of his voice, 'What have you done with my wife?' and he kept on shouting until the manager of the hotel appeared on the landing in his night-clothes waving a letter from Mrs Warde, which had in it the address of the house in Broad Street.

Mr Warde set off angrily in pouring rain to find out what the devil his wife thought she was up to.

When he found Broad Street he banged on the door and shouted for Mrs Warde for so long that he woke the whole neighbourhood, but Mrs Warde had given orders for no one to be admitted, for all the beds were occupied, and no one came down to let Mr Warde in. In the end he went away, angrier than ever, soaked to the skin, thinking he must have gone to the wrong address, and sat up all night in the smoke-room back at the Albion Hotel drinking glass after glass of Henekey's Cognac Brandy and feeling rather foolish.

When he returned to Broad Street the next morning he was surprised to find he had not been given the wrong address, and he found a pokey house, hideously furnished, smelling of stale cabbage and dead rat, and jammed from top to bottom with the fifty-three enormous leather trunks which they had hauled all the way from Warwickshire in order to keep up the appearance of affluence, spilling his wife's dresses, shoes and jewels all over the floor. And he found his wife flying everywhere, trying to supervise the unpacking and trying to bring order out of chaos. Every room was full of screaming children or quarrelling servants, or both, and every time Mr Warde went in or out of a room he banged his head on the door-frame.

'I hate this house,' he shouted. 'I hate this stinking house.' And while Marianne sponged his bloodied head with Burnett's Disinfecting Fluid (long since the saviour of the family) he shouted at her for not telling him what she was going to do, and for not letting him in the night before.

He shouted at her again because there was no separate room for him to sleep in, and he shouted at her yet again because he was faced with sharing with Mrs Warde and the baby, who was awake and grizzling at all hours of the night. He asked her what she intended him to do, he would not stop talking, and he shouted at her once more, 'Where the devil do you intend me to sleep?'

Marianne bit her lip and said she had got her calculations wrong.

'I am very sorry,' she said, 'I have mistaken the number of

72

rooms. I thought you would not mind sharing a room with me. I thought it would please you.'

Already Meller was having to share a room with Fuller the valet and Mathieu the footman, a potentially explosive situation which Mrs Warde proposed to defuse by arranging as many of the fifty-three trunks as she could down the middle of the room in order to preserve Meller's modesty and to prevent Fuller or Mathieu from climbing into the wrong bed in the middle of the night.

When Charles ran out of breath and had said everything six times, Mrs Warde quietly suggested, 'Perhaps after all you had better keep on your room at the hotel, where you will have more space and less bother. As for me, I shall stay where I am, for I really am determined to economize.'

Charles agreed at once, as if he was anxious to get away from Broad Street as soon as he could, and Marianne breathed a sigh of relief at the thought of a rest from his constant haranguing about his troubles.

The arrangement was, after all, nothing very new, for they had slept in separate bedrooms for years on account of Marianne's delicate health. It was no coincidence that all her children were born in the month of February, as if on some pre-arranged day once every two years she had left her door unlocked for Mr Warde to get in, for this is exactly what had happened.

But Marianne could not imagine *that* had anything to do with Charles's angry behaviour. She constantly told him that she loved him. He could not be in any doubt about that. She did her best not to resent his abuse or his bad temper and she put it all down to being away from home, and to the strain of the Railway business.

Every afternoon, therefore, according to plan, Marianne and the children were collected in the carriage and driven to the Albion Hotel to visit Mr Warde. They all trailed up and down the grand staircase like a happy family, walked on the beach, bathed from a bathing machine, and the children rode in turn on their papa's shoulders. They took tea together, were all perfectly content, kissed each other affectionately goodbye and returned to their separate lodgings to sleep.

But in private, out of the public eye, things were different.

When Charles went to the cramped Broad Street house he would always be awkward and irritable. He complained constantly about the children's noise and said their chatter made his head ache and prevented him from concentrating on the documents he now took wherever he went, so that before long Marianne had to keep the children hidden away when he was coming, or ask the nurse to take them all for a long walk whether it was raining or not.

Mr Warde pored for hours over his correspondence with Lord Bute, who kept asking when Mr Warde intended to complete the contract for Luton Hoo, and kept writing, 'I should like my One Hundred and Sixty Thousand Guineas by the end of the month.'

Mr Warde puzzled and brooded for weeks over his impossibly tangled financial empire which was so complex that no one understood it, least of all himself, and at the same time he wrestled with complex legal papers relating to the County of Warwick, and interminable documents relating to half the Railway Companies in Southern England.

He was snowed under by piles of dog-eared papers, which kept losing themselves, or got out of order, or were knocked on to the floor by five children playing blind-man's-buff, or were gathered up as rubbish and thrown away by the servants, or were simply too abstruse for him to understand.

He had so much on his mind that he began to say, 'This will drive me to Bedlam' and he talked away angrily nineteen to the dozen about his problems until Marianne retreated into herself and stopped listening to him, and tried to think about sewing, or the Warwick Dispensary Ball instead.

She wrote to her sister, 'We have *never* slept under separate roofs before, and I fear we are becoming strangers to one another.'

At the end of the summer the fifty-three trunks were packed up and the Wardes returned home to Warwickshire on the Railway, hardly the better for the change of air, and life returned to normal, or as normal as it could be.

Mr Warde went back to walking the estate all day and made sure that he opened his mail promptly and read his way assiduously through *The Times* every morning. But his manner towards Marianne continued, more often than not, abusive. He would often appear to be the worse for wear from drink during the day, something that had happened only rarely in the past, and he had begun to neglect his appearance, returning in the evenings looking more and more dishevelled, with his collar and cravat awry, and straw in his hair, and grinning mysteriously.

Mrs Warde wrote to her sister, 'Mr Warde is still not himself.'

After the return from Brighton Mr Warde's behaviour grew more and more eccentric. One morning he refused, to Mrs Warde's astonishment, to have anything more to do with family prayers, and there was a gap of a fortnight while she tried to think what to do, and while the servants gossiped about it, until Mrs Warde decided that her husband's eyesight was impaired and announced that she intended to read the prayers in future herself. And she did.

While all the servants were lined up behind the chairs in the dining-room with their eyes tightly closed, praying for peace, or rain, or for whatever was required, Mr Warde would lie upstairs in bed with his eyes tightly closed pretending to be asleep, and only emerged when he was sure that Religion was over for the day.

On Sunday mornings he would try to do the same, pretending to have a stomach-ache instead of going with Marianne to church, and only going when there were visitors, so that she began to keep a calendar of his attendances, and waved it in his face when he refused to go. But he ignored her studiously until she stamped her foot and left the room in a passion.

One winter, Mrs Warde calculated, Mr Warde showed his face in church only eight times in the course of three months, whereas she and the children had clocked up twenty-four appearances, trudging through snow and rain and mud, walking beside the carriage if necessary, in order to hear sermons lasting upwards of an hour or two.

'What am I to say to our neighbours who ask if you are ill?' she demanded. 'What will people think?'

'I do not care what people think,' he replied.

'Am I to tell them lies? Am I to tell them that you are tired of saying your prayers? That you have become an infidel?' But Charles Warde just lay in bed grinning and hid his face behind the Prospectus of the London & Warwickshire Brick Company, and ignored her completely, so that more than once she ended up shouting at him, 'Why can't you talk to me?'

Some Sundays Mrs Warde would be ready for church and standing at the door with a liveried footman to carry her Prayer Book, only to find that her husband had driven out in the carriage not five minutes before and that she would not be able to get to church at all.

When he came back, grinning broadly, Charles would slap his head, frantically consult his pocket watch, exclaim, 'I didn't know it was Sunday!' and squeeze her so hard that she had to tell him to stop. And he would spend the rest of the day talking at her very excitedly at the top of his voice, about the progress of his Railway Shares, or about Ground Rents in Manchester, or the price of corn, going on for as long as six or seven hours without a break.

He waved away servants who came to announce meals, saying, 'Later, later, my wife and I are discussing matters of business,' so that Mrs Warde had to keep on pretending to listen and went hungry.

Sometimes Mr Warde's sentences began but never seemed to end, and the flood of words went on and on. Sometimes he talked so fast that his words fell over each other and did not make any sense at all. When Mrs Warde could bear it no longer and ran weeping from the room Mr Warde would shout after her, 'You see, my dear, I can talk to you. I will talk to you.'

Every Sunday evening Mrs Warde would sit by the fire in the little drawing-room and read the Evening Service to her children, but every Sunday without fail Charles would interrupt them and bang and crash about the room looking for his pocket watch, or pretend to wind the clocks and make them all chime without stopping. He would never join in the service but sat behind Marianne making sucking noises with his cigar, or blowing smoke-rings, or breathing down her neck, or making faces, so that the children giggled and his presence was a constant source of disturbance.

One of these Sunday evenings in particular stood out in Mrs Warde's mind from all the rest. She had been teaching the children the Catechism and they were all laboriously repeating after her the part which contained the words 'The renunciation of the Devil and all his works, the pomp and vanity of this world, and all the sinful lusts of the flesh' when something made her look up and she saw Charles's face leering round the door, and he began to shout at her, 'Before they are very much older I will put a stop to the damned stuff called religion that you are teaching my children' and he banged the door so hard that all the pictures bounced on the walls, and was gone again.

Later, when the children were asleep in bed, Mrs Warde remonstrated with him, 'I was most distressed at your unkindness and I think that if it were not for the children I should go away to my mother and not return.'

Chares Warde smiled a great smile of joy and roared, 'Oh, I wish you would go, and take all the children with you, for it would be a great relief to me to get rid of you all.' And he danced round the room clapping his hands. Then he ran out of the room and down the stairs four at a time and dismissed Harriet Meller and all five housemaids on the spot, shouting 'I am pleased to inform you that your mistress is going away and that your services will no longer be required.'

He threw a handful of sovereigns at them, saying, 'Go on, get out, we don't need you any more. Go and shift your traps. The carriage will be at the door to take you all away in ten minutes' time.'

He then ran upstairs and could be heard pounding along the passages in search of the nurse and nursery-maids, and shouting at them to quit his service as well.

When all the female servants were gathered in the entrance hall, weeping uncontrollably, and Mrs Warde was pulling at her husband's sleeve to try and make him change his mind, he shouted at her in front of them all, that she was 'a damned fool' and he yelled at the top of his voice, 'The sooner you give me a divorce and the sooner you leave me the better,' and he turned on his heel and stormed into the noble library and slammed the door so hard that all the chandeliers in the house tinkled for five minutes.

Mrs Warde, in tears herself, begged the servants to take no notice of Mr Warde, and pleaded with them not to get into the carriage which was waiting to take them to the Railway Station at Coventry. 'He does not know what he is saying,' she sobbed.

'He is ill,' and she ran upstairs wailing and locked herself away in her bedroom yet again.

Shortly afterwards Charles was on his knees announcing to her through the keyhole that he had changed his mind. He said he was sorry, shed some tears himself, begged Marianne to forgive him and to take no notice of his outburst, and said, 'I am going insane' so many times that she agreed to stay with him and look after him, and promised that she would never leave him, and retired relieved and exhausted to bed.

An hour later Charles Warde hurled himself through the door into her room, breaking the lock, and burst out in a strain of very violent language, cursing and swearing at her with such vehemence that she rang frantically for Meller, afraid to scream for fear of what the servants might say down in Stratford, but thinking that this was the end, the end, and that she would be bludgeoned to death with the poker.

But Meller did not come, for she had gone off to the Shakespeare Hotel for a secret meeting with Emily Mathias, and Mr Warde was able to rave and roar uninterrupted until his voice was hoarse. In the candlelight his face was purple with anger, his wrists jerked and shook uncontrollably and made huge shadows on the wall behind him as he shouted, beside himself with rage, 'I do not believe in any religion or any future state. It is all a parcel of damned nonsense, and as I believe that this world is our all I shall take care to make the most of it by enjoying myself in every way I can, for I neither care for God nor for any human being.'

Mrs Warde ran away sobbing to Meller's room in the attics, regardless of the ghosts, found Meller was not there, and collapsed on to the iron bed, where Meller found her still weeping two hours later.

Mr Warde went off to bed as usual, quite calm, as if nothing had happened.

While she was locked away for the night armed with a shotgun Mrs Warde made up her mind to leave Charles for good, but when she emerged from hiding in the morning she found him quite his usual old self: charming, polite, considerate. He made his usual apologies, seemed to have recovered from his rage and was most attentive. Mrs Warde fell in love all over again and put off the evil day, and kept on putting it off.

For another year and a half Mrs Warde dithered between staying and going as Charles's manner alternately improved and deteriorated. He would always apologize for his outbursts, and he always made her the most extravagant presents of diamonds, emeralds, rubies and pearls that she knew he could not really afford, and he made her extravagant promises: that he would keep his temper; that he would consult Dr Pritchard about his health and about his uncontrollable rages, and about his heavy drinking; he promised to drink less and to go to church more, and that he would try to be a good husband to her.

On the one hand Marianne could not bear to live with his unpredictable temper any more. On the other hand she could not bear the thought of life without him either, and she could not bear the prospect of dragging the children away from the Papa they adored. And so she allowed matters to drag on as they were, and did not really know what to do about Charles at all.

When she was ordered by her family not to return to Clopton in April 1847 she was led to think that no Court of Justice would allow such a monster to retain the custody of such tender infants, and she was led to believe that her evidence provided quite sufficient grounds for Charles to be deprived of the custody of his children for ever.

Mrs Warde's solicitors told her she had a very good case, and she at once handed over without a murmur all the money they asked for, before the case of Warde *v.* Warde ever reached the Court of Chancery.

In due course Mrs Warde gathered together her witnesses, trained them up in the art of saying what they had to say, and paid for them to be brought to London so that they could give their evidence against her husband.

Joseph Callaway, yeoman, aged about fifty years, appeared in court in his best suit of corduroy and clutched the edge of the witness-box tightly as he said that he was formerly Bailiff to Mr Warde but was now an independent farmer at Oak Farm, a few miles from Clopton.

His face was grim and his voice shook as he told the court, 'I witnessed my former master doing those things that he ought not to have been doing.'

It was a summer afternoon, 3 June in the year 1841, and Joseph

Callaway was walking along the Coach Road that led up through the park to Clopton House, minding his own business, when he heard the sound of laughter and giggling and was surprised to see a figure so large that it could not have been anyone but Mr Warde lying under the trees at the top of the bank beside the road, and in full view of the road.

Mr Warde was not alone but in the company of a woman who was most definitely not Mrs Warde. Callaway said, 'I knew her by sight and I think her name was Harriet Gilbert. She had on her bonnet. Her face was towards the road. I am certain it was her.'

The two figures were lying down, but they were not lying still.

'My eyesight is not so bad,' said Joseph Callaway, 'that I could not recognize the fact that Mr Warde was in the very act of committing adultery with this girl, for he was lying on top of her. The movements are unmistakable. There can be no possible doubt about it.'

Callaway thought it was most extraordinary that the pair were on view to anyone who should happen to pass by. If they had been two or three feet further up the bank no one would have seen them for they would have been over the top and hidden from the public gaze.

It was as if Mr Warde wanted to be seen, for he knew very well how regularly the carts and carriages came up the Coach Road. It was as if he did not care who saw him, as if he had no shame. Joseph Callaway thought it was all very odd.

Even odder was the fact that Mr Warde *saw* Callaway but made no attempt to get his head down, or cover up his face so that he would not be recognized, but he actually paused in his exertions and waved and nodded most civilly to Joseph Callaway, and raised his hat, for he still had on his hat, and very odd that looked too.

'I was too embarrassed to wave back at him,' said Callaway, 'I didn't know what to do with myself. I turned red in the face. I just looked away immediately and kept on walking up the road as if this sort of spectacle was an everyday occurrence, something that I saw every day of my life in the countryside. There was nothing else I could do.'

Callaway shook his head, as if the story was too much for him to understand even six years afterwards.

'Mr Warde had on all his clothes,' he said, 'and I could hear the jingling of money in his pockets. It is not a thing a man can easily forget. It is still crystal clear in my memory.'

And he testified further, 'Since I have known Charles Thomas Warde Esq. I verily believe that he has been, year after year, plunging deeper and deeper into immorality and vice, and I have frequently heard the same opinion expressed by other people who knew him. Bad women constantly loitered about his grounds and I supposed that they were there for immoral purposes.'

Mrs Warde thought there could be no more damaging testimony than Joseph Callaway's, and she was convinced that she had a very strong case indeed.

And in addition to Mr Callaway's story Mrs Warde had now squeezed out of Harriet Meller the most extraordinary tales about Charles Warde, and she had gone to great lengths to train Meller in the art of throwing her voice and enunciating her vowels properly, so that the gentlemen of the law would not only be able to hear what she said but also to understand it. Mrs Warde had rehearsed Meller's speech and cross-examined her about it every day for a month, so that Meller was as ready as she ever would be for her ordeal, though she quaked in her boots all the same.

Meller told first of an innuendo about Maria, a young kitchen-maid whose surname she never knew, but who went away from Clopton House some years back looking very *stout*.

It was rumoured at the time that it was Mr Warde, the Squire himself, who was responsible for Maria's stoutness; that it was Mr Warde who sent her away; that it was Mr Warde who set her up in a house all of her own at Leamington, and paid all her expenses and gave her a handsome sum of money towards the upkeep, upbringing and education of her child.

But that was not all Meller had to say, for she told next a story that directly concerned herself. It was about the same time – about the year 1838, she thought – that Mr Warde had attempted to solicit her chastity, and she launched into the story of how one afternoon he had grasped her round the waist, how he had thrust his hand under her dress in a most indecent manner, and how she had struggled with him and, in the end, run away.

And there was more than that, for on quite another occasion, when she had been told to take the hot water to the master's dressing-room, he had deliberately and wilfully exposed his person to her.

It was all designed to present Mr Warde in the most unsavoury light and to provide Mrs Warde with the keystone of her case: that Mr Warde had been unfaithful to her with a variety of women, and had committed adultery, and that such a man was wholly unfit to have the care and custody and bringing up of five infant children.

In addition to Callaway's evidence and Meller's testimony Mrs Warde had also what she thought was the tremendous advantage of some seventeen ordinary working women of Stratford-upon-Avon who were sitting outside the court in their Sunday clothes, ready and waiting and fully trained to tell the truth, the whole truth and nothing but the truth about Mr Warde: that he had been unfaithful to his wife with every one of them, and had committed adultery or attempted to commit adultery with all of them in the plantations on the Clopton estate.

Mrs Warde could not imagine how Charles could possibly have had anything to do with such women. They were women she would have had nothing to do with in normal circumstances; women she found disgusting to contemplate and distasteful to talk to. But the women were on her side and supported her case, and these were not normal circumstances.

She had spent the entire month of October travelling in her mother's ancient pony phaeton in her efforts to track down these women in their disgusting hovels in the worst slums of Stratford-upon-Avon and the villages round about, offering the women money and talking them into speaking out on her behalf.

'I don't care how much it costs me,' she said, 'it will be worth every penny if I am enabled to keep my children.' And the field women's stories were so extraordinary and so horrifying that *undoubtedly* the case would be decided in Mrs Warde's favour.

Mr Bury had been quite confident. 'Of course you are going to win, Mrs Warde,' he said, 'you have nothing to worry about, nothing to worry about at all.'

But Mr Bury was quite wrong.

FIVE

In court Mr Warde denied almost every word of his wife's story and refuted almost every bit of her evidence.

'My wife,' he said, 'is a lady of delicate health, which has unfortunately required us to sleep apart for very many years, though these are delicate matters which a Court of Justice cannot enquire into further. Suffice to say that my wife is suffering from a nervous complaint complicated by a number of women's complaints. Her delicate health has been such that during the course of our married life – a period of some thirteen years – she has been obliged to consult so many doctors and medical gentlemen that I cannot say how many there have been in all.

'But the result of it all is this: that my wife is now in a worse state of health than at any other time since our marriage.

'She is unfortunately given to delusions. She had been, until she left me, constantly under the impression that I, her own husband, was on the point of driving a knife into her ribs and seeking to murder her in cold blood.

'My wife is now unfortunately addicted to a very considerable number of medicinal preparations, and also, and most deleteriously, to laudanum, and she is labouring under the delusion that it is these preparations alone which prevent her condition from becoming any worse.

'My wife is now accustomed to spending her days in a darkened room with the blinds drawn from dawn to dusk in a trance induced by a surfeit of medicines. Her judgment is impaired. She no longer knows her own mind. My wife is an incurable invalid.'

Mrs Warde drew the sympathetic glances of everyone in court, and looked indeed the invalid that Mr Warde said she was.

'It is unfortunately true,' Mr Warde continued, 'that I have from time to time been unfaithful to my wife since my marriage, though it was never to the extent that Mrs Warde's counsel would like to believe. And what husband, locked out of his wife's bedroom month after month and year after year on account of his wife's delicate health is so strong-willed that he would not be driven, from time to time, to seek the consolation of women besides his wife, however much he might regret it, however much he might abhor it and find the very idea wholly repugnant, wholly distasteful and wholly disgusting?'

Mr Warde did not appear to be excited at all. He was cool and calm, eloquent and plausible. He was impeccably dressed, and he did not appear to be the monster that Mrs Warde made him out at all.

In contrast Mrs Warde was visibly shaking, hardly able to stand, and had to be supported by Mrs Mathias on one side and Meller on the other, and Meller was armed with the largest bottle of smelling-salts that she could lay her hands on, and was afraid she was going to have to use it.

It was Mr Warde's case that not one of his wife's allegations was true.

Mr Warde's extremely expensive counsel, the eloquent and distinguished Mr Richard Bethell QC, proceeded to attack Mrs Warde's evidence and discredit it systematically bit by bit, for, he said, her evidence was false evidence, her charges were trumped-up charges, and her allegations were the product of a fevered imagination and a deluded mind.

First Mr Warde produced James Beech Esq., a Justice of the Peace and his neighbour in Warwickshire, who swore that he had visited the Wardes every day while they were staying at Brighton and that he had noticed no sign whatever of any unkindness of manner or any irritability of temper on the part of Mr Warde towards his wife, but quite the contrary: they seemed to him to be living on the most affectionate terms and very happy.

Four venerable silver-haired clergymen then came forward to testify that they had known Mr Warde all his life, and they bore witness in glowing terms to the odour of sanctity in which Charles Thomas Warde Esq. lived and moved and had his being.

The clergymen were unanimous in their opinion that Mr Warde's manners became his station in society.

Not one of them had ever had the slightest reason to suspect him capable of any conduct that would be degrading to a gentleman.

They never ever had the slightest reason to think Mr Warde a gentleman of irreligious habits or irreligious notions, for he was a regular worshipper and he was only too pleased to donate the most handsome sums of money – fifty or a hundred pounds at a time – to church funds.

Not only did Mr Warde come to Divine Service with his wife and children most regularly, but he came with all his numerous servants as well, sometimes forty or fifty of them, which the clergy took to be the sign of a very well-conducted household. It was hard to miss Mr Warde in church on a Sunday morning, for he was the largest member of the congregation, had the loudest voice, and his household filled up a very considerable portion of the church.

The Vicar of Stratford, the Vicar of Snitterfield and the Rector of Hampton Lucy had known Mr Warde in public and private for years and years. Between them they had christened all his offspring. They had never once heard the slightest hint or suggestion of Mr Warde indulging in blasphemous or profane or indecent language.

Mr Warde's father, the mild-mannered aged clergyman, was brought forward to swear that his son was educated as a Christian and was taken to church very regularly twice every Sunday throughout his childhood.

He said, 'Mrs Warde's charge that I have brought up my son to believe that this world is our all and that there is no such thing as eternal life, is a charge that is most cruel, most unjust and most untrue.'

Charles Warde himself swore that it was a rule with him *never* to use the carriage on a Sunday, and he could recall only one occasion when he had broken his rule, which was when he had been obliged to travel up to London in order to present a petition in the House of Commons against a Railway Bill which would have brought the Railway Line right through the middle of his pleasure grounds at Luton Hoo.

Mr Richard Bethell QC maintained that it was a common habit for gentlemen to use their carriages on a Sunday and that Mrs Warde's claim that Mr Warde's use of the carriage on a Sunday was evidence of irreligion was an absurd claim. For her to say that Mr Warde was an unnatural parent because he read and wrote opinions on what he read on a Sunday was quite absurd and ridiculous. It was the common habit of almost every lawyer in the kingdom to read and write on a Sunday: many thousands of gentlemen would be guilty of such a charge.

As for the allegation that Mr Warde wilfully absented himself from church during the winter months, Mr Bethell knew from bitter experience what country churches could be like in the winter, and again there were many thousands of worthy gentlemen – and ladies – who would be guilty of this charge of irreligion if Mrs Warde's complaint were to be upheld.

It was an unjustified complaint, and it was a false complaint, for all the clergy testified that Mr Warde's attendance at church had not been irregular at all, but quite the opposite.

Mr Warde was the son of a clergyman; all his own children had been brought to church to be baptized; he was a most liberal and generous supporter of church finances: there was no evidence at all for what Mrs Warde held to be her husband's irreligious outbursts and blasphemous remarks. Mr Warde's habits were not at all the habits of an irreligious man. No one had witnessed anything of the kind.

And the reason for that, of course, was that Mrs Warde had imagined them, or invented them, in order to advance her case, because she knew very well that if she did not do something of the kind she would herself be declared unfit to have the care and custody of the children.

Mrs Warde's charges relating to her husband's bad language were equally without foundation, for not only all the clergy but also all Mr Warde's gamekeepers denied any knowledge of it. The gamekeepers were with a gentleman when he was most likely to be off his guard – if a dog misbehaved, or if one shot very badly, for example – occasions when the temptation to use bad language was so great that many gentlemen were not in the habit of resisting it altogether. And all Mr Warde's gamekeepers particularly drew attention to the fact that Mr Warde was not a gentleman who used profane language, but that he abstained from the foul expressions which were familiar to so many men's mouths.

There was only one voice raised in dissent, which was that of Henry Dunchley, now coachman to the Earl of Lichfield, but formerly Mr Warde's coachman. And what Dunchley had to say was this: 'I did on one occasion hear Mr Warde make use of the word *Damn*, but I have never heard Mr Warde make use of any other words that could be called improper.'

As for Mrs Warde's complaints about her husband's evil conduct and profane language at Brighton, and later, when they returned home, when his extraordinary outburst against the Christian religion was supposed to have taken place – there was not one servant who felt able to come forward and make an affidavit about it. There was not one domestic. Not even Harriet Meller, the lady's maid, who was a person who might normally be relied upon to support her mistress in every difficulty. Not even Harriet Meller could point to one instance of Mr Warde's evil and violent verbal assaults.

There was not a single witness to any of it, and the reason why was the same reason: it was because the charges were false, the stories were fictitious and the alleged offences never ever happened.

What Meller did have to say about Mr Warde was completely discredited, for his so-called assault on her virtue and his so-called assault on her chastity, and the so-called indecent exposure of his person, and the idle story about Maria the kitchen-maid whose surname nobody could remember, were events that took place, if they took place at all, so many years ago, so many years before the present difficulties and disagreements arose, that they could have no possible bearing on the case in question and were quite irrelevant to it.

Not only were these events of more than *ten years before*, but Meller was quite unable to remember exactly when they occurred, and her memory was so bad and her details so few that her complaints were wholly unacceptable in an English Court of Justice.

Not only were there no dates, but Meller had not breathed a word about these extraordinary happenings to anyone. She had not even told Mrs Warde. She had done nothing about her horrid experiences at all. She felt she was so safe and she felt that her honour was so secure that she could continue in her situation. She mentioned what had happened to not a soul. And the sole reason for that was the fact that these were experiences she had invented not six months ago. She had made it all up.

Furthermore, for anyone to even dream of soliciting the chastity of an individual so grotesque as Harriet Meller was quite unthinkable. Meller was at least fifteen years Mr Warde's senior; she was almost old enough to be his mother; some forty years old to his twenty-five at the time when all this was meant to have taken place.

'Miss Meller was not at all a person to inspire thoughts of that description,' said Mr Warde. 'She is not at all a person to inspire amorous thoughts. What she alleges never took place at all.'

The fact was that Meller was almost blind, so blind that she put her eyes in the plate at dinner, and she was quite incapable of seeing any object the size of a man's hand at the distance of two or three yards even with the aid of the strongest eye-glasses in the County of Warwick. So that even if Mr Warde, perhaps by accident, did expose his person to her she could not have seen it. She could not be telling the truth. The evidence made it seem more and more unlikely that Mr Warde could even have dreamed of doing such a monstrous thing.

The charges brought by Miss Meller were so ridiculous that they could not be entertained for a moment longer, and Meller had to retire hurt, before she got a chance to enter into all the horrid details, for the needle brain and eagle eye of Mr Richard Bethell QC had swept on and turned in all their fury in the direction of Mr Joseph Callaway before Meller could collect her thoughts and open her mouth to protest.

Under Mr Bethell's fierce scrutiny Joseph Callaway's evidence collapsed as well, for although he could say precisely when Mr Warde's supposed adultery with Harriet Gilbert took place, it turned out that he was able to supply the precise date only because on the same day he had gone home and made a *memorandum* of it, and he had gone to the trouble of writing down all the details of what he saw.

'Is not this Mr Callaway a most malignant character?' demanded Mr Bethell. 'For he has surely endeavoured to treasure up against some future day the means of assailing Mr Warde and wreaking his vengeance and gratifying his spite against him.'

No man of ordinary honesty went about the countryside witnessing such things – perhaps by accident – and then went home and wrote about them as Mr Callaway had done.

The fact was that Mr Warde's property was crossed by a number of public footpaths which had existed for years, hundreds of years – since the time of Shakespeare – and it was on these paths that the bad women referred to by Mr Callaway had been seen.

Any gentleman whose land was thus traversed by a public path might therefore be accused of being an abandoned character if the kind of accusation made by Mr Callaway was to be given any credit. He would have to produce better evidence than that. No man could be guilty simply because women of ill-repute had been *seen* loitering near his house.

But Joseph Callaway had no evidence apart from what he had already testified. He had only his opinions: 'I believe Mr Warde to be a man without religion or feeling.' It was not enough. Such words could have no weight in a Court of Justice unless they were supported with and backed up by something more concrete than '*the reports I have heard*'.

Mr Callaway's testimony bore all the marks of a man whose only thought was to do Mr Warde an injury. His testimony was utterly unworthy of anything but the strongest condemnation, and his story was cast aside and forgotten.

If Joseph Callaway was 'a most malignant character' what could be said for his daughter, Emma? For he had sent her out into the fields and hedgerows to root about and dig up and collect whatever evidence she could from the women who might have known something about Mr Warde's activities that would be of use to his wife in her campaign.

Elizabeth Lock, a labourer's wife, told the court how one afternoon Emma Callaway had knocked on her door and tried to talk her into speaking out against Mr Warde.

What Miss Callaway said was this: 'Mr Warde is a shabby, dirty fellow and the more you can say against him the better it will be.'

But Mrs Lock said she did not know any harm of Mr Warde.

Miss Callaway then offered her five sovereigns if she would say what she knew, and Mrs Lock asked what it was that she wanted to know.

'Mr Warde pulled out his person and showed it to Mrs Grimes,' said Miss Callaway, 'and we want to know if you ever heard of him showing it to anyone else. That's all we want to get hold of – if we could get hold of that one thing we should not care.'

But Mrs Lock said, 'I never heard anyone say such a thing. I know nothing at all about Mr Warde and I've never set eyes on his person.'

Mrs Lock was none the less dragged down the street by Constable Reason to give the evidence it had been said she could give, and to be interrogated at the house of Mr Lane, the Stratford magistrates' clerk.

A Mr Tibbits read a document to her in a low voice.

'I am very hard of hearing,' said Mrs Lock, 'and I could not hear a single word he said. A Mr Finch gave me a book to hold. I did not know it was a Bible. I did not know I was swearing to anything. They must have muddled me up with someone else. I will swear that Mr Warde never insulted me. He never did me any harm and I know nothing wrong of him.'

Other women told similar stories of being manhandled by the policeman down to Mr Lane's house and of being forced to sign their names to false confessions.

Mercy Houghton, a spinster, of Russell Court, one of Stratford's most notorious slums, was taken to Mr Lane and kept against her will for more than an hour while he fired questions at her.

'Did you not have connection with Mr Warde?' he demanded.

Mercy Houghton denied it indignantly. Mr Lane insisted it was true, and said, 'Ann Davis told us quite plainly that you were up at Clopton every day.'

But Mercy Houghton said, 'I swear that I never had connection with Mr Warde. I swear he never touched me in my life and he never spoke to me but once, which was when I was gleaning in a field belonging to Mr Fisher Tomes during the harvest.'

The tears streamed down her face. 'I know nothing of Mr Warde,' she wailed, 'I have only ever been up to Clopton to pick up sticks.'

Mrs Elizabeth Hodgkins, a labourer's wife, also of Russell Court, told how Joseph Reason had banged on her door one day and said, 'I wants your daughter, Ann Hodgkins.' And she told how she had gone down to Mr Lane's house with her daughter, thinking it must be a matter of some importance if the policeman was involved, and of how Mr Lane had smiled and snapped at her daughter, 'You have been with Mr Warde and had connection with him, is it not so?'

And he had threatened to get Dr Pritchard to examine her if she would not confess it.

A week later Mrs Smith the Stratford midwife had been sent to examine Mrs Hodgkins' daughter and declared, 'Your daughter has never had connection with any man. She is unquestionably a virgin.'

And it was Mrs Smith who had to lead Ann Hodgkins by the hand down to Mr Lane's house the second time because Mrs Hodgkins was too ill to go, and Mr Lane had had to write down Ann Hodgkins' statement all the same:

> I have seen Charles Thomas Warde Esq. but I have never spoken to him in my life and nor did he to me. He never touched me in my life. My Mother has told me and I believe that I was eleven years old last November.

Not one of Mrs Warde's allegations would stick. The charge of irreligion did nothing to advance her cause. The charge of blasphemous and profane language was wholly without the support of witnesses. A charge of cruelty towards the children on the part of Mr Warde was quite out of the question.

It was Mr Bethell's theory of the case that when Mrs Warde's advisers discovered that Mr Warde's confession that he had committed adultery was not on its own enough to win the case for his wife, they were at a complete loss until someone had a bright idea, and that bright idea was this: that the only thing left to do was to try to pin upon Mr Warde some criminal charge and bring him before a Criminal Court.

Thus Mrs Warde's advisers hurried down to Stratford-upon-Avon with the object of proving, or cooking up, two things: first, that Mr Warde had had criminal connection with a child under the age of puberty, and second, that he was guilty of indecently exposing his person to a variety of women.

Both these attempts were miserable failures. There was no question that Ann Hodgkins was anything but a victim of an attempt to pervert the course of justice on the part of Mrs Warde's advisers. There was no proof at all that Mr Warde had exposed his person to Harriet Meller, or to anyone else, for however hard Emma Callaway tried to prove it and however many women she interviewed, all her efforts to help Mrs Warde were unsuccessful.

Mrs Warde's advisers had then opened an office at the house of Mr Lane in order to gather all the vile accusations they possibly could drum up from all the abandoned women of the town, raking about in all the filthy kennels to dredge up the most disgusting stories they could find, in order to prove Mr Warde guilty and to ensure that Mrs Warde was granted the custody of her children.

Every single prostitute in Stratford-upon-Avon had turned up on Mr Lane's doorstep, one after another, every one of them thinking that she too would not mind earning an extra five shillings and being helped to a glass or two of red wine in exchange for making up a tall story about Mr Warde of Clopton House.

The whole case was got together by raking about in the filth of the neighbourhood: there was nothing to be gained by going in detail through the evidence of these seventeen women, whose lies and fabrications could not be taken seriously by any Court of Justice.

And so all Mrs Warde's seventeen low and abandoned women, who had come to London at her expense and on her behalf, had come for nothing, and they had to return to Stratford without having been called to give their evidence at all.

'There is one thing never to be forgotten,' said Mr Bethell. 'So far is Mr Warde from being a notorious evil-liver that he not only enjoys and possesses the respect of the whole County of Warwick, who have come forward to support him in his trouble, but also that Mrs Warde admits out of her own mouth that before she went away to her mother's house in April she never dreamed of any immorality on the part of her husband, or heard the slightest whisper of it.'

All Mrs Warde's actions and all her charges subsequent to quitting Clopton House were governed by the desperate need to justify her removal of the five children, for which, in law, there was no justification at all.

The only thing that could be said against Mr Warde was that on

94

a number of occasions he had been unfaithful to his wife, but that alone did not give Mrs Warde just cause to abduct his children, and it did not give her the right to be granted their permanent custody.

Mrs Warde sat in court with her mind spinning, and felt victory slipping away from her. She shook her head slowly from side to side as she gradually realized what was going to happen.

Mr Warde had spent every afternoon during the month of October 1847 travelling up and down the County of Warwick in his newest carriage in order to visit all his most distinguished friends, and all his colleagues on the Bench of Magistrates.

He knocked on the doors of upwards of a score of luxurious country-houses, all set in extensive parkland, and he was warmly received, and had his hand pumped, and was filled with madeira cake and sherry wine wherever he went.

'My wife has left me,' he announced, as if his hosts did not know already, 'and I am fighting her for the custody of my children.'

The same reply came back every time: 'What can we do to help?'

And out came Mr Warde's pen and paper, and all his distinguished friends and all his colleagues on the Bench found themselves agreeing on the spot to testify in the most glowing terms to the impeccable reputation, the spotless character and the perfect behaviour of Charles Thomas Warde Esq. JP.

A dozen Justices of the Peace travelled to London to testify that they had known Mr Warde intimately for seven years, ten years, for years and years, had met him at Clopton House and elsewhere in society, and at each other's residences, and they were unanimous in their good opinion of him.

Mrs Warde sat in court watching them come forward one by one. She knew them all, and all of them knew her, and yet not one of them so much as glanced in her direction or acknowledged her existence: not James Roberts West Esq. of Alscot Park; not Gustavus Thomas Smith Esq. of Goldicote; not George Skipwith Esq. of Newbold Hall; not even Darwin Galton Esq. of Edstone. And John Branston Freer Esq., who had been so warm and friendly whenever she met him, and always asked so kindly after her children, stood up like all the rest and painted her husband in glowing colours.

Mrs Warde squirmed in her seat as they all said the same thing and made her husband seem as good as gold.

'Mr Warde is a gentleman of an honourable and manly character . . .'

'Mr Warde is altogether a gentleman in his manners and deportment . . .'

'Mr Warde's manners and conversation have always been such as become his station in society . . .'

'Mr Warde has always regarded low or profane language only with disgust . . .'

'Mr Warde has never deviated from the ordinary rules of genteel society . . .'

'Nothing like blasphemy, profaneness or indecency has ever escaped Mr Warde's lips in my presence . . .'

'It is perfectly monstrous to represent Mr Warde as unfit to have the care and custody of his children . . .'

'Mr Warde is of the most manly and straightforward character . . .'

'Mr Warde is a gentleman of the highest honour and integrity . . .'

The Justices of the Peace had all, over the years, donned their smoking-jackets and smoking-caps and played billiards and drunk their brandy and water with Mr Warde in every substantial country house in the County of Warwick. Mr Warde was excellent company and there was not a word to be said against him.

All the Justices of the Peace were impeccably dressed and all of them looked very distinguished indeed.

Mrs Warde's name was not mentioned once, and as she sat there, stunned and shocked by what the Justices were saying, something wound up like a spring inside her head and it crossed her mind that all of her witnesses looked very shabby.

Everyone in court wondered what Mrs Warde could be doing bringing up such a collection of low characters, whom they had passed sitting in a row outside the court looking very gaudy and very out of place, with their faces painted and caked with make-up, and chattering and laughing and squealing at the tops of their voices. Nobody doubted that the Justices of the

Peace were telling the truth about Mr Warde, and nobody doubted that the prostitutes of Stratford-upon-Avon were out to do Mr Warde an injury and to exact their revenge against the magistrate who represented the Law that fined and imprisoned and transported their friends and relations and, from time to time, themselves.

Twelve immaculately dressed servants from Clopton House provided an equally perfect picture of Mr Warde's domestic life, scotching once and for all Mrs Warde's picture of Charles Warde as an unnatural parent.

All the servants had worked at Clopton for very many years, or had known Mr Warde all his life, or had worked for his uncles, and all of them agreed that Mr Warde could do no wrong.

Mrs Roberts, cook and housekeeper, had seen the master scores of times playing with his children. 'He would carry them about on his back,' she said, 'and be as happy as any of them, and as for swearing I don't believe he ever did such a thing.'

Mrs Roberts never ever heard of Mr Warde's women or maidservants complaining that he had taken or attempted to take liberties at all.

'I never heard anything of the sort,' she exclaimed.

Richard Callaway, Joseph Callaway's brother, was Mr Warde's gamekeeper and had known him since he was a child in petticoats. 'I've spent half my life out shooting with Mr Warde and I've seen him hundreds of times playing with his children in the plantations,' he said. 'They would play at hide-and-seek and Mr Warde seemed to be remarkably fond of them. They certainly never appeared to be afraid of him. It is nonsense to say that they might be in any danger from his violence. It is not Mr Warde's habit to swear but quite the contrarary.'

William Brown, Mr Warde's gardener, had also known the master from his childhood. 'I never saw a man, gentle or simple,' he said, 'fonder of his children than Mr Warde was. He was most indulgent and kind to them in every way, wheeling them about in a wheelbarrow, drawing them in their little carriage about the grounds, carrying them upon his back and playing with them just as if he was a child himself.'

Brown went on, 'I have never seen a father and children fonder or happier than Mr Warde and his children was. I have seen him daily when he was at home; I have seen him with his gamekeepers and dogs; I have seen him with his workmen and with his indoor and outdoor servants; I have seen him both when he was angry and when he was pleased, and I solemnly state that I never knew a man less likely to swear than Mr Warde.'

All the servants agreed: Mr Warde's conduct was irreproachable.

Captain Edward Walhouse, of the Army and Navy Club, St James's Square, London, had shot and fished and drunk and visited with Mr Warde and advised and commiserated with him about his marital problems, and he stood up to say, 'I have known Charles Warde since my childhood and I have had ample opportunities of observing his character as a gentleman, as a husband and as a father.

'Unfortunately I know from his own admission to me that he has often had connection with other women besides his wife since his marriage, and that he is, in fact, more addicted to the pleasures of sexual intercourse than most men, but all indecency, even to the extent of talking about such pleasures is, I believe, disagreeable, if not disgusting, to him.

'I utterly disbelieve every one of the charges of indecent exposure. Mr Warde is decidedly a gentleman and would regard the beastliness with which he has been charged with nothing but loathing and abhorrence.'

Jevon Perry Esq., of Goodrich Court in the County of Hereford, testified that he knew Charles Warde perhaps better than any other man. He had travelled with him to Belgium and Paris, had stayed at Westover, Welcombe, Clopton and Luton Hoo and had never perceived either in his general character or in his personal habits the slightest want of manliness or gentlemanliness in Mr Warde.

'I have heard of the charge of beastly indecency,' Perry said, 'with nothing but loathing and contempt and am certain that Mr Warde would regard such things with nothing but disgust. I have seen him countless times playing with his children. I have seen him dancing with them while Mrs Warde played the organ or piano, when he appeared as much a child as any of them. No man could appear a fonder or more affectionate father than Mr Warde did.'

Miss Purefoy Lloyd, Mr Warde's Aunt, had known her nephew all his life and recalled staying at Clopton for months at a time, when Mr Warde always appeared to her to be a most kind and indulgent parent.

'I gave him a child's carriage,' she said, 'and I often saw him pulling all the children round the grounds in it, all of them laughing and squealing with delight. Mr Warde's children had their liberty as other children did. Mrs Warde often spoke of Mr Warde's kindness to her, and she always appeared to be most happy whenever Charles was present.' And she sighed, 'They were always such a very happy family.'

As for Dr Sutherland's investigation into the state of Mr Warde's mental health, he found him by no means in a state to require his medical care, did not order Mr Warde to be kept quiet or free from excitement, and his black carriage and his burly assistants were not needed at all.

'The case was quite out of my line,' said Dr Sutherland, 'for Mr Warde was not mad or anything like it, and he is not mad now.'

Mr Bethell drew particular attention to Mr Warde's remarkable self-restraint, saying that many gentlemen of his acquaintance on being visited by a mad-doctor and being informed that they were proper subjects for his medical care, would without a doubt have immediately kicked the mad-doctor downstairs.

But Mr Warde did not react in an extravagant manner. Mr Bethell found it hard to believe that Mr Warde was the same man as the monster of depravity that Mrs Warde complained about and vilified throughout her evidence.

Mr Warde was not the monster of depravity that Mrs Warde made him out to be at all: he was, as all the Justices of the Peace affirmed, a perfect gentleman.

The Vice-Chancellor of England, presiding over the case of Warde *v.* Warde, lost no sleep worrying over who was to have the custody of the five Warde children. He had already made up his mind.

There was no sign that the children's morals had been damaged by living with their father, and no suggestion at all that their morals would be damaged if he continued to bring them up.

Mrs Warde *said* that such and such a thing was true, but there was no proof.

It did seem to the Vice-Chancellor that Mr Warde had been very excited at the time of the collapse of the Railway Shares, but the Vice-Chancellor thought that the idea of any man talking away for *six or seven hours* at a stretch was an idle story and must be a mere exaggeration on Mrs Warde's part. In fact he thought the whole case against Mr Warde was exaggerated to the highest degree.

The Vice-Chancellor could not forget that the distinguished-looking gentleman standing before him was a Justice of the Peace, a Deputy-Lieutenant and a former High Sheriff of Warwickshire. Mr Warde was in the prime of life, with everything before him to achieve, and he was said to be thinking about standing for Parliament. It would be a severe blow to Mr Warde's career for him to be labelled as The Man Who Could Not Be Trusted to Look After His Own Children. Such a man's career would be completely destroyed at a stroke.

Looking at Mr Warde the Vice-Chancellor thought that the very idea of labelling him as an unnatural parent was completely absurd.

It was true that Mr Warde's fortunes had now recovered, and that his financial difficulties were now over, for Luton Hoo had been resold and Mr Warde was once again in the enjoyment of a very considerable income.

It was true also that Mrs Warde and the Lawes family still did not appear to have the means to educate Mr Warde's children in the most fitting manner for their station in society, and it was true that Rothamsted Park leaked, and its crumbling masonry was a danger, and the house was draughty and unsuitable for children, whereas Clopton House was very well appointed and had every modern convenience.

It would be a great pity if Mr Warde's eldest son were to be brought up away from Clopton and ignorant of the duties he would have to perform when he inherited his father's estates and his father's position in society.

Moreover, Mr Warde did appear to be a most affectionate father. He was wearing a most engaging smile. There could be no doubt that he was a kindly man, the perfect parent that everyone said he was.

Mrs Warde on the other hand looked ill and weak and her delicate health must also be taken into account: how could an incurable invalid take charge of five boisterous children?

The Vice-Chancellor's mind was made up.

Mr Richard Bethell QC spoke his last words on the case: Here were people of rank and station in the County of Warwick who swore that though they had known Mr Warde in public and private for years they knew nothing against him and could declare him with one voice to be incapable of anything degrading to a gentleman. There was nothing like a clergyman or a magistrate on Mrs Warde's side: all her witnesses were discarded servants and low and abandoned prostitutes, who, on account of their conduct and their station in society, were utterly unworthy of credit, so that if the Vice-Chancellor acted on the evidence of these women, or on the testimony of characters like Harriet Meller or Joseph Callaway, he would be doing what all the magistrates of Warwickshire and all the gentlemen who had known Mr Warde and could speak with authority of his habits of life for a very considerable time would unanimously declare a thing monstrously unfit to be done.

The Vice-Chancellor called all five children into court, where they stood in a row gazing up at him with blue eyes, a row of angels with yellow hair, to hear the Vice-Chancellor say that they were *all to be delivered to their father*.

Mrs Warde's frail body seized up like a stopped clock and refused to obey her orders. She let out a prolonged moan and fainted away to the floor of the court with a thud that was muffled by thirty yards of expensive silk dress.

Harriet Meller reached too late for her smelling-salts and screamed for help.

Mr Warde was oblivious to what was happening to his wife. He threw his hat into the air with a whoop, and danced with the five children, whom he had not seen for more than six months, and gathered them up: George Lloyd Warde on his shoulders, Henry Lloyd Warde and Charlotte Purefoy Lloyd Warde under each arm, Ada and Emily Lloyd Warde clutching at his coat-tails, and cried tears of joy.

As the Vice-Chancellor passed them in the vestibule on his way home for Christmas ten minutes later they were still dancing about, beside themselves with delight, and he beamed a broad smile in their direction, went up to Mr Warde and shook him warmly by the hand, patted the little girls on the head and knew that he had come to the right decision.

As Mr Warde's highly polished carriage careered too fast down the Strand, sliding from side to side in the snow, extraordinary howls and whoops of delight could be heard coming from it, so that the passers-by turned their heads and looked at it strangely.

SIX

When Mrs Warde's tears finally dried up she changed her solicitors and lodged an appeal with the Lord Chancellor against the Vice-Chancellor's decision, saying, 'I am convinced that the field-women's reports of my husband's behaviour are true,' and feeling that there was still more to the whole horrid business than she had yet discovered.

She threw all her remaining energy into employing spies to infiltrate the kitchens at Clopton House so that they could report back to her every incident that was in the slightest degree out of the ordinary.

And thus Mrs Warde was informed at once of everything that went on, for everything was out of the ordinary: from what the children ate for breakfast to the number of times they did not say their prayers; from the number of times Mr Warde said *Damn* in front of the children to the number of times he failed to take them to church. And in return Mrs Warde sent the spies sovereigns and half sovereigns, as arranged, and got through a small fortune in loose change.

Meanwhile she instituted proceedings for divorce, stuck to her story and had the low and abandoned women pumped for information and for more details of the monster that was her husband, so that on the morning of 4 January 1848 when the Commission issued under the Seal of the Arches Court of Canterbury opened in the parish church at Stratford-upon-Avon in order to hear and collect the evidence for the divorce, the low and abandoned women, and others, all made sense, did not contradict themselves or each other, and filled their testimony with precise dates and exact locations, while still telling the stern-faced Commissioners nothing but the truth.

Rumour said that Mrs Warde had parted company with very large sums of money in order to get the women to speak out on her behalf at all. Counter-rumour said there had been an unprecedented run on sovereigns, and that Mr Warde had broken the bank of Messrs Oldaker, Tomes & Chattaway at Stratford in order to line the pockets of everyone who could promise to keep his or her mouth shut about what Mr Warde had been doing.

A third rumour circulated the town to the effect that the low women had been very happy to accept payments from both Mr *and* Mrs Warde, and the Commissioners were intrigued to notice that all these pauper women appeared to be wearing brand-new boots, which squeaked as they walked about trying to keep warm, and that they were all sporting new bonnets, which looked incongruous with their worn dresses, though every one of them fiercely denied being paid so much as a farthing for their attendance and their trouble.

The women shivered and complained loudly about the icy church until the Commissioners agreed to adjourn the proceedings to the Shakespeare Hotel, where there was a fire, and there the women sat in a long line on hard chairs outside the chamber of interrogation, adjusting their ill-fitting bonnets, preening themselves, chewing their nails, uncomfortable in their Sunday clothes on a Tuesday, with their stories running through their heads as vivid as lantern slides.

Mary Ann Perkins, a wheelwright's wife, said she was thirty-four years of age and that she did anything she could get in the way of laundrying and dressmaking, though sometimes she did not get any work to do at all, and her husband, who earned seventeen shillings a week, was often out of employ in the winter.

Mr Finch and Mr Bathurst, the Commissioners, asked Mrs Perkins if she knew Mr Warde, and if she had been with him.

'Yes,' said Mrs Perkins, 'I do know him, and yes I did go with him.' And she told how she used to go for a summer walk across the fields to Welcombe, and how she often used to see women of bad character there, just wandering about aimlessly in the fields, pretending to pick up sticks.

'I thought it was more of an excuse to see Mr Warde,' she said, 'there was plenty of winter fuel nearer the town.'

She told how she first went there with a Mrs Brown; that they met Mr Warde, who said they were trespassing on his land, and that they were to go back.

'The next time I saw him,' she said, 'was during the haymaking season in the year 1845, when Eliza Johnson, a girl I had passed the time of day with a few times, came to my door and asked me to go for a walk with her to Welcombe to see Mr Warde. We set off up the Maidenhead Road together.'

'And did Johnson tell you *why* you were going to see Mr Warde?' asked Mr Finch.

'She didn't say why in so many words,' said Mrs Perkins, 'but I guessed partly what it meant. I knew what Mr Warde would do. I knew what he would pay me. I needed the money.'

'And what did he do?' asked Mr Bathurst.

'When we reached the Blue Cap Coppice Mr Warde met us. He was looking at his pocket watch as if there was an appointment made and we was late for it. He didn't say much but straightaway he threw me to the ground and –'

Mrs Perkins was at a loss for words.

'Shall we say "He had the carnal use and knowledge of my body and committed adultery with me"?' asked Mr Finch.

'Yes, sir,' said Mrs Perkins. 'I remember that the ground was very damp and that I caught a chill. It was quite dusk and there was owls swooping about and hooting, but there was light enough to see Mr Warde by, and I will swear it was him.'

'And what did he pay you?' asked Mr Bathurst.

'He give me a half a sovereign, sir,' said Mrs Perkins.

'And what did your husband say to that?' asked Mr Finch.

'Oh, my husband never knew nothing about it!' she exclaimed. 'He was down the Sir John Falstuff all the time getting drunk.'

Ann Davis was put out because she could not get the mud off her dress and had to go in to the Commissioners looking like the agricultural labourer that she was. She wondered when Mr Finch and Mr Bathurst were going to produce their bottle, for the last time she had been through this ordeal by questioning about Mr Warde Mr Lane had given her glass after glass of red wine. This time she could see no sign of anything alcoholic to loosen her tongue at all.

Ann Davis decided not to answer any questions until she was given a drink. She sat with her arms folded and her mouth shut. She was tired of giving evidence about Mr Warde and his affairs.

But when Mr Finch wearily placed five shillings on the table in front of her Ann Davis started talking at once, and her hand closed over the silver.

'I do field-work and such like, sir,' she said, 'and I used to work up at Lower Clopton for Mr Tomes, and during all the time I worked there Mr Warde used to come into the fields where we was weeding and such like and he used to hail us women as we was working, and beckon to us. One time in the winter time he stood at the side of the field in the mud beckoning and heighoing to us nearly all the day.'

'And what did you think of that?' asked Mr Finch.

'Well, I thought it was very strange conduct,' she said, 'but most of the women used to ignore him and say he was half crazed, or did he not have a wife to go home to, or did he not have a job of work to do – and things like that.'

Then Ann Davis stopped talking until Mr Finch produced another five shillings.

'My getting mixed up with Mr Warde all began one day in the haymaking season in the year 1845 when a girl called Ann Dale asked if I would go a walk with her. It was a wet day, I remember, so as we couldn't work. I thought it was strange conduct to go for a walk in the rain so I asked Ann Dale wherever she wanted me to walk to on such a day. Ann Dale says to me, "I'll tell you when I gets you out of the town." And so off we went, up the Maidenhead Road, and when it was too late to turn back Ann Dale says to me, "We be going to Welcombe and we shall meet somebody when us gets there." I stops dead in my tracks and says, "If it's Mr Warde I dare not go with him," but Ann Dale says to me, "If he asks you to go anywhere with him, do you go."'

'And what happened?' asked Mr Bathurst.

'Well,' said Ann Davis, 'I was afraid, as it was the first time, but Ann Dale said I was not to be afraid as she was sure Mr Warde would give me something for my trouble. When he appeared I stood at a distance trembling, getting wet from the rain dripping off the trees, and Mr Warde asked me, "What are you afraid of? I won't do you no harm." And so I went with him into the Coppice and he threw me down and had connection with me upon the ground. My dress got filthy. I screamed and hit out, but there was nobody there to help me and he was squeezing me tight. My hair was full of spiders. Afterwards I ran all the way back to Stratford with my sovereign.'

'And when did you see him next?' asked Mr Finch.

'It was some weeks later,' she said, 'and Mr Warde asked if I could by chance bring him up a fresh young girl or two. I wondered if I wasn't fresh enough or young enough for him any more. I am now only twenty-five years of age. I was put out, so I said I knew of ne'er a one. Then Mr Warde pulled out a half a crown and promised me a half a crown more if I brought him up someone, and half a sovereign for the girl. I thought of Mary Jane Moore, who wasn't very young, or very fresh, but Mr Warde wasn't to know that, and I knew she would be willing enough and I knew she could do with the money. So I took her to Mr Warde. I needed the half a crown.'

Mr Bathurst looked at Ann Davis's boots and asked what she did for a living.

'I do field-work, sir, when I can get it,' she said, 'but I have been out of employ ever since a fortnight after Michaelmas. Mr Gibbs of Avon Hill has promised mother and me work among the turnips as soon as the weather is fine.'

Mr Finch asked about her criminal record.

'I was taken before the Magistrates on two occasions,' she said, 'once for drinking on unlicensed premises, and once in connection with a Mrs Tomkins, who was guilty of keeping a disorderly house. I was kept in Warwick Bridewell for a month to be a witness and after that Mrs Tomkins was sent to prison for nine months and I was set free. When I was let out I turned over a new leaf. I would not now commit any crime. I wouldn't take a girl to the best man that stepped in shoe leather.'

'And what did you tell Moore about Mr Warde?' asked Mr Bathurst.

'All I told her,' she said wearily, 'was that Mr Warde wanted to see her. Nothing more. I didn't say what she'd get from him but she know'd she'd get something, for everybody a'most was talking about him. All these girls, they hadn't a need to go without they'd have liked it. They know'd who Mr Warde was, and what he was, and that he was quite a town's talk. They had themselves to please, but they didn't want much persuading. I wouldn't do anything of the kind now. I've become much better since I was let out of prison last Lady Day. I will swear I am not a common prostitute, and that I haven't been since last Lady Day.'

Mary Jane Moore was just twenty years of age, and a spinster. She wore a gaudy bonnet, a velvet mantle, pink silk stockings, and lifted her dress to her calves, and smiled and smiled, and seemed to be the worse for drink.

'Tell us about yourself,' said Mr Bathurst drily.

Mary Jane Moore took a deep breath and said, 'I am a gay lady and I maintain myself by prostitution. I lodge in Leamington and give my landlady five shillings out of every pound I earn.'

'And tell us about Mr Warde,' said Mr Finch.

'There's not much to tell,' she said, 'except that I had connection with him in the plantations up at Clopton House, but I don't remember much about it. He was not the first man by one or two that I've been with. But I do remember that we argued about the price and in the end he gave me only ten shillings for myself, and two shillings for Ann Davis. It wasn't as much as I was expecting, I can tell you. I could have earned much more by staying put in Leamington.'

Mary Cooper, twenty-six years old and a native of Stratford-upon-Avon, said she first saw Charles Thomas Warde when she was eighteen and walking across the Welcombe fields with a Mrs Worrel, a washerwoman.

'She was telling me all about how Mr Warde gave girls money to go with him,' said Mary Cooper, 'when who should appear but Mr Warde himself. He came up to us, smiling, and he asked my name and address and wrote them down, then he followed me along the Coach Road and sat on a bank holding out four sovereigns to me in his huge hand. I was tempted to take the money but I was afraid. Then Mrs Worrel said, "You'd better take the money, as it will do us both good," and so I went with Mr Warde straight away into the Coach Road Coppice.'

Mr Finch wrote down, 'Had the carnal use and knowledge . . .'

'The money jingled in his pockets and fell out all over the ground, and we crawled about together picking it all up. But Mr Warde never give me the four pounds at all. I got only a sovereign and a half and the half I had to give to Mrs Worrel, who was waiting for me. I was disappointed, but I didn't like to mention it in case he took it back and never give me nothing. The second time it was a sovereign. The third time he give me twelve shillings and sixpence. But that was the last time, for I wasn't going to do it for less than twelve and six. I had my dignity to keep up. I was a respectable girl.'

'And when', asked Mr Finch, 'did you last go to Clopton?'

'Most times I met Mr Warde by accident,' she said, 'but I swear that since I was married to George Cooper six years ago I haven't been nowhere near the place. I was too scared of Mr Warde to go on my own. Mrs Worrel always went there with me. I always expected to see him somewhere about on his estate, though there was no appointment for me to go there – that is, not every time. But I swear I've not been nowhere near Mr Warde for six years now. Once he tried to get me to bring him up Harriet Cox, a girl he seemed to take a most particular interest in, I don't know why, but I wouldn't have nothing to do with it, and I did not take her to him at all.'

Harriet Cox looked pale and drawn and could hardly stand up. Mr Bathurst offered her a glass of water and she sat down and smiled wanly.

'Tell us all about yourself,' said Mr Finch gently, 'and all about Mr Warde.'

'I was born and bred in Stratford-upon-Avon,' she said, 'and as a young girl I used to go to Welcombe to play. It was a favourite place with the children because there were apple trees and crab trees to gather fruit from and to climb up. When I grew out of play I used to go there instead to pick up sticks and it was picking up sticks one afternoon on the Welcombe estate with a girl called Elizabeth Neal that first I set eyes upon Mr Warde. He was sitting upon a block of wood and smoking a big cigar. He had on a talk silk hat.'

'Go on,' said Mr Bathurst.

'We carried on picking up our sticks and working our way right round the field till we came near to where Mr Warde was. He was watching us all the time. Then he stood up and climbed over the gate into one of his plantations. It was a round one. Then he beckoned to me and wanted me to go over and speak to him. I put down my sticks and did as I was asked. I was shaking all over with fright. He asked me lots of questions and asked two or three times how old I was and stood talking to me for over an hour. Then he took out lots of money from his pocket and asked me to go with him.'

'And then?' asked Mr Finch.

'I was afraid to go in among the trees and I just stood there rooted to the spot when Elizabeth Neal came up. I said I would go into the plantation if she could come too. We both started to climb over the gate but Elizabeth Neal turned back when she was halfway over. Mr Warde grabbed me by the arms and dragged me over the gate. My dress ripped. I was shrieking and screaming, but I couldn't get away from him. He had got me tight. He took me into the very darkest part of the plantation, threw me down and had connection with me. I screamed, but not much. There was no one there to hear me except Elizabeth Neal and she would be the last person to come running.'

'And that was the last time you saw Mr Warde?' asked Mr Finch.

'No, sir,' said Harriet Cox, 'a fortnight after that I was walking along the Coach Road on the Welcombe estate with my sister and a Caroline Uwins when we met Mr Warde out walking. He had a great big grin on his face and he said "Good afternoon" in a very eager sort of way, and asked me at once if I was at service.

'"No, I'm not," I said.

'"Would you like to go?" he said.

'"That depends upon the service," I said.

'"Would you like to go and live at my house at Leamington?" he asked. "I will allow you *fifty pounds a year*."'

Harriet Cox's eyes still widened at the thought of it.

'I squealed and said he should be ashamed of himself, for I thought he meant a bad house. I might have been a bad girl but I wasn't going to become a prostitute. Mr Warde looked like a dog that had burned his tail and he just turned on his heel and strode away without another word and that was the last I heard or saw of my fifty pounds a year. I found work instead at Warwick, as assistant to Mr Clark the baker there, and I spent the next twelve months wishing I had asked more about Mr Warde's house at Leamington, for Mr Clark paid me just five pounds ten shillings a year. One September I saw Mr Warde at the Warwick Races and he sent me a note on the race-course, saying I was to go over to Clopton at once about becoming a servant there, but my master, Mr Clark, forbade it, and I never did go.'

'And instead you became a common prostitute at Warwick,' said Mr Bathurst.

'I'll swear I was *not* a common prostitute before I went into service at Warwick, or indeed while I was there,' she said. 'I'll swear I've never had connection with any man, except twice with Mr Warde, and also twice, nine months ago, when my master, Mr Clark the baker, came into my room on two separate occasions and took advantage of me while I was asleep.'

Harriet Cox wiped away her tears.

'Mr Clark turned me out on to the street just before my confinement, a few weeks ago. I am now living at Stratford with my mother, who is a widow with eight young children. Dr Pritchard said I was not fit to be moved and shouldn't come down here to the Shakespeare at all, but I was fetched here with a summons and told I must come down whether I was fit to come or not.'

Mr Finch asked Harriet Cox how old she was.

'I am seventeen years of age, sir,' she said.

Elizabeth Southam, a milkman's wife, had known Mr Warde ever since he came to live at Clopton as she lived in one of his cottages.

'It was in the damp misty weather of the year 1841,' she said, 'that Mr Warde called on me while I was in the middle of milking my cows, and my husband was away delivering milk to our regular customers. I let Mr Warde into the house to inspect some repairs that had been finished a few days before, but no sooner was he over the threshold than he grabbed hold of me round the waist and whispered in my ear, "You are a nice little woman, but I suppose you are aware of that." He then sat down upon a kitchen chair, grinning all over his face, and he pulled me upon his knee and thrust his hand under my skirts in a very indecent manner. I screamed blue murder and my free hand flew up to scratch his face. There was five lines like railway lines right down his cheek, oozing blood. He put up his hand to protect himself and I managed to pull myself away from him and run screaming out of the door into the garden. It was pouring with rain but I stood out there until I was quite soaked to the skin. I wasn't going to risk going inside. I'd heard a lot of stories about Mr Warde. My hair was bedraggled. My dress stuck to me. But there was no one about to hear me screaming or come to my help. There was not a sound but the lowing of the cows and the rain beating on the tin roofs.'

'What happened?' asked Mr Bathurst.

'Mr Warde then came to the door of my cottage with a cigar in his mouth and he stood there quite calm, holding a large white handkerchief to his bloody cheek. He seemed in no hurry to go away. He just stood there in the dry of the doorway and pulled out a quantity of money from his pocket and held it out to me. He said, "I will give you anything you like if you will give up to me." I could see he wanted to have connection with me.

'But I said, "No, sir, it's not money that would tempt me to do any such thing."

'He then asked me if the upstairs rooms had been repaired as well.

'I said, "Yes, sir, they have been whitewashed," and he asked me if I would be so kind as to show him what had been done, but I wasn't going to fall for that one and I said, "I will do no such thing, but there is the door and you can go up on your own if you please."

'But he didn't bother going upstairs. He put half a crown upon the table and said, "There's something for the trouble I've given you." I screamed at him then, for I was in a great passion. I said, "No, sir, I don't want your money, you may take it away."

'Then he said, "You may come inside now, for I'm going." But I didn't trust him an inch and I said I would go in when he had left. At last he went out of the front door and I went in at the back, and I slammed and bolted both doors and just sat down in my wet clothes in the kitchen, dripping water all over the floor until my husband came home. I told him all about Mr Warde's visit.'

Mr Bathurst enquired about Mrs Southam's religion.

'I am a Baptist, sir,' said Mrs Southam, 'and I attend Chapel most regularly four times a week.'

Isabella Grimes' complexion was famous in Stratford-upon-Avon as surpassing that of any lady, and was achieved without resorting to artifice of any kind, and was enough to make Mr Finch and Mr Bathurst sit up.

'Tell us what Mr Warde did,' said Mr Bathurst.

'Well,' said Mrs Grimes, 'he came to visit me at Clopton Cottage, didn't he? The first time was not long after his return from Italy, about the year 1840 or 1841, and then he behaved himself like a proper gentleman. The next time I remember was in the great heat in the year after my baby was born, so it must have been about 1846. Mr Warde came right up to the privet hedge that separates my garden from one of the plantations, about a quarter of a mile from Clopton House, and he spoke to me while I was hoeing in the garden.

'He said, "What a nice young woman you are, to be sure. You didn't ought to be working in the garden. What a prize your husband has," and a quantity of rubbish such as that. He asked me, "Why do you always hide when you see me coming? What are you afraid of? I won't do you no harm," and I told him I thought his intentions wasn't any good. Then he held up five pounds in gold and said to me, "I'll give you this if you'll come to the gate and give me a kiss." Five pounds for a kiss! It was as much as my husband earned in months. But I told him I was not to be tempted by his money, for that I was poor but I was determined to be honest. But Mr Warde kept talking to me over the hedge and told me I was a silly woman. He didn't seem to want to go away and he didn't seem to want to take no for an answer. After ten minutes I got tired of being stared at and went indoors, but he was still there half an hour later, hanging about, grinning away and whistling, and rattling the money in his pockets. The sweat was pouring off him for it was a very hot day.'

'And what happened after that?' asked Mr Finch.

'He came to my house many times after that, and he used to stand outside singing, and dancing up and down upon the spot in order to get my attention. When he saw me looking out at him from the door or window he would hold up his five pounds and wave it at me, and grin and beckon to me. He had a desperate way of beckoning with his head, backwards like, like this.'

And Mrs Grimes demonstrated, contorting her neck round and jerking it backwards repeatedly.

'I thought it was a very strange way of carrying on, sir,' she said. 'Mr Warde's last visit was one evening in April 1847, about six o'clock, when I was on the point of going to draw some water up from the well, when I caught sight of Mr Warde waiting for me in the waggon hovel, which I would have to pass on the way. I put off getting the water for as long as I could, but I was annoyed with him for interfering with me all the time, and so I ran across the road to Mr Tomes's farmyard where my husband, Joseph Grimes, who was then Mr Tomes's waggoner, was grinding beans for the horses in the loft over the stables. I told my husband, "I am going to fetch up some water and I hope you will follow me to see if Mr Warde insults me." And then I set off. As I passed the waggon hovel sure enough Mr Warde called out, "Come here, come here" to me several times over. I put down my buckets and said, "Now, sir, you've insulted me a great many times without reason, and now I'm determined to have a stop put to it and I want you to tell me what you mean by it."

'I'd hardly got the words out when I glanced down and I saw that Mr Warde's trousers was unbuttoned and his private parts was exposed in a most indecent manner, and I saw that he had lots of money in his hand. I thought, "Oh my Lord" and my hand sprang up without my thinking about it and I slapped the Squire's stupid grinning face. I turned away immediately and at the same moment my husband came up out of the rick yard round the corner of the waggon hovel and he was not in the best of tempers. I didn't stop for an instant but went on to get my water.

'My husband was in time to see Mr Warde fumbling at the fore part of his trousers and said, "Hollo! What are you up to here?"

'Mr Warde said, "I was only enquiring about the baby," and smiled a lot.

'My husband said, "The baby's nothing to you. It's not that you're after, you're after my missus, and if you can't keep away I'll see if I can't make you," and he picked up a pitchfork and said he would have used it, only Mr Warde was at his most terribly polite and grand and charming.

'Mr Warde said, "I didn't mean no harm to Mrs Grimes by offering her money. It was all a joke." But my husband roared that it was not a joke at all and it wasn't the first time by a many that he had offered me money. He had tempted me in every way to take it. Mr Warde just smiled his most superior smile. He didn't deny he'd offered me money, but he just laughed it off. He said, "Pooh, pooh!" and smiled down at my husband and said, "Don't you say nothing about it, and I won't, and I'll give you a handsome present," and he held out half a sovereign to my husband, who touched his hat and took the money, and said, "You are a gentleman, sir, thank you, sir."

'Mr Warde said nothing more than this: "I will forfeit ten pounds if ever I come on such an errand again," and he went off towards Clopton House still trying to do up his trousers. Two weeks later Mr Tomes gave my husband the sack, saying he found no fault with him, but must get rid of him "for other reasons" though he never told us what they was. My husband was convinced he was dismissed on account of Mr Warde, who made up some story about me receiving stolen butter from Mr Tomes's larder, which was quite untrue. My husband now works for Mr Hardy, the corn and coal merchant in Stratford, and he is much better pleased, for he never liked his old situation very well and he never liked Mr Tomes very well, nor Mr Warde neither.'

'What is your religion?' asked Mr Finch.

'We are Wesleyan Methodists,' said Mrs Grimes, 'and we attend the Class Meeting regularly every Monday night, the Lecture regularly every Thursday night, and we go regularly to Chapel twice on the Sabbath day.'

Catherine Goodwin, formerly upper housemaid at Clopton House, told the Commissioners that it formed part of her duties to go into Mr Warde's bedroom at eight o'clock precisely every morning in order to light his fire.

'I remember that in general Mr Warde slept apart from his wife, sir, and in a different part of the house, and that he used to lock himself in for the night. When I knocked on the door Mr Warde would in general get out of bed, unbolt the door, get back into bed again, tell me to come in, and I would go in and spend the next fifteen minutes wrestling with the pages of the *Warwick Advertiser*, which never seemed to be quite dry, trying to light the fire. I never liked lighting Mr Warde's fire, sir.'

'Why not?' asked Mr Bathurst.

'I was afraid, sir,' said Mrs Goodwin, 'and I'll tell you why. I can remember quite clearly three separate occasions when Mr Warde raised himself up in bed grinning all over his face, and held up a sovereign in his fingers, or between his teeth, and said, "Wild, come here, come here" to me (Wild was my maiden name, sir) and beckoned to me to go over to him. He never said any more than that, but I understood from his manner that he wanted me to go over to him for an improper purpose, I suppose to have sexual intercourse with him.'

'And what did you do when he said that to you?' asked Mr Finch.

'Sometimes I just didn't answer him, sir,' she said, 'but I used to pretend I hadn't heard. Sometimes I said, "No, sir, I'd rather not" or "No, thank you, sir." I was so scared of what might happen to me that the footman, George Goodwin, used to have to come and clean the lamps on the stairs while I went in to light the fire. I thought Mr Warde would be less likely to interfere with me if he could hear the menservants whistling and banging about outside his room. I was continually afraid of Mr Warde's violent manner, and George Goodwin was there expressly to protect me, and he had the poker by him ready to rush in and rescue me the moment he heard me scream.'

'And did Mr Warde ever lay his hands on you?' asked Mr Bathurst.

'I can't say as he did, but he used often to say "Come here" when he passed me in the passages, and he would grin a lot and leer a lot and he hissed indecent suggestions in my ear as I went by.'

Mr Finch asked, 'If life at Clopton was so terrible, why did you not leave Mr Warde's service?'

'I only stayed because Mrs Warde was such a good and kind mistress to me,' said Mrs Goodwin, 'but I did leave when Mrs Warde went away, and now I keep a beer shop with my husband, George Goodwin, who I married two years ago, in London.'

'And why,' asked Mr Bathurst, 'did you never tell Mrs Warde of what went on, or complain to her about it?'

'It was for fear of hurting her feelings,' she said, 'and for fear of causing unhappiness between Mr and Mrs Warde. They was unhappy enough as it was, sir, I didn't want to make it no worser.'

*

Ann Parsons had also been a housemaid at Welcombe and Clopton for longer than she cared to remember, but she recalled Charles Thomas Warde often visiting his uncles as a boy.

'I don't remember Master Charles taking no liberties with me back in them days,' she said, 'but I do remember his very impudent tongue. It was later that the trouble started. Later, when I was taken into Mr Charles's service, one day – it would have been 1837 or 1838 – I was sent over to Clopton House to prepare for the moving in. I was sweeping the floor in the big drawing-room upstairs when Mr Charles stuck his head round the door and grinned at me. He then crept into the room on tiptoes and shut the door carefully behind him. And then he suddenly grabbed me round the waist and began to pull me about. He was saying, "Thorns, Thorns (Thorns was my maiden name, sir) – Thorns, you are so beautiful, oh Thorns" all the while, and he tried to throw me down upon the floor and pull up my clothes. I was determined not to let him do anything of the kind. I remember there was no sofa in the room at the time and no carpet down on the floor. The room was quite bare. I screamed the house down, but it was no use for the place was quite empty and he knew it. My voice just echoed back to me. Mr Charles hung on tight and kept on kissing me, and I kept on screaming, and he was saying, "Oh Thorns, Thorns" and a whole lot of rubbish about my soft soft skin. I scratched him and fought him off for ten minutes or so till at last he gave up fighting me and ran off down the stairs. I didn't tell nobody what had happened but after that he left me quite alone and didn't try to interfere with me no more for a long time, not until I was married to William Parsons, who is an agricultural labourer, and then Mr Charles started again coming down to my house, Welcombe Lodge, which was down on the main road, in order to pull me about, or try to. He used to try to put his hand up my dress and he used to offer me huge sums of money. He would come to the door and ask me, "Thorns, what o'clock is it?" in spite of my name not being Thorns no more but Parsons, and if he saw there was no one inside with me he would march in as bold as brass and put his arms around me and sweep me off my feet and try to kiss me.'

'Is that all?' asked Mr Bathurst, for Mrs Parsons had stopped talking.

'No, sir, that is not all,' she said. 'One time he came down and his trousers was unbuttoned, and I saw his private parts. I do remember that his trousers was not like most gentlemen's trousers, which have a kind of flap – what they calls "pigsty doors" – but his trousers buttoned straight up the front. Anyway, as soon as I saw his private parts was exposed I used to run straight out the door and into the road, the *main road*, and I stood there until he got bored and went away. I always told him he should be ashamed of himself and that I would go directly and acquaint Mrs Warde with what he had been doing, but I never did, for I was afraid no one would believe me and think I was making up idle stories about the Squire, and I was afraid of losing my situation, you see. It was such a very odd thing for a respectable gentleman like Mr Charles to be doing. My husband always used to say to me that Mr Warde was a madman. I don't think as he ever said anything on those occasions but "Ann, what o'clock is it?" and then he began to unbutton his trousers and bring out his person.'

Harriet Meller complained that it was not a lady's maid's job at all to take hot water to the master's dressing-room, but the butler was away in the Isle of Wight seeing to the packing up of all the boxes and boxes of things to be brought to Warwickshire.

'I only took the water under protest in the first place,' she said, 'but there was no one else to take it but me, and so I stood there outside Mr Warde's door with the jug burning my fingers afraid to go in. I knocked and waited. It must have been the year 1838, when I was nearly forty years of age, but I cannot now remember for the life of me whether it was morning or evening, daylight or candlelight, or whether Mr Warde was dressing for dinner or undressing for bed, or anything about when it was, except that it might have been June or July, and the water was hot water, and that Mr Warde had rang for it and it was me what took it to him. As I turned to go Mr Warde stood up (he was sitting at the dressing-table) and came close up to me. I was astonished to see that he wasn't wearing nothing but his day shirt and he didn't have on no trousers at all – no stockings, no shoes, nothing – and that his private parts was quite exposed to me. I could see them distinctly. I won't swear that he lifted the shirt-front up, at least I didn't see him do it, but the shirt-front was raised up and his private parts was exposed to my view. It was one of his Ford's Eureka Shirts that he always swore by. The tails of them was so very long that they don't never come untucked. I do remember that before he got those kind of shirts that his shirt-tails was always a-hanging out.'

'And what did these private parts look like?' demanded Mr Finch, as if he doubted whether Meller had seen them at all, and doubted whether she could have seen them.

Meller paused in the flood of words, wondering whether she should say it, not knowing how to say it. And then she blurted out, 'They was big, sir. If they hadn't of been I shouldn't hardly have been able to see them should I? They was very big indeed.'

Mr Bathurst cleared his throat loudly.

'Go on, Miss Meller,' said Mr Finch.

'Well, sir, Mr Warde didn't utter a single word and I wondered what on earth was going to happen. I was very much hurt and flurried at what I saw and I turned away at once to get out of the room as quick as I could before anything did happen, before he could try anything. I knocked over the water-jug, the wash-hand stand, the towel rail and two chairs in my hurry and panic, and I broke my eye-glasses in two so I couldn't see nothing at all. I stood outside the door panting. I didn't know what to do.'

'Did you scream?' asked Mr Bathurst. 'Did anyone hear you?'

'I don't remember,' said Meller, 'I don't know. I hardly knew what I was doing. But I will swear that Mr Warde's exposing his person to me was not an accidental thing at all, but quite deliberate, and that he must have done it on purpose. I never saw anything like it in my life.'

Before she went on Meller was given a glass of water, which she gulped down before taking a deep breath and launching into the tale of her second adventure.

'It was a Sunday afternoon when we was still living at Welcombe, and all the family had gone off to church at Snitterfield and there wasn't nobody left at home but Mrs Roberts the cook and me, and Mr Warde. I spent the afternoon quietly reading the newspaper in the housekeeper's room, with my new eye-glasses and a magnifying glass in my hand until I heard Mr Warde come into the room. His shoes made a particular creaking noise of new leather. I didn't take no notice for he used often to stand quite still at the door while I was there a-reading or a-sewing, and he would sometimes stand for ten minutes without uttering a single word. *Why* he did it I can't imagine. I don't think I can explain why he did any of the odd things he did. He was a proper conundrum. Anyway, this time it was different. Mr Warde came over to me and all of a sudden put his hand round my neck. His hands was quite smooth and silky, not like a working man's hands at all, for he hadn't never done a day's work in his life time. I froze stiff. All the horrid stories that people whispered about him came flashing through my head all at once. My newspaper flew up in the air. My new eye-glasses was smashed on the floor and my only thought was to get away from him, to get away, and my nails – specially sharpened for such an occasion as this – flew up to Mr Warde's face to scratch his eyes out. But he was too quick for me and he caught my hand as it went up. He passed his hand round my waist and squeezed me very tight up against him and asked me to go with him. I think his actual words was, "Meller, come with me and let us go and do it" or words to that effect, but I quite understood from his manner altogether that he requested me to go with him for an improper purpose, namely to have sexual intercourse with him. I could not allow that to happen. I could not. I said never a word but I just wrenched myself away and tried to get out of the room. Without my eye-glasses that was not very easy. I banged about the room and knocked over most of the furniture before I found the door and flew up the stairs to my room. I sat panting upon my iron bed, thinking I was safe, trying to get my breath back, but five minutes later I heard the door-handle slowly turning. I had forgotten to turn the key in the lock. I felt like all my hair was standing up on end. Then there was a loud creak and Mr Warde's grinning face came round the door and the rest of him came after it. He nearly filled my tiny room. I screamed and screamed and sprang up, thinking this is the end, there's no escape, and I tried to push past him and get out of the room, but he put up his arm to stop me.

"'Meller," he said, "I will not hurt you," and he held out his great hand to me. I am not so blind that I cannot see the glint of

122

money, and I could see quite clearly that there was two gold sovereigns in his hand. His hand was close up to me, almost touching me. I was scared to death. I shrank back against the wall, screaming my head off, shouting, "No, sir, No. No, sir, No. Pray leave the room, sir."

'And then he said, quite calm and innocent, "I have only come to bring you your eye-glasses, Meller," and he brought them out from behind his back. They were not smashed at all. And then he left the room and I slammed the door and locked it. And then I could make out the shape of the carriage coming back from church, with Mrs Warde and the children walking beside it, and the next minute the house was full of people again and I was safe. After about an hour I composed myself and went downstairs and went about my business, though I didn't go nowhere near Mr Warde. I was upon my guard after that. Later Mr Warde swore he left two sovereigns upon the painted chest of drawers in my room, but there never was a painted chest in my room, for the simple reason that the room is too small for anything but a bed and a chair. The sovereigns must have been still in his hand when he left the room and I was damned if I could find any money in my room at all. I will swear that I never took no money at all from Mr Warde for my trouble and I never received nothing from him in return for my upset.'

Joseph Callaway told the Commissioners it was only when Mr Warde was at Clopton that his estate was infested with women of bad character, and that when he was in London or abroad they would come as usual for a day or two, until they discovered he was away from home, and then the whole property would be quite deserted until he came back.

'I have often seen Mr Warde making signals to these girls,' said Callaway. 'They would often come to a place called Greenhill, from where it was possible to look down on to the gardens of Welcombe House and see Mr Warde playing with his children. But he would be quite happy to stop playing hide-and-seek and send the children away when one of these women appeared up on the hill. He would point in a certain direction with his stick, the girl would move off in that direction, the children would run indoors and Mr Warde would hurry off in hot pursuit of his bad woman.'

'You seem to have spent a good deal of your time observing Mr Warde's behaviour,' remarked Mr Finch.

'I have,' said Mr Callaway, 'and I should observe that it was always a rule that I followed and which all the gamekeepers and outdoor servants followed – that we were never to watch him, and never to follow him ourselves. It was I that ordered them not to. And in consequence whatever I did see was always quite by accident. It was impossible not to see what was going on, for Mr Warde was quite open about it, and it went on almost every day of the week, for the place was quite overrun by women of bad character. At times they were almost queuing up to see Mr Warde. I don't know the names of all of them but I've heard the farm labourers call them by various nicknames. They would say, "There goes Gabby Goole, or Chocolate Shuke" or, "Gooseberry Eye has just gone by" or there would be a sighting of "Nutty" or "Ducking Dale" on the horizon going towards Mr Warde. It was common knowledge and the talk of the whole town of Stratford that these women were always hanging around Mr Warde. I swear that what I observed on 3 June 1841 was quite accidental, and it is quite untrue that I was following Mr Warde and quite untrue that I was spying on his private affairs. Mr Warde and the girl Gilbert were some twenty-five yards away from me. I saw them quite plain. The girl's petticoats were all up and I could see her bare legs exposed and thrashing about wildly, and Mr Warde's legs all tangled up with them. They were both laughing and making such a lot of noise that it would have been hard not to notice them. Mr Warde was as busy as a cat in a tripe shop.'

'And what about the writing down of all the details?' asked Mr Bathurst.

'It was the result of my having seen Mr Warde so many times with one or other of these women that I decided to keep a count of them all, but my son discovered my notes and asked me what they were, so after a time I stopped making any notes at all. I will swear that I bear no grudge against Mr Warde. I never tried to talk William Brown into speaking out against him. I never asked him any such thing, for he was quite in his dotage, but what I will say about Brown is this: He had been a kind of labourer about the gardens at Welcombe and there were two girls under him that we used to call Brown's Girls, though their names were Johnson. One of these girls died suddenly and our conversation was about them. I asked Brown which of the two girls it was that died and Brown said, "It's the naughty one – not Eliza but Harriet." What Brown said to me was this: "Well, Mr Callaway," he said, "all the time I was in Mr Warde's service I never saw any harm of that man, but if that girl was alive she'd have something to say."'

William Fuller, now of the George the Fourth Public House in Brixton, licensed victualler, but formerly butler and valet to Mr Warde, was examined on the subject of Mr Warde's linen.

'I have looked after Mr Warde's wardrobe,' he said, 'in France and Italy, in London and Paris, at Brighton and at home at Clopton and Welcombe, and at a score of other places. His clothes was the most handsome and most expensive clothes money could buy, but it was a cause of great worry and trouble to me that his clothes were so often plagued with mysterious stains and marks, irrespective of whether he was at home or abroad, or on his estates in Ireland.'

Mr Finch asked Fuller about the women of evil reputation.

'I have seen them, sir,' said Fuller, 'very often, but I always used to avoid watching them. It was none of my business. I know nothing about Mr Warde's employing procuresses to find him young and fresh females, but I will say this: that I have observed that when Mr Warde returned home from his walking, his clothes would invariably be soiled and stained in such a manner that it left no doubt upon my mind that he had been having sexual intercourse upon the ground, for there was green and dirt and other stains upon his trousers, and upon the flaps of his coat, and upon his hat, which could not have got there in any other way. It was my job to deal with these stains, though there was never ever a word spoken about it between us. Mr Warde would just step out of his trousers and leave them lying upon the floor of his dressing-room for me to pick up and take away. Or he would just say, quite brisk, "Fuller, clean up these trousers."

'I have observed these marks at different times, and, I may say, repeatedly throughout the whole time of being in Mr Warde's service. In fact there was no mystery about the marks on his clothes at all, for it was quite obvious what he had been up to.'

The Commissioners' last visitor was a witness of a very different calibre. When John Bennet Lawes Esq. came into the room Mr Finch and Mr Bathurst stood up for the first time, shook Mr Lawes warmly by the hand and invited him to sit down.

'Upon my oath,' said John Bennet Lawes, 'I have never entertained any animosity at all towards my brother-in-law. I have never expressed any such thing and would be glad to serve him even now. Far from wishing to disgrace or vilify him I have done everything in my power to avoid unpleasant publicity and to get an amiable settlement of these proceedings if possible.'

Amongst other things he told Mr Finch and Mr Bathurst of his visit to Charles Warde at the Grosvenor Hotel on the night of 6 May 1847.

'I had an interview of nearly three hours with him upon that occasion, and he was in a most excited state throughout. He spent a third of the time upon his knees, and talked and talked as if he was never going to stop. He admitted to me in the course of this interview that he had carried on an adulterous intercourse with various females and said to me, "I didn't think there was any harm in it, for that my wife was the only woman I ever loved or cared for. I used these women in the same way as I might smoke a cigar." These were as nearly as possible Mr Warde's actual words. His conduct was very candid at that time. He said to me last of all, "Make me as bad as you please, you can't make me worse than I am."'

In March 1848 Mrs Warde was granted a divorce by Sir Herbert Jenner-Fust in the Court of Arches on account of her husband's most profligate course of adultery, about which there could be no doubt, for Mr Warde had himself admitted his guilt.

All the evidence proved that Mrs Warde was an amiable lady of irreproachable character, who had sought to promote her husband's happiness in every way she could.

The learned judge said it was in vain for him to go in detail through the countless disgusting scenes in which Mr Warde had taken part, for there could be no question that Mrs Warde's witnesses were telling the truth.

Some dispute arose as to exactly what Mr Warde's income was. Mr Warde did not know. 'I have not the faintest idea what it is,' he said. 'The money just flows into my bank without my having to lift a finger. I never have to think about how much things cost.'

Ultimately the court agreed to fix his income at something in excess of £5,000 per annum, and awarded Mrs Warde the sum of £1,200 per annum permanent maintenance, a sum that was beyond the imagination of most of the people present in court, and which seemed to be vastly in excess of any lady's requirements.

Mrs Warde retired exhausted but triumphant to Rothamsted, spent a week in a darkened room recovering from the strain of *everyone* knowing what had been going on, and was able in due course to pay for the complete re-roofing of her mother's house, the replacement of the crumbling masonry, and for the restoration of the suite of very grand rooms that had been occupied by the Prince Regent and had been damaged by damp and wet rot.

She fitted out a brand-new nursery wing and spent five consecutive days closeted with her new solicitors discussing how she was going to get her children back.

Mrs Warde's mother suddenly started appearing in new dress after new dress and disappeared one day on an extended tour of Italy, leaving a note which said she did not know when she was coming back.

Mr Warde, his finances now fully restored, and with an income one thousand times greater than that of Harriet Cox the baker's assistant, was now free to devote his endless spare time to the woman who had brought about the collapse of his marriage in the first place: The Woman from Brighton whom he had supposedly promised to marry.

Miss Anna Maria Cobden Hooper was a young lady who, like the young ladies in the plantations up at Clopton, had been tempted by Mr Warde's money, and she too was looking forward to her first taste of luxury.

SEVEN

On 9 May 1848 raven-haired Anna Maria Hooper, known to some as The Brighton Belle, dressed up to the nines and left her mother's house for the last time, thinking she had made her fortune, and was driven in style to the railway station in order to join the assembled household of Charles Thomas Warde Esq., who had been staying at the Albion Hotel in a suite of the grandest and most expensive rooms with all his children but without any wife, and was now on his way home to Warwickshire.

A mountain of the finest leather luggage, fifty-three trunks in all, was piled upon the platform with a dozen liveried servants to attend to it. When Anna Hooper made her entrance all eyes turned in her direction, for she was resplendent in the most expensive scarlet silk from head to toe.

Nobody knew who Miss Hooper was, but Mr Warde condescended to introduce her as the new nursery governess, and then wandered away, more interested in the arrival of the train, and went off to talk to the engine-driver.

Miss Hooper's fellow servants looked her up and down curiously, wondering where a nursery governess got the money to pay for such a dress, and they interrogated her about her past, received a few off-hand answers, and quickly came to the conclusion that Miss Hooper's qualifications for the post of nursery governess were precisely nil.

They had no illusions about who the scarlet woman was, or what she was, for Miss Hooper showed little interest in the five children who raced squealing about Brighton railway station quite out of control; she showed little interest in education and no interest in her new acquaintances, whose existence she seemed keen to ignore altogether. She was interested only in Mr Warde and could not keep her black eyes off him.

Miss Hooper received her first blow very quickly, for it soon became clear that Mr Warde would, of course, be travelling in a First Class carriage with his children, whom he refused to let out of his sight in case Mrs Warde kidnapped them again, and that Anna Hooper, contrary to her expectations, would be travelling Third Class with all the servants.

She did not open her scarlet lips all the way to Leamington, except to yawn, but sat wondering and wondering whether she had done the right thing, and what she had let herself in for.

Her travelling companions played rubber after rubber of whist and chattered away, thinking that it would only be a matter of time before the sparks began to fly.

Anna Hooper arrived at Clopton in pitch darkness and was received without ceremony of any kind. Mr Warde studiously ignored her presence and shut himself up in his library with Scrope's *Art of Deer Stalking*.

After a few weeks Miss Hooper began to enjoy the children's confidence, but she fought a losing battle from the start, for the children were already set in their ways and had different standards from any other children she had ever met. Her haphazard attempts at teaching them their letters and reading with them grew daily more vague and as the months went by grew shorter and shorter.

When Ada Warde swore at the nurse Miss Hooper spent some days persuading her charge to use a vocabulary more becoming to young ladies, but ended up swearing at Ada Warde herself.

When Emily Warde refused to taste her vermicelli pudding Miss Hooper spent an hour trying to persuade her to change her mind, but ended up throwing the vermicelli pudding out of the window.

When Miss Hooper found Charlotte Warde cutting round the scarlet birds in a handsome book called *Birds of America* she did what she could to stop her, but ended up helping herself to an eagle for her own album.

When she found George and Henry Warde engaged in colouring in all the handsome plates in Piranesi's *Vedute di Roma* she rebuked them, but ended up helping, until the Pantheon was bright blue, the Pyramid of Cestius a fetching pink, and the church of S. Paolo fuori le Mura a brilliant orange.

The children got up when they liked and went to bed when they liked, rang bells for meals in the middle of the night, blew trumpets when everyone was asleep, and, when the fancy took them, climbed into bed in their muddy boots.

The Warde children were completely free to do and say exactly what they liked whenever they liked.

In the evenings they would all eat at their father's table, wide-eyed at the splendour, sitting up on cushions, their noses just above their plates, wielding silver forks and spoons that were too big for them, and falling asleep before the pudding arrived, so that they had to be carried off to bed by the footmen, only to be awake again at midnight, playing Murder in the Dark.

Anna Hooper did her best. She joined in the children's games. She sometimes read to them out of *The Headlong Career & Woful Ending of Precocious Piggy*, and calmed their tantrums, tucked them into bed every night, listened to them sobbing themselves to sleep, and tried to take the place of their mother.

But she woke up each morning to find that during the night every one of her boots had been mysteriously filled with urine, and in time she became accustomed to finding excrement in her bed, but when she remonstrated with the children they went running to their papa, who refused to believe that either of these outrages had anything to do with his children.

'Miss Hooper,' he said, 'my children do not do wrong things.' And in time Miss Hooper got used to life at Clopton and accepted such events as a matter of course. Ultimately all the children began to speak with Anna Hooper's voice, and they would toss their heads when they were cross just as Anna Hooper did, and got all their vowels wrong, so that when Mrs Warde saw them a year later she gasped when they opened their mouths and was obliged to search for someone to give them elocution lessons.

A year after Miss Hooper arrived at Clopton Mrs Warde's appeal was heard before the Lord Chancellor in His Lordship's private room, in order to prevent differences of a most unpleasant nature between Mr and Mrs Warde being made public.

But the Lord Chancellor's judgment did not have to be delivered in private, largely because Mr Warde had already published most of the evidence at his own expense in a special supplement to the *Warwick Advertiser* running to four full-sized pages, or fifteen yards of newspaper column, which showed that he was quite innocent of every one of his wife's charges.

When Mr Warde heard what the new evidence was that Mrs Warde had got hold of and planned to put before the Lord Chancellor he filled his britzka with trunks and boxes, sent all the family silver to the bank, drew out all the money he could lay his hands on, ordered the children to gather up their prized possessions, dismissed all the servants on the spot except Mrs Doughty the housekeeper, investigated the Channel tides and set off at top speed for France.

He was in the act of loading the luggage on board ship at Dover with the children wrapped up in anticipation of a long and rough crossing, clutching their musical boxes, and a scarlet parrot in a cage and a dozen favourite dolls, when a gang of hirsute policemen appeared from nowhere and served an order on Mr Warde from the Lord Chancellor, which restrained him from taking the children out of the country in anticipation of an adverse decision.

In the scuffle that followed Mr Warde delivered four black eyes and the children's parrot escaped and flew off towards Cap Gris Nez and disappeared from view.

The police turned the Wardes back, and they unloaded all the luggage and trailed all the way home to Clopton escorted by six Constables and an Inspector, who placed lookouts on every road leading away from Clopton House until the Lord Chancellor's decision was announced.

In the former case of Warde *v*. Warde the personal conduct of Mr Warde was not of itself sufficient to deprive him of his children's custody for there was no proof that he had brought them up improperly, and no proof that any of his irregularities had been allowed to reach the children's ears or eyes.

Since then Mrs Warde had filed horrifying new evidence, which chronicled countless disgusting scenes in which Mr Warde had taken part, and it seemed that the grossest immorality was almost a daily occurrence. It now appeared also that Mr Warde's way of bringing up the children was expressly calculated to demoralize their minds.

Mealtimes at Clopton House were irregular and table manners were ignored. Lights burned all over the house at all hours of the night. A doll's house set on fire by the children had nearly caused the destruction of the nursery. The eldest boy, George

Warde, had a parrot which he was teaching to swear. The children were permitted to play with the labourers' children and their education was seriously neglected. The Warde children spent most of the day running wild on the Clopton estate, wreaking havoc wherever they went.

Mr Warde's servants stayed only a month or two and then left in disgust, for Clopton was a house in which the normal rules of genteel society no longer applied. The housemaids would drink Mr Warde's brandy all morning and be too drunk to perform their duties in the afternoon. The butler and valet would be found sitting half way up the grand staircase smoking Mr Warde's cigars or sitting with their shoes on Louis XIV fauteuils that cost hundreds of pounds.

Mr Warde's household was in complete disorder.

The Lord Chancellor said there was no need for the court to puzzle itself over any inquiry about Mr Warde, for he had placed his misconduct beyond doubt in a letter to John Bennet Lawes Esq., in which he unburdened his mind to the extent of saying, 'My folly and wickedness have deprived me of my best friend – my wife – who is a woman of the highest excellence and has borne much from me patiently.'

The Lord Chancellor was most deeply concerned about the welfare of Mr Warde's eldest daughter, Miss Ada Warde, who was now ten years old and just at the age when good or bad government would in all probability seriously affect her future development.

Mrs Warde's fresh information was of such a revolting nature that the Lord Chancellor said, 'I am sure that if the Vice-Chancellor had known of it he would have come to a different conclusion,' for it appeared that Mr Warde's conduct in Stratford-upon-Avon and the neighbourhood for miles around was so notorious and so objectionable that no modest woman dared to go anywhere near him.

People crossed the street when they saw him coming. Shops closed as he passed by. The appearance of his distinctive carriage in the town brought all cattle and sheep auctions, all traffic and all business to a halt as people stared after Mr Warde and whispered about him. Everywhere he went Mr Warde was shunned as little short of a monster.

In addition to all this there was too good reason to suppose that Mr Warde was now living with a woman of improper conduct.

His own statement regarding this woman – a Miss Hooper – was that he hired her at Brighton in the menial capacity of a servant, but had later promoted her to the office of housekeeper. However, the evidence supplied by Mrs Warde stated that this Miss Hooper was very often the sole companion of Miss Ada Warde, and that she invariably took her seat with the family at the dining-table, something that in normal circumstances and in any normal household no mere servant would ever be permitted to do.

It was, moreover, by no means an uncommon sight for Mr Warde and his daughter and this Miss Hooper to be seen strolling in the grounds of Clopton House, all three of them with large cigars in their mouths, smoking away, and to find Miss Warde and Miss Hooper dressed in men's clothes.

'The habit of smoking', said the Lord Chancellor, 'is at all times and by all persons bad enough, but it becomes truly disgusting when practised by a young lady of Miss Warde's station in life.'

It was a fact that she had a very large supply of the very best Havana cigars piled up beside her bed for her own exclusive use, and several servants testified that she would often be found sitting up in bed in the morning blowing smoke-rings, and that she had on more than one occasion narrowly escaped being burned to death when her bed-clothes caught fire.

It was pretty plainly to be implied that Miss Hooper was a bad influence and pretty plainly to be implied that she was not living with Mr Warde in the capacity of either cook or house-keeper.

It was true that various visiting masters taught Miss Warde the usual accomplishments of young ladies – French, the pianoforte, and so on – but there was no evidence at all to suggest that her moral or religious education was under the control of any individual except this Miss Hooper. The clergy had long since ceased to visit Clopton House and Miss Warde was never taken to church.

With such evidence of her father's grossly immoral conduct, and his failure to show anything other than irreligious habits, and taking into consideration the great probability that he was now carrying on an improper intercourse with Miss Hooper, the Lord Chancellor said, 'I feel it is always better that children should be brought up together, and not educated half to side with one parent and half with the other, and thus I feel bound to order that *all Mr Warde's children should be delivered up to their mother.*'

Mrs Warde's troubles lifted instantly from her shoulders and floated away, and she was seen to smile for the first time in more than a year.

Harriet Meller screamed with delight, quite forgot herself and where she was, and the smelling-salts, from which she had already removed the stopper so as to be ready when Mrs Warde fainted away, spilled unnoticed all over the floor of the court as she ran exclaiming to gather up *her* children, one on her shoulders, one under each arm, and two clinging to her skirts, as the court burst into a round of polite applause at the decision.

It was Mr Warde who had to be led away from the court, numb with grief, blinded by tears, to spend a month in a darkened room at Clopton, unable to bear being spoken to, unwilling to eat, unable to do anything but weep for the loss of his children.

And it was Anna Hooper who took it upon herself to supervise Mr Warde's return to health. She took him all his meals and fed him with a spoon as if he was one of his own recalcitrant children. She was his sole contact with the outside world and did her best to persuade him to return to it.

But Mr Warde would do nothing. 'I have lost everything,' he said, 'wife, children, Luton, all my pretty ones gone in one fell swoop.' And he stayed where he was, turned his face to the wall that was papered with elegant strawberry-coloured wallpaper, and groaned that he wanted to be left alone to die.

Anna Hooper continued to smarten herself up before she knocked on Mr Warde's door even though he refused even to look in her direction. She appeared in a different dress every day, borrowed from Mrs Warde's redundant wardrobe, and her expenditure on scent bore no relation to her meagre income.

By the end of the month it had become clear to the indoor servants, who only stayed on because they had not been paid, that Miss Hooper had succeeded, whether by accident or design, in interesting Mr Warde only in herself.

When Mr Warde finally emerged blinking into the light of day Anna Hooper was to receive an allowance for clothes, an allowance for jewellery, an allowance for everything she asked for, and for everything that money could buy, all made with only one condition – that she never handled the money, for Mr Warde was afraid he would lose her and that if he gave her money she would run away. But Anna Hooper did not mind that. She was only too pleased to stay and be showered with presents and spend as much of Mr Warde's fortune as she possibly could. All she had to do was to present Mr Warde with her bills and he would pay them without a murmur, however outrageously large they were, and whatever they were for.

One morning Ada Warde's French tutor turned up at Clopton, not having been told that, alas, there were no longer any pupils for him to teach. As he drove disgruntled down the carriage-drive Anna Hooper ran after him calling, 'Come back Monsieur Croûton, you can teach me French instead!'

When the pianoforte tutor arrived Anna Hooper began to take lessons on the chamber organ that had stood silent since Mrs Warde left Clopton and she was soon able to pick out half-remembered tunes with one finger.

She began to take herself off to London with Mr Warde's free Railway pass and to frequent Howell & James's Regent Street shop, from which she would emerge laden with fine silks and priceless jewels and expensive lumber that she had no use for and did not really want, and she went everywhere in her finery, dressed in the height of fashion, dripping emeralds and rubies, putting every other woman in her shadow, and leaving behind her a tidal wave of the most expensive scent she could lay her hands on, and, in Stratford, a tidal wave of gossip about who and what she was.

The dogs looked up and sniffed as she went by, and half the adult male population of Stratford-upon-Avon found themselves at one time or another following her involuntarily down the street.

One evening Anna Hooper appeared at dinner radiant in a sumptuous ball dress of black gauze with a crimson garniture, and wearing the Warde diamonds, which Mr Warde had thrown out of a window in some fit of temper, and which she had found being kicked about the gardens by the coachman's children.

She could no longer pretend to pass as the nursery governess for there were no longer any infants to take care of and the nursery was locked up just as it was, with Mr Warde's strictest orders that nothing was to be moved: Anna Hooper had become in all but name, and almost without realizing it, Mr Warde's wife.

When Mr Warde's racehorse Romance was refused entry to the Leamington Stakes he went off to Paris in disgust, and it was there in the autumn of the year 1849 that Anna Hooper was safely and easily delivered of her first child, a strapping girl, who was named Maria Charlotte. Wherever she went Miss Hooper passed as The Lady of Charles Warde Esq. Her French was fluent, if spoken with an English accent. Her manner was bold. Her looks were striking. All Bohemian Paris noticed how she swore like a trooper, smoked like a chimney and drank like a fish, and all Mr Warde's Parisian friends congratulated him on his new wife and thought she was so much more suited to him than the last one.

When they asked what had happened to his old wife, Charles Warde just shrugged his shoulders and said, 'She was so silent, so shy, so retiring, so religious, that one day she was not there at all – she just faded away.' And he snapped his fingers and roared his head off.

In Paris, which did not know all the details of Mr Warde's career and would not have cared if it did, Mr Warde was his usual roaring success. Back at home in Warwickshire things were different. All the doors that had so readily opened to admit him for ten years and more now closed against him at once.

All the social occasions he had taken for granted for so long refused to acknowledge Mr Warde's existence and no longer wanted to admit or know him, for now the whole County of Warwick was talking about him behind his back, and knew who he was, and what he was, and what he had been up to.

There was no more blind-man's-buff at Warwick Castle with the Earl and Countess. No more commands to Buckingham Palace. No more glittering parties. Mr Warde's prospects were destroyed at a stroke, his ambitions cut off and his hopes of glory demolished for ever.

Mr Warde could not have cared less. 'I couldn't care if I never speak to Her Majesty again in my life,' he declared. But he was subdued and more morose than usual, and he was more subject to black moods and violent changes of temper.

One by one all his servants trudged down the Coach Road to new situations in Stratford, Warwick or London, or to Mrs Warde at Rothamsted, in a slow exodus from a house where it was no longer to anyone's advantage to say they had worked, until the only servant left from Mrs Warde's time was Mrs Doughty, who had been there for so long that it was unthinkable that she should go anywhere else.

'I've been here since the Battle of Trafalgar,' she said, 'and I'm not going to leave now.'

But Mr Warde's isolation from society was not quite total, for there were some doors which could not slam in his face. He continued to frequent the Warwick Quarter Sessions and made known his views on New Prisons, New Highways, County Rates, Local Constables, Poor Law Administration and the Pauper Lunatic Asylum, and became notorious for the irrelevance and inordinate length of his speeches.

His face was often pointed out at the Assizes, where the more interesting cases were tried – Murder, Assault, Felony and Capital Offences. But try as they might, the Justices could not ignore Mr Warde, or keep him away by sending notes to say that the Sessions would be held at Coventry instead of Warwick, and he kept on turning up time after time, looking sleek and distinguished, stuck in the awkward limbo between disgrace and respectability, a gentleman who could neither be introduced nor overlooked, for he was still the most handsome ornament to the Bench of Magistrates, still the richest man in Stratford, still one of the richest men in the county, still turned out in spotless frock-coat, stove-pipe hat, gold-topped cane, stroking his side-whiskers, grinning away like a cat, displaying himself in public at every opportunity, making himself as conspicuous as he could. Still almost the perfect gentlemen.

Time passed and Anna Hooper spent much of her new life bearing Mr Warde's children, child after child, one every fifteen months. As time went on she gradually learned, with the aid of *The Gentleman's Pocket Book of Etiquette*, never to convey food to her mouth with her knife; not to make disagreeable noises when drinking soup; not to pick her teeth at table unless from absolute necessity, and that the proper attitude to servants should be condescension without familiarity.

For a time Mr Warde's name and activities disappeared almost completely from the pages of the *Warwick Advertiser*, and he was thought to be living a retired and respectable life with his new family, having turned over a new leaf, untroubled by lawsuits or solicitors.

In the winter he visited Paris as he had always done, and Anna Hooper's diamonds outsparkled everyone else's.

In the summer they visited Mr Warde's Irish estate, Augher, in County Leitrim, where Mr Warde fished and shot and hunted every living thing in sight, and then returned home to do the same at Clopton, where in the end no birds sang, for Mr Warde had killed them all.

He whiled away his time purchasing acres and acres of agricultural land and several farms adjoining the Clopton estate. He purchased a handsome and distinguished residence in Curzon Street, Mayfair, for use in conjunction with visits to the opera and to house the spoils of Anna Hooper's ever more reckless shopping expeditions.

There were priceless jewels and countless expensive dresses, which she would wear only once and then put away in her giant wardrobe, only to be heard complaining bitterly a few days later that she had nothing to wear. Mr Warde's spending power knew no bounds. His resources were unlimited and his money kept on flowing, so that Anna Hooper was resplendent in the latest fashion, whether it was crinoline or bloomers, or ball gowns, in all the colours of the rainbow, and it was acknowledged everywhere she went that hers was the finest collection of clothes in all Warwickshire, so that when she appeared in public, always in the very grandest shining new carriage, all heads turned to look, and American visitors to Shakespeare's Birthplace would ask who she was, thinking at the very least she must be The Lady So-And-So, or The Countess of Blank.

When Miss Hooper graciously stopped her landau to bestow

her favours upon the local tradespeople grown men would fight to be allowed to hold her horses.

Time passed and Joseph Reason found that devotion to duty had its rewards when, in spite of Mr Warde's loud objections, he was promoted to Chief Constable of the Hundred of Barlichway. Joseph Callaway, always so keen to mind other people's business for them, was flattered to be appointed a Special Constable.

Mr Warde no longer stopped to speak to anybody but drove round and round in circles before returning to Clopton without having called anywhere and without having visited anyone. On wet afternoons he had nothing better to do than to wander through his extensive glasshouses and crush the scarlet flowers between his fingers and pull the tops off all the chrysanthemums, while the rain drummed on the glass roofs and the flies buzzed against the window-panes.

Miss Hooper was fully occupied with her children, or fully engaged out spending Mr Warde's money, or busy making Clopton run as nearly like clockwork as it could under her haphazard and disorganized supervision.

One autumn Mr Warde and his colleagues on the Bench imprisoned John Russell for fourteen days for stealing a pair of scissors; John Wilson for a month for stealing a shirt; Mary Dugan for two months for stealing a frock; William Turner for three months for stealing a pair of boots; Sarah West for four months for robbing her master of various articles of woman's apparel, and Bolding Watkins for six months for an assault. Thomas Lees was put away for nine months with hard labour for stealing three planes and Charles Mills was transported for seven years for stealing a pound of bacon.

Charles Warde could do nothing but smile with delight to see Justice done. Chief Constable Reason, who was on duty in court, was overheard to say, 'I am not surprised the Justices have their enemies. I'm not surprised they are now and then the target for resentment.'

On a moonless night not long afterwards a ragged procession made its way through Clopton Park carrying a bizarre collection of makeshift musical instruments – saucepans and ladles, hammers and tongs, kitchen utensils and farm tools, intent upon making known their disapproval of Mr Warde's irregular household and their resentment against him as a magistrate.

All Hell was let loose around Mr Warde's house. The mob screamed and shouted abuse, beat their instruments as hard as they could and yelled for the Squire to come out and show himself.

Mr Warde, watching from an upper room, was unable to prevent himself from seeing his own effigy go up in flames, and unable to drag himself away from the window, and unable to avert his eyes from the image of Anna Hooper in straw that lit up the gardens.

A roar went up when they saw him, but the mob stood its ground, unsure whether to advance and smash windows or whether to fire ricks and stables, or whether to lay hands on the man himself.

Mr Warde railed at them from his open window but was not idle for long. In the capacity of magistrate he summoned the Police, the Yeomanry Cavalry, the Militia and the Riot Act, which he shouted through a speaking-trumpet over the heads of the rioters.

Anna Hooper, unaware that this was anything but the serenading of a popular squire by a devoted and boisterous tenantry, slipped on a carnival mask and danced with the members of the crowd in the shrubbery.

But not for long, for the mob was soon cut off from behind, clubbed and batoned, trampled and truncheoned into flight, forced to disperse and make its way home across field and track, mud and briar and marsh and pool.

As time went on Mr Warde himself became the ghost that haunted Clopton, himself the reason why people did not like to go there after dark if they could help it, or even in broad daylight: himself a bogey for small children to add to the perils and dangers of the night, and for the mothers of recalcitrant infants a useful bugbear: 'Eat up your dinner or Boney and Squire Warde will come and get you.'

Shortly after the Battle of Clopton Fisher Tomes Esq., tired of being pointed out at market as Mr Warde's neighbour, put the contents of Lower Clopton Farm up for auction and moved to an area with a more savoury reputation.

143

About the same time Mr Warde buried his father, the aged clergyman, at Snitterfield, where Mrs Charlotte Warde had been interred six years before, and a Gothic monument, all spikes and crocketed pinnacles, was sent from Paris with an inscription which read: *Leur fils unique reconnaissant a fait ériger ce monument à leur mémoire.*

About the same time George Lloyd Warde, now thirteen years of age, was sent away to school at Charterhouse but was sent home to his mother after only half a term, suffering from influenza and laryngitis, and died a few weeks later in the arms of a distraught Meller.

Mr Warde was still in Paris with his mistress, spending a great deal of money, and did not learn of the death until some time after the funeral had taken place. He had hardly seen his son for five years.

Such meetings as Mrs Warde would allow had to take place on a deserted road precisely halfway between Rothamsted and Clopton, and were supervised and overshadowed by the forbidding Puffy, Mrs Warde's trusted go-between, and a brace of bailiffs armed with shotguns, who timed the meetings, holding a pocket watch, so that the monster did not exceed his allotted thirty minutes or start eating his offspring.

Such meetings were less than satisfactory, for Mrs Warde stipulated further that father and children were not to embrace or touch each other, but were to remain at all times exactly six feet apart. And Puffy the go-between stood over them with her tape-measure, glowering at Mr Warde and interrupting his stilted conversation with the five children in order to keep them apart and make them stick to the Rules.

Mr Warde thus became a stranger to his children, and passed out of their affections, for they were set against him by their mother and were quite unable to comprehend his wilful absence from home. They behaved as if he were the victim of some frightful contagious disease, and on one occasion Mr Warde overheard Henry Warde, aged six, solemnly telling the coachman, 'The heat drove our papa insane.'

Mr Warde no longer knew what to say to his children, and they were, if the truth were told, scared of him, so that in the end he discontinued the meetings altogether and tried to forget that his children had ever existed. A death in the family was almost without meaning, elicited little emotion and brought forth no great show of tears.

'Children of mine have died before,' he said, 'I am quite accustomed to bereavement.' But he banged about more than usual and raged behind locked doors for a long time, and lay awake night after night even so.

After a month he climbed into his carriage and went down to see his solicitors. 'Henry Warde will be the heir to Clopton,' he told them, and then he returned home again.

One December Mr Warde was seized with a sudden new philanthropic zeal and pressed the sum of £10 into the Mayor of Stratford's hands, saying, 'The necessitous poor will be grateful for some roast beef for their Christmas Dinner.'

Towards the end of 1856, after much petitioning by the educated and intelligent classes about the lack of an easy and cheap mode of visiting so hallowed a spot as the Birthplace, Home and Grave of the Immortal Bard, the Prospectus of the Stratford-upon-Avon Railway Company was published, amid great celebration, with the object of linking the town to the Great Western Railway at or near Leamington.

Mr Warde, mindful of his last Railway Extravaganza and unfortunate crash, thought long and hard for some weeks, and then rushed out and purchased a very large number of shares and became immediately the principal shareholder in the scheme.

When the Public Dinner to celebrate the passing of the Stratford-upon-Avon Railway Act was held at the White Lion Hotel, the Mayor gave the health of C.T. Warde Esq., who had kindly presented a haunch of venison, and he went so far as to devote the end of his speech to him: 'Mr Warde,' he said, 'has come forward to aid every single charitable cause that I have brought to his attention.'

The toast was drunk with three times three cheers, and the clapping continued for some fifteen minutes. Mr Warde, who was present, for he could hardly have been kept away, having provided the victuals, sat smiling and nodding, acknowledging the applause, in spite of being seated between two empty chairs in a dark corner of the room because no one was willing to be seen sitting next to him.

A year later Mr Warde's announcement that he would

increase his number of shares in the Railway Company by fifty if the directors would double theirs was met with the frenzied banging of fists on tables, continued cheering and the wild stamping of feet.

At the Grand Opening of the Stratford-upon-Avon Railway Mr Warde was almost given pride of place, and the Directors permitted him to ride, garlanded with evergreens and roses, on the front of the engine from Hatton Station to Stratford, hallooing and shouting and cheering all the way, and waving his top hat, so that everyone who did not know that Mr Warde was not really a gentleman who was going to change his spots might well have been forgiven for thinking that the reformation and rehabilitation of the Liberal Proprietor was well under way, if not complete.

Rumour, however, in Stratford-upon-Avon at least, never lies down for very long, and there were people who were talking about Mr Warde again, and they were not only the grateful poor, who had been on the receiving end of Mr Warde's bounty yet again in the form of 400 pounds of best beef. There were people whose tongues still wagged about events at Clopton House, and whose tongues, in fact, had never stopped wagging. There were people who said that the legal profession had by no means finished making a most handsome living out of Mr Warde's affairs, and who said that it could only be a matter of time before Mr Warde's name brought shame and disgrace upon the town of Stratford all over again.

On 5 November 1856 Mr Warde descended on Stratford-upon-Avon, saying, 'I see no reason why I should remain a social outcast for the rest of my life. I am tired of being shut away up at Clopton.'

Darkness had fallen on the water meadows beside the River Avon before Mr Warde set off, and a crowd of 3,000 Stratfordians had already gathered in celebration of Guy Fawkes before Mr Warde left his carriage incognito.

Faces flitted to and fro, lit up from beneath by torches, and then disappeared again. Lights blazed suddenly in the dark and then were extinguished. And in the dark Mr Warde was able to go to and fro among the crowd, unrecognized and unseen.

The Stratford Brass Band struck up the tune that had come to be Stratford's anthem, and 3,000 voices joined in the words.

Our Shakespeare compar'd is to no man
Nor Frenchman, nor Grecian, nor Roman,
Their Swans were all Geese to Avon's sweet Swan
And the man of all men was a Warwickshire man
    Warwickshire man
    Avon's Swan
And the man of all men was a Warwickshire man.

The song was wafted back and forth on the wind, and Stratford threw caution to the winds and indulged in the nearest it ever got to Bacchanalia, while a procession of torchlit boats moved down the river, with four gentlemen in each, holding up streamers and lights and discharging rockets into the air.

Mr Wilder the Pyrotechnist let off gerbs and maroons and lit massive fixed pieces in multi-coloured fireworks on the island near Lucy's Mill: a Shakespeare, a Guy Fawkes, a Florence Nightingale, the hero of the Battle of Inkerman – a figure that was mistaken for Mr Warde and was cheered on a gale of wild laughter – all consumed in gunpowder and coloured lights and a blaze of sparks.

An immense illuminated air balloon rose slowly over the town and salted fires lit up upturned faces in all the colours of the rainbow. Later a monster bonfire was lit and the 3,000 revellers drew near to it like a vast swarm of bees. The torchlit procession made its way back up the river: boats, torches, Mayor, Brass Band, dogs, boys, aldermen, fallen women, field women, screaming girls, shouting youths, singers and dancers, all moving in the same direction and all bursting their lungs with

Each shire has its different pleasures
Each shire has its different treasures
But to rare Warwickshire all must submit
For the wit of all wits was a Warwickshire wit
    Warwickshire wit
    How he writ!
For the wit of all wits was a Warwickshire wit.

And the procession made its way past the church with its sacred bones, past private houses whose occupants feared for their windows and trembled at the uproar, to Waterside and the

Basin, where scores of small boats rowed back and forth, each lit up to reveal a stout farmer, a lover and his lass, a boatload of merry wives, ordinary people floating about in the moonlight, beneath the monster balloon, all squealing and dodging sparks and spent rockets, all reflected in the glassy stream, until the Stratford Brass Band marched off up Bridge Street and disappeared, followed by the crowd, who had quite forgotten by this time about Guy Fawkes, and a grinning Mr Warde made his way back to his carriage, where the horses and coachman were still waiting for him, stamping their feet in the frost to keep warm.

Early in 1857 all polite Stratford was shocked and surprised and intrigued to learn that Mr Warde had hauled his own butler before the Stratford Magistrates charged with threatening to shoot him.

Thomas Williams, a dashing young fellow with moustachios, appeared in court respectably dressed in black clothes, with his round face scrubbed and shining and his curly yellow hair plastered down with Fred Lewis's Electric Oil, ready to defend himself, but the magistrates adjourned the case for a week for further evidence to be collected, and no one in court was privileged to know the details of what had happened or why it had happened, for a week later Mr Warde dropped the charge and the prisoner was free to go.

The affair remained a mystery as far as the genteel public was concerned until two years later, when the same Thomas Williams, now described as formerly butler at Clopton House, was brought up in custody by Mr Warde a second time, charged with trespassing on the Clopton Estate.

'The prisoner has not actually done any damage yet,' said Mr Warde in court, 'but he is up at Clopton every day of his life, lurking in the shrubbery and plantations and spying on me with a telescope, and he has made frequent threats against me. He is doing all he can to annoy me.'

The ordinary working women of Stratford, who filled the public gallery, and who seemed to have abandoned work for the day, began to whistle and jeer and stamp their feet. A larger crowd of women, who could not be crammed in, waited outside in the snow, stamping their feet, shouting and chanting and making such a noise that they could be heard quite clearly inside the building.

John Branston Freer Esq., the presiding magistrate, had a sinking feeling in the pit of his stomach that something unpleasant was going to happen.

Mr Warde sat bolt upright, pretending to be deaf, smiling a little, and the proceedings went on as smoothly as they could when no one could hear what anyone else was saying.

'The charge against my client arises from jealousy,' said Mr Greves, who was Williams' solicitor, and he urged Mr Freer to investigate the case fully. 'It will become clear,' said Mr Greves, 'if only you would take the trouble to ask a few questions, that it is Mr Warde who should be bound over to keep the peace, and not this unfortunate boy, whom Mr Warde has led astray.'

Mr Greves then referred in hostile terms to Mr Warde's moral character and reminded the magistrates of Mr Warde's former history.

But Mr Warde said, 'This is nonsense. Williams has threatened me repeatedly. I know he is contemplating doing me an injury. I am perfectly confident that his behaviour will lead to a breach of the peace.'

'And will the breach of the peace come from Williams or from yourself?' asked Mr Greves, but he got no direct answer to his question, for Mr Warde just said, 'Pooh, pooh,' and blustered, and his voice was drowned by the tumultuous noise from the women in the gallery.

'It is not true that I threatened to murder Williams or tear him limb from limb,' said Mr Warde. 'Miss Hooper advised me to thrash Williams and said she wished he was dead . . . I may have said that if Williams pursued such a course it might lead to murder.'

The public gallery was in uproar and it was several minutes before order was restored, for the field-women were drumming their stout boots on the wooden floor, refused to leave the court, and had to be manhandled and dragged, screaming and shouting obscene remarks about Mr Warde at the tops of their voices, out into the street.

Mr Warde sat trying to look as if butter would not melt in his mouth and as if he could not understand what all the fuss was about.

Mr Freer ordered the whole court to be cleared and even the silent members of the public were evicted.

Mr Warde then produced a witness, a page, who hotly denied Mr Greves' suggestion that he had been promised a handsome sum in return for saying what Mr Warde told him to say.

'I was travelling along in the carriage with Miss Hooper and the children,' said the page, 'when I saw the prisoner standing by the first milestone on the Birmingham Road. He was blowing kisses at Miss Hooper. She stopped the carriage to speak to him. She kissed the prisoner several times and told him to go away, for Mr Warde was threatening to give him a good thrashing and was going to prosecute him for trespass. Thomas Williams kissed Miss Hooper full on the lips with a smack and I heard him say, "Let him thrash me. I can use my stick as well as he can."'

The page stopped talking and looked at Mr Warde, who nodded at him to go on.

'Then Miss Hooper kissed the prisoner again, and she turned round in the carriage and saw Mr Warde himself striding towards us through the cornfield, waving his stick at us. She said, "Look! See there, the old devil stands watching us." And she kissed Williams goodbye and told the coachman to drive on. She didn't stop to speak to Mr Warde. The children were there all the time. I never heard Mr Warde make use of no threats against Mr Warde except that time. I have never heard Mr Warde threaten to shoot Thomas Williams.'

Mr Greves pressed Mr Freer again that Mr Warde ought not to meet with the magistrates' sympathy for one moment, but he was prevented from calling evidence.

Mr Greves repeated emphatically, 'I should have been able to prove that Mr Warde is the real offender; that Williams went to work for Mr Warde as an innocent boy and has been led away from the paths of rectitude by his master.'

But the magistrates ignored Mr Greves as much as they could.

John Branston Freer Esq. was one of the worthy gentlemen who twelve years before had been only too pleased to testify that Mr Warde was a manly character, capable of nothing degrading to a gentleman, and Mr Freer was not specially keen to take the lid off the box of snakes that he knew very well would escape if he permitted Mr Greves to call witnesses and ask embarrassing questions and to investigate the case properly. Mr Warde was, after all, still a magistrate.

'Really, Mr Greves,' said Mr Freer, 'you would bother us to death. Mr Warde's behaviour in the former case of Warde v. Warde is quite irrelevant to the present proceedings and has not the slightest bearing upon a case of simple trespass.' And Mr Freer turned to Thomas Williams and said, 'I advise you to keep off Mr Warde's property altogether. Even if the offence was ever so slight this court is bound to protect Mr Warde. No matter what he is, you have no right to improperly intrude upon his premises. In fact you have no business to be there at all.' And he bound Williams over to keep the peace to all Her Majesty's subjects, but especially to Mr Warde, for the next twelve months.

Williams pulled the required sum of £40 from his pocket and had no trouble producing two sureties of £20 each, and Mr Freer was left wondering how a butler without employment had laid his hands upon such a sum, that was twice his former annual income, and Mr Freer kept on wondering about it, knowing very well that there was much more to this case than met the eye, and wondering just what the field-women were doing abandoning their fields for a whole day, and who had paid them to come, and just what was going to happen next.

But Williams was free to go, and Mr Warde was free to go, and the proceedings were over, and the women outside the court, who had expected to see Mr Warde arrested and removed to Warwick Gaol to await his trial in a higher court, were disappointed, but threw their eggs and tomatoes and domestic rubbish and jeered and shouted abuse at him all the same, so that Mr Warde arrived back at Clopton House much as usual, in need of a bath and a complete change of clothing.

It was about this time that Caroline Sutton arrived at Clopton from Coventry, on foot and soaked to the skin, in the middle of what the *Warwick Advertiser* described as an Awful and Destructive Storm, the worst in living memory, with crashing peals of thunder, flashes of lightning and a deluge of rain and hail that smashed all the windows at Clopton House for the second time in Mr Warde's occupancy.

No one took any notice of Sutton except the new butler, who

let her in, showed her where to go, and left her to her own devices in the scullery, for she was to be the scullery-maid. And there, in the absence of anyone to tell her what to do, she set about clearing up the broken glass from the floor, and dried her frayed bonnet, and was found by Mr Warde as she stepped out of her sodden dress before the kitchen fire.

Sutton learned, as time went on, to deliver Miss Hooper's hot water at precisely the right temperature; to polish Miss Hooper's boots in just the way she liked; to brush Miss Hooper's raven hair with the Revolving Hairbrush into the most fashionable hairstyles, and she learned to wait on the mistress and watch over her and attend to her every whim every day, day after day and night after night, and in the middle of the night.

Times had changed since Anna Hooper arrived at Clopton, and Sutton was from time to time splashed by Miss Hooper's hot tears, lashed by her sharp tongue, and, from time to time, flecked with Miss Hooper's strong blood.

Sutton stored up in her heart all Miss Hooper's mistakes, wondered what all the trouble was about, for there was trouble, and watched and waited. She returned daily to her scullery, plunged her red arms into boiling water up to her elbows, and dreamed of all the remedies that would soften her hands and make them as white and smooth and delicate as Miss Hooper's.

Sutton noticed how Miss Hooper drank her way through a pint of Henekey's Cognac Brandy every day of the week, at two shillings and sixpence the pint, and she calculated that in the course of two months the mistress drank her way through as much money as a mere scullery-maid could earn in a year.

Sutton watched and waited and Miss Hooper was bloodied over and over again so that in the end Sutton had to keep herself in a state of permanent readiness, expecting to fly with her bandages and disinfectant at any moment, and to have to send Horseley the coachman off to fetch Dr Pritchard to stitch up Miss Hooper's livid wounds yet again.

Sutton practised her kind words in front of her cracked looking-glass and learned to disguise her real feelings. She kept the smelling-salts by her bedside and steeled herself to cope with the murder that seemed inevitable.

When Miss Hooper went out on one of her spending expeditions Sutton would steal into her bedroom and try out the contents of bottle after bottle from Miss Hooper's laden dressing-table. She would sniff at jars of miracle-working creams and ointments, and plaster them on to her chapped hands, a fruitless exercise she knew, for she had to return within the hour to her sinks. But Sutton dreamed none the less of the day when she would be able to escape the scullery, and she told herself it could only be a matter of time before Miss Hooper was no longer there to be waited on hand and foot all day every day and abuse the scullery-maid who had to double as lady's maid and do the work of two women, and who had to attend to her every want and whim and call her 'Madam' even though she thought in her private thoughts that she did not deserve it.

Sutton did not have to wait very long for in May 1859 Anna Hooper walked out of Clopton House for the last time, leaving her children behind her much as Mrs Warde had done twelve years before, only Anna Hooper had no intention of returning to Mr Warde, and told him so, and spat in his face.

If Anna Hooper could have skipped and danced all the way down the carriage-drive to Stratford-upon-Avon and freedom she would have done. As it was, she went on her way limping, black and blue all over, with the greater part of her body bandaged and scarred, and with two black eyes and a bloody nose.

She limped as far as she could and then had to beg for assistance at a washerwoman's cottage where once before Mary Bafact had taken her in. She collapsed on the doorstep in tears.

In April 1860 the Registrar of Births, Marriages and Deaths at Stratford was visited by a striking girl of eighteen with blue eyes and golden hair, who reminded him for some reason of Mrs Charles Warde, and who said she had come to register a birth.

The Registrar asked the name of the child.

'Charles Aprilius,' said the girl.

'Father's name, surname and occupation?' asked the Registrar.

The girl's scarlet lips remained closed.

'Name and surname of mother?'

'Caroline Sutton,' said the girl.

'Father's name?' the Registrar asked, trying again.

There was a profound silence.

'Place of Birth?'

'Clopton House, Old Stratford,' she said.

The Registrar could put two and two together as well as anyone else, and he shook his head sadly as he filled in the certificate with the customary blank spaces that indicated illegitimacy.

He held out a pen for Caroline Sutton to sign her name.

She took out one red hand and signed her shaky cross on the paper.

By the end of that year Mr Warde found he was once again spending more time on the road going to or returning from his solicitors than he seemed to be spending at home, and he found himself in court yet again, this time as the defendant in a case brought by Anna Maria Cobden Hooper, who charged him with assault, and which was tried in the Court of Queen's Bench, Guildhall, London, at considerable expense and amid great publicity, before Lord Chief Justice Cockburn and a Special Jury sitting after Term.

Mr Edwin James QC and Mr Honeyman appeared for Miss Hooper, the plaintiff.

Mr Serjeant Pigott, Mr Hawkins QC and a Mr Coleridge appeared for Mr Warde, the defendant.

A gallery full of newspapermen appeared on behalf of the curious and scribbled as fast as they could in order to take down every detail.

They described the case of Hooper *v*. Warde as one of the most extraordinary causes of modern times.

EIGHT

The gentlemen of the press wrote that the case contained a fearful amount of immorality, the greater part of which was totally unfit for publication, but they also said that their duty was to the public and they were therefore quite happy to print all the horrid details.

Miss Hooper charged Mr Warde with assault, with detaining articles of jewellery which belonged to her, and with failing to repay money which she had lent him.

Mr Warde pleaded guilty to the assaults, but said he had committed them in self-defence.

Miss Hooper claimed that Mr Warde had assaulted her with far more violence than was necessary for the purpose of self-defence.

Mr Warde denied that the jewels were Miss Hooper's property and claimed that he had already repaid the money she lent him.

This was the outline of the case.

Mr Edwin James QC, who was said to earn more than £10,000 a year, was the most expensive counsel Anna Hooper could find.

'Mr James is the most expensive,' she said, 'so he must be the best.' And Mr James was determined to fight his hardest for Miss Hooper not only because he believed she was in the right and had been grievously wronged, but also because there was some doubt where she was going to find the money to pay his enormous fee, and he feared she would not be able to pay it at all unless he won the case.

'It is a painful story for me to have to submit to the jury,' said Mr James, 'for if the documents I have in front of me are reliable Mr Warde seems to be a gentleman of most violent passions.'

All eyes in the crowded court swivelled to look at the defendant, and they saw a powerful middle-aged man with greying hair, who was upwards of six feet tall, straight as a ram-rod, and who sat looking very innocent indeed, as if he could not think what all the fuss was about; as if he could not imagine why everyone was looking at him. Mr Warde was quite calm and collected, and presented his usual distinguished appearance, as if he might have been Her Majesty's Ambassador to Such-And-Such, or The Lord So-And-So, and not a shabby, dirty fellow, not a gentleman of violent passions at all.

But Mr James went on: 'Mr Warde's conduct during the whole time Miss Hooper lived with him as his wife – a period of more than ten years – was so intolerable that, lest I be thought to exaggerate, I will leave the plaintiff herself to describe it.'

'Miss Hooper,' said Lord Chief Justice Cockburn gently, 'tell the court all about yourself, and tell us what it is that Mr Warde has done.'

All eyes swivelled now in Anna Hooper's direction, identifying her as the injured party. And she stood up and swore in a voice that had been refined by years of genteel living, to tell the truth. She wore the same scarlet dress she had worn for her journey to Clopton, and the dress still fitted her like a glove. She was still a handsome and attractive woman at thirty-one years of age. Her black eyes still flashed like diamonds and sparkled like stars. Her black hair still turned every head.

> I first met Mr Warde when I was living at Brighton with my mother and sisters. My father was a greengrocer, deceased, but my mother still ran the business. We lived over the shop, above the cabbages and cauliflowers. When I met Mr Warde I was standing under a gas-lamp in the street, waiting for a Mr Cheeseman, the man I should have married, but Mr Warde thought I was waiting in the street for altogether different reasons. He was the handsomest man I'd ever set eyes upon. He was a lovely man. I could tell at once that he was a gentleman. I forgot all about poor Mr Cheeseman and never gave him another thought.
>
> Mr Warde wanted to know my name. I saw no harm in telling him that. He asked where I lived, and he wrote down my address in his pocket-book. He asked a whole lot of questions about my mother and he said to me, 'What a handsome woman you are. What a prize your husband will have' and he said he'd like to buy me a present.
>
> He followed me home to my mother's door and refused to go away. He kept up a watch under my window into the small hours, singing and whistling and jingling his money in his

pockets and dancing about. He made so much noise that I couldn't get to sleep. My mother thought it was very strange conduct indeed and wanted to send for the Police but I said to her, 'Mother, think of the money.'

I didn't set eyes on him for a whole year after that and then one day he suddenly appeared again and asked if I was interested in a proposition. I asked what that might be, and it was this: that I should go to Clopton House to live, and be a nursery governess to his children. He said he would allow me the sum of £16 a year as wages. It was a very tempting offer. It was more money than I had in the world. It was more money than I have now. I will have to admit, however, that I never really went to Clopton to look after the children at all, though I did look after them. I always understood that if Mrs Warde should die Mr Warde would marry me. He always said he wanted to. But his wife did not die, and he never could or did marry me, so I remained his mistress. It was better than nothing. It was better than cabbages for the rest of my life.

Shortly after the children were taken away by order of Lord Cottenham Mr Warde's housekeeper left Clopton in disgust and I was appointed in her place. Mr Warde spent a whole month after that confined to his bed in a kind of hysterical fit after the loss of his children, and it was then that an improper connection took place between us for the first time. I have had seven children by Mr Warde. Four of them are still living, all daughters, but I have not set eyes on them since I left Mr Warde. He has not allowed me to go near them. They are not allowed to write to me. They could be dead for all I know. They are Mr Warde's prisoners, just as I was his prisoner.

I finally decided to abandon my children and leave Clopton House once and for all in the month of May 1859, after Mr Warde savagely beat me with a cartwhip, an archery bow and a billiard-cue.

Mr Warde is a Hercules, and capable of doing anything wrong, and there he is – sitting straight in front of me on purpose to annoy me, smiling away as if none of this had ever happened.

At first we lived together very happy and I have no complaint about the first six years or so of our living together as man and *wife. The troubles all began around the year 1856. In September there was a large shooting party on the Clopton estate during which Mr Warde and his friends shot dead almost every living thing and the game larder was full of dead rabbits and pheasants dripping blood all over the floor.*

Well, Mr Warde's gun went off – by mistake, he said – and one of the visitors, a Captain Walhouse, was badly injured in the arm and came back to the house in quite a state, dripping blood all over the carpets.

Mr Warde came in and wanted a sponge to clean the wound with, but he couldn't find one. He didn't know, of course, where that sort of thing was kept. All he knew was how to ring bells and order people about. And he couldn't find anyone to ask because all the menservants were out acting as beaters and all the women were away plucking feathers in an outhouse, up to their elbows in blood and gore.

I heard Mr Warde shouting his head off and I went to see what on earth was the matter. When he saw me he said, 'Where the Devil have you been?' and I said, 'I was in the little drawing-room all the time.'

Mr Warde said, 'I don't believe you,' and he knocked me down. I fell against the pedestal of a huge marble vase he had brought back from Italy and I split my head open. I lay unconscious on the floor, but Mr Warde, I learned afterwards, just turned on his heel and left me lying there, weltering in my blood. It was Mr Jevon Perry, another guest, who picked me up and bandaged my head.

As soon as I could stand up I ran away to Mr Greves the solicitor, who I regarded as my friend. I collapsed upon his doorstep and he sent at once for Dr Pritchard, who was with me the whole night.

I refused to return to Clopton after that but Mr Warde begged and pleaded and pestered me so much, and showered me with emeralds and expensive gifts, that I gave in and agreed to go back to him on condition that he never did anything of the kind again. I could not leave my children anyway. They needed me. So, like the fool I was, back I went.

Some months after that I was sitting quietly one afternoon minding my own business in the housekeeper's room, reading to Mrs Doughty from the newspaper, when Mr Warde burst through the door and complained that no one had answered the bell.

I said I didn't hear a bell, which was the truth, for my hearing was impaired after my fall on to the marble vase. Mr Warde expected me to answer the bells like a servant half the time, and the rest of the time he expected me to sit about on a sofa playing at being Lady of the Manor. But he still paid my wages, my £16 a year, though he never could quite make up his mind whether I was to be his housekeeper or his wife. I never quite knew where I stood. It depended upon his mood whether I answered the bells or not. I did resent being at his beck and call. I resented him calling me 'Hooper' like one of the servants, as he sometimes did. I thought I deserved better than that, but I was not so foolish as to say so. I put up with it all on account of the emeralds.

Anyway, on this occasion Mr Warde said to me, 'Hooper, I want some boiled eggs.' He was pretty cross.

I said again, 'I didn't hear any bell rung,' and then without warning he knocked me out of my chair on to the floor. I fell with a great crash onto the fender with my face in the coal-box. My shoulder was dislocated and I was screaming with pain. I must have looked a pretty sight, all covered in coal-dust.

Mrs Doughty could not stop screaming blue murder as if it was she that had been assaulted and not I, and she gave in her notice on the spot, but Mr Warde just walked off. It was Mrs Doughty who sent for the Doctor to attend to my wounds. I could see no reason for Mr Warde's violence. It wasn't my fault if I didn't hear, was it?

Mr Warde swears, I know, that on that occasion I was drunk, but that is not the truth. It is a lie. I was not drunk then or on any other occasion. I have never been intoxicated by strong liquor.

A few days after that incident Mr Hobbes the lawyer was fetched up to Clopton in order to see me. Mr Warde said he wanted me to sign a Deed, but he wouldn't tell me what was in it or anything at all about it. He refused to read it to me, for it was 150 pages long, and he would not let me read it for myself.

161

I was afraid there was something in it about the custody of my children. They knew very well that if I discovered what it was I wouldn't sign it. And I wouldn't have if it had meant signing away all my rights to see my daughters. I was determined not to be put upon.

So I refused to sign the Deed and I refused to see Mr Hobbes at all. Mr Warde was annoyed for Mr Hobbes had come all the way from Stratford for nothing, on a wild-goose chase. I retreated upstairs to my room, and I locked and bolted the door, fearing what might happen.

But Mr Warde would not let the matter rest. He sent Horseley the coachman off to get the Police and they tramped upstairs in their boots, leaving a trail of muddy footprints across the carpets, and they shouted to me through the keyhole. I was terrified.

Inspector James said, 'Miss Hooper, you must come down and do as Mr Warde says.'

I shouted back, 'I will not come down for 50,000 Hobbeses.'

So Mr Warde ordered the Police to cut away the panels of my door, and he sent for an axe. The door was made of the finest mahogany but it was smashed to splinters in two seconds. The Policemen were inside my room in a flash. I was sitting there on the edge of my bed holding a pistol in each hand – I wasn't taking any chances – I knew now how Mr Warde could behave when he was annoyed. And I sat there and said to the Policemen, 'If you come anywhere near me I'll shoot you to pieces.'

But the Police were not to be put off by threats like that. They were upon me in no time. Inspector James was wrestling with me to get the pistols away. I put up quite a fight, I can tell you. One of the pistols went off through the ceiling and brought down a ton of carved cornice about my ears. In the end Inspector James took both pistols away and gave them to Mr Warde, who fired them off out of the window at the deer, which were grazing close up to the house. He gave the Police a haunch of venison.

The Police said I must go down and sign the document and they threatened to handcuff me and take me off to Warwick Gaol if I refused to do as they said. I had no choice but to obey. I was never allowed to forget that Mr Warde was a magistrate and could have me locked up for the slightest offence. He used to recite all the penalties and punishments to me over the breakfast table. In the end I did sign Hobbes's dirty Deed, but without reading it. I have not seen the Deed since and nor have I seen my children. Mr Hobbes's Deed is the reason why.

In the winter of the same year Mr Warde turned me out of the house and I was forced to take shelter in the Coach House in the back of one of the carriages, with nothing but straw to keep me warm. It was bitterly cold. There was snow upon the ground. Mr Warde alleged some reason for his action but I forget now what it was. He was in such a passion. I might have retaliated. The Police might have been called. Mr Warde sent for them so often that I simply can't remember whether they came on that occasion or not. But I do remember that Mr Warde struck me that time. He was in the habit of striking me for the least offence. It was so frequent that I may say he struck me almost every day.

Another time he locked away all the family silver because he was afraid of burglars and one or two pieces had gone missing. He suspected the servants might be helping themselves to it. He wanted me to eat with a steel fork, but I refused. I didn't see why I should eat off anything but the best silver. I had borne all Mr Warde's children. I was his wife in all but name. I told him I would not use a steel fork if he paid me to.

He knocked me down. I cracked my head open on the corner of the dining-table. There was blood everywhere. Dr Pritchard had to be called out to stitch me up.

A little while after that I ran away to my mother at Brighton because of Mr Warde's violence, but he came hurrying after me, suddenly terribly sorry for what he had done. He showered me with diamonds and quantities of exotic flowers, and he begged and begged as usual for me to come home. He said he loved me and couldn't live without me. Like a fool I believed him. I went back of course. I still loved him too. I thought he was genuinely sorry.

On Christmas Day in the year 1856 there were more diamonds. They must have cost a fortune. I went off happily to church in the carriage, with the footman to carry my Prayer Book, and I thought, this is a new beginning, all's well that ends well, he has turned over a new leaf and we shall be happy. For Mr Warde was that morning very pleasant and friendly and attentive, quite his old self.

He did not go to church with me of course. He said there was no God, no Heaven and no point in saying your prayers at all. He used to swear about it a lot. When I got back from church I found Mr Warde standing upon the doorstep waiting for me. His eyes flashed. He was quite hopping mad. My heart sank right into my boots and I wondered whatever had happened and whatever I had done wrong now. He said, 'There is something the matter with the grapes in the conservatory – it is your damnation flowers.' And he ordered the gardeners to carry all my flowers out into the garden. I remonstrated with him for making such a fuss about such a little thing but that only made him even angrier. His grapes were prize-winning grapes, the vine was upwards of 100 years old, and everything had to be just so.

Mr Warde then boxed my ears. My head was ringing. He boxed my ears so often that I was deafer than ever. He then rushed outside into the snow, quite beside himself with anger, and ordered the gardeners to burn all my plants on the spot, and the whole contents of all the glasshouses as well. There were all manner of rare and exotic specimens. All the house flowers were destroyed. I was very fond of my flowers. I was very upset.

The bonfire blazed late into the evening, with the men, all thirty of them, in spite of it being Christmas Day, piling on more and more plants. Every so often Mr Warde would throw up a window and shout orders to them in the darkness. He was in a blinding rage, cursing and swearing at everyone.

I was very weary by that time, but I went into the dining-room to finish the preparations for our Christmas Dinner with my three daughters. But Mr Warde's tantrum was not yet over. He followed me into the dining-room and began cursing and swearing at me violently. I really couldn't say why. He smashed all the china and glass we were about to use and swept everything on the table on to the floor with a crash. The meal was ruined. Christmas was ruined. My three daughters were very upset and very disappointed. And so was I.

They witnessed the whole of Mr Warde's outburst and they were very frightened.

We all went off to bed without having any Christmas Dinner at all. We were too upset to eat a thing. The servants spent half the night clearing up all the mess.

In the New Year of 1857 I went with Mr Warde to London on the Railway and we spent some days spending money and staying at Hatchett's Hotel, where I was always known as Mrs Warde and where we had, of course, nothing but the best of everything.

One night Mr Warde came in from his club, the Conservative Club, in St James's Street, and ordered me quite sharp to hand over the diamonds he had given me for Christmas. I could tell there was trouble on the way, but I was determined to stand up to him. I refused to give up the diamonds and I refused to tell him where they were. I said to him, 'They are my diamonds and you shall not have them.'

He overturned all the furniture in a frenzy but he still didn't find my hiding-place. He went off instead in a rage to ask Sarah Carter, a nurse girl who was with us to look after my children, where I had put them. Of course the stupid girl told him at once that the diamonds were under the mattress where I had put them.

Mr Warde stormed back into my room, pulled all the bed-clothes on to the floor, took out the jewels, stamped and jumped upon them repeatedly, swearing and cursing, and I will even swear that he was growling and snarling like a wild animal as well, and the diamonds were all mangled and smashed to pieces so that I was obliged to wear paste instead.

Sarah Carter just stood there with her mouth hanging open like a fly-trap and her eyes popping out of her head. She was afraid it was all her fault. There were diamond earrings, a diamond necklace and diamond bracelets in bits all over the carpet. I had to crawl about the floor with Carter trying to find all the pieces. We were both weeping, but at least this time the violence was not directed against me.

Later I protested to Mr Warde, who did say he was sorry, though he didn't really sound like he meant it.

*

Two years later, in January 1859, I refused to sleep in the same bedroom as Mr Warde on account of his shameful treatment of one of the female servants. It was Ann Allcott, a housemaid, and she had broken a valuable Venetian looking-glass and Mr Warde locked her in a dark broom cupboard to teach her a lesson and refused to let her out. She was screaming and panicking. She was quite hysterical and broke all her nails scratching at the door to get out. Her fingers were all bloody. She was in a dreadful state.

I thought Mr Warde should apologize to her for what he had done at the very least, and I told him what I thought. It was disgraceful treatment. I went off to my own room and was undressing for bed when Mr Warde burst through my door and made me jump out of my skin. I had not locked the door or bolted it. He said to me in a very loud and rough manner, 'Hooper, unless you come into my room this instant I will knock out all your windows.'

I said to him, 'Very well, then, you will have to knock out all the windows, for I am not coming,' and I alluded again to the reason why.

Mr Warde then very calmly picked up the brass fire-irons from the grate and smashed every pane of glass in the room. I still refused to go with him though, in spite of the snow and hail pouring into the room and in spite of it being a bitterly cold night.

Mr Warde then picked me up and put me over his shoulder and took me forcibly into his bedroom. I was struggling and screaming all the while, and biting him upon the arms to make him put me down. He kicked the door shut and locked it behind him. His treatment was very violent, but I still refused to get into bed with him. He then knocked me down and I lay upon the floor panting and crying with rage and frustration, but I refused to get up. I could not get up because of the blow he had given me.

Mr Warde was wild-eyed. I had never seen him in such a fury. His eyes flashed round the room and lit upon an archery bow that for some reason was in the room. He picked it up and snarled at me, 'Unless you get into bed with me at once I will cut you to pieces with this bow.'

I refused.

166

Mr Warde then struck me blow after blow with the archery bow. I was severely wounded about the back and face for I was wearing only my night-clothes. He only stopped striking me when the bow was broken all to pieces and he could strike no more. I was very much injured. If the bow had not broken I should have been dead. There was blood all over the sheets and bed-clothes and blood all over me. My nose bled everywhere but even then he did not stop. I have the marks of the beating still across my back and could demonstrate to the court if necessary. Mr Warde behaved like a complete madman.

My eldest child, Maria Charlotte, who was then just nine years of age, was in Mr Warde's bedroom the whole time and witnessed the whole assault. She was whimpering in a corner. She was very much upset.

When Mr Warde was done he went to the door, took out the key and went to sleep as calm as you please, with the key under his pillow so that I could not escape.

I remained upon the hearth-rug all night long, in front of the fire, planning and plotting my flight, and trying to pluck up the courage to murder Mr Warde with the poker while he slept. But I had not the strength to do it. I was too much injured. I could not lift my arm above my head. I was afraid I would only manage to wake him up, and start him off fighting me again. I knew I should come off worst in a battle. Mr Warde was so strong.

I was in so much pain I could not sleep, but Mr Warde slept as soundly as he always did, snoring away regularly, as if nothing at all had happened.

In the morning he got out of bed and went to the door to receive his coffee from William Murphy, the houseboy. I sprang up quickly and banged the tray from below and upset it all over Mr Warde. His hands were scalded. The blue and gold coffee-service was smashed on the floor, but I managed to slip through the door and away, though I could hardly stand, let alone walk.

I took medical advice from Dr Pritchard and never turned in my bed for eight days. When I recovered I forgave Mr Warde for the sake of my children. I had no means of supporting myself. I had nowhere at all to go to. There was no alternative but to stay and put up with his treatment. I was a prisoner. But *in spite of it all I loved him still, even though I had done nothing to deserve such violence.*

Two months after that, one evening in April 1859, I walked down the Coach Road to Stratford-upon-Avon in order to post a letter. When I returned to Clopton I found the whole house locked up so that I could not get inside. It was only seven or eight o'clock and I could not understand why on earth everyone had gone to bed so early. I knocked and banged and called and shouted, but I couldn't get anyone to answer or let me in. The place was silent as the grave and it was getting dark. It was cold and the wind had started blowing a gale. I continued banging upon the doors, ringing and screaming at Mr Warde to let me in, but every window was shuttered and barred and there was no one to be seen. I thought I should have to spend the night in the Coach House again. I kept on banging though. I knew the house was full of people. I could not understand what had happened and I shouted the names of all the servants in turn.

After what seemed like hours and hours Mr Warde himself appeared in the stableyard. He was wearing his nightshirt and red flannel dressing-gown. He had a cigar between his teeth and a cartwhip in his hand. It was an ordinary carter's whip, with a handle heavily bound in brass. He was very angry. His eyes flashed. I dreaded to think what he would do, but I had done nothing wrong. I had done nothing to deserve any ill-treatment.

Mr Warde said to me, 'Have you been to Stratford, Hooper?'
I said, 'Yes, I have.'
He said, 'Posting letters?'
I denied it. It was none of his business what I was doing.

He then said, 'Now take this whip,' and broke it over me with all his might, like a lion-tamer from the Menagerie. He was smiling a great grim smile all the time. And I was screaming my head off, but nobody came out to rescue me from him. No one lifted a finger to help me.

He said, 'The more you beat them the better they like it,' and he struck me with that terrible whip for as long as he could. The end of the whip licked about my face and arms. The blood flowed in torrents but that did not make Mr Warde stop. He beat me all the harder. I was covered in weals from head to toe. I could do nothing. I did not even attempt to run away. I could not. If I had he would have chased after me even in his night-clothes. I'd never seen him so brutal.

When he was finished he strode into the house and slammed the door behind him with all his might, leaving me lying upon the ground outside. He couldn't have cared less whether I was alive or dead.

After ten minutes or so I managed to crawl over to the door to try to get into the house again, but he had locked the door behind him. I was devastated. The place was like a fortress. I could not get inside. I was weeping. I didn't know what to do. I looked up at the attic windows and could see all the servants' faces looking out at me, but not one of them dared to defy Mr Warde's orders not to open the door to me. And so I set off. I couldn't stay there could I? I could hardly move. I was hobbling and crawling along. I could not spend the night in the open after that sort of treatment. I had to get my wounds seen to. I went towards Stratford-upon-Avon where my friends were. I was sobbing. My dress was torn and soaked with blood. I must have looked a sight. It was a long way to Stratford. When I could walk no further I took shelter for the night in a servant's cottage. The next morning I sent for a carriage to take me to a hotel in Stratford. It was the Shakespeare Commercial Hotel, the best hotel there is in Stratford. The Wardes never have anything but the best. And I sent for Dr Pritchard to attend me as usual and I remained at the Shakespeare for three days.

Dr Pritchard asked no questions but I told him what had happened. He said nothing as he bandaged me up. All he said was to ask when his bill would be paid. I said I had no idea. I wasn't going to pay his bill. I had no right to pay it and I never did pay it. I felt sorry for old Dr Pritchard and I told him to send the bill to Mr Warde, listing all my wounds in detail. He charged for fifty feet of crêpe bandage. I looked like an Egyptian mummy at the end of it.

I went back to Mr Warde again, cursing myself for a fool. I had no money, you see. I had diamonds and emeralds and rubies, every kind of precious stone you care to mention, but what use were precious stones when they were kept locked up in Mr Warde's safe in the corner of his bedroom and only issued to me two minutes before dinner, or when we went out visiting? Mr Warde used to hold out his hand after dinner, or when we got home, and I would have to give up the jewels for safe keeping. I could not go off and sell them!

I had clothes and jewellery worth hundreds of pounds but as for money I had hardly a penny to my name. If I left him I should have starved. I had got used to a life of luxury. I had got used to spending money like water. I had grown accustomed to spending upwards of £20 in a day whenever I felt like it. There was no going back to my old life, earning less than £20 in a year. I had to stay with Mr Warde. I had to stay where I was. I had to stay rich.

On 19 May 1859 there were several guests to dinner at Clopton House. There was the Honourable and Reverend Cornelius Griffin, who was Chaplain to the Stratford Union Workhouse, only he had been in Warwick Gaol for debt as a result of putting up a rich stained-glass window in his church and not being able to pay for it; there was Mr Hillyer the land agent; Miss Grey, who was governess to my daughters; a Mr Wrightman from London, and Mr Lattimer the builder and his wife, and my daughters – Maria Charlotte and Georgina Louisa, and myself and Mr Warde.

At the start all went well. Mr Warde was quite his old charming self and very friendly, but in the middle of dinner he started to complain that the vegetables were badly dressed, and he blamed me for it. He said it was my fault and he wanted to know what I proposed to do about it. He ordered me in fact to go and fetch some more from the kitchen garden.

I refused to go, because I was wearing my best dress and it was dark already and in any case it was pouring with rain. I refused to go digging in the garden in my diamonds. I had my dignity. I would not be humiliated in front of visitors. But the dressing of the vegetables was my doing, and Mr Warde was angry because I would not do as I was told. He was always angry after he had taken wine. You could never predict what he might not do under such circumstances; you could be sure of only one thing – that he would be violent.

I was fearful of what he might do, but I could not and would not let myself be insulted or ill-used in front of the guests. I had to stand up for myself.

Mr Warde suddenly tipped the whole of the gravy out of the gravy dish into a tumbler, and without any warning he threw it all over me in front of everyone. The gravy dripped through my hair, down my face and into my bosom, and scalded me badly. I screamed at him. Some abuse, I don't remember what. I was livid. Then Mr Hillyer threw a jug of water over me to ease the pain.

Miss Grey hurried Maria Charlotte and Georgina Louisa out of the dining-room and away, as she always did when she saw trouble brewing.

I screamed at Mr Warde, 'I will not go into the garden on such a night.' He then picked up a billiard-cue and started to beat me over the back and arms with it. He gave me a great many blows and hurt me fearfully, but not one of the visitors moved a muscle to help me. Not one of them remonstrated with Mr Warde to stop. I was lying on the floor covered in blood. They just sat round the table and carried on drinking their wine, as if this sort of thing took place every day. They could not have stood up to Mr Warde anyway. He would have attacked them too. The Reverend Cornelius Griffin had had too much to drink to even notice what was going on. It was Mr Hillyer in the end who picked me up and carried me up the stairs to my room.

I made doubly sure I locked and bolted my door and shuttered all the windows. I wouldn't have put it past Mr Warde to climb up the drain-pipes in order to get at me again.

The next morning I went downstairs. All the guests had gone. Mr Warde was sitting at the breakfast table with his cold ham, reading The Times as if nothing had happened the night before.

He smiled at me and said, 'Good morning' in his usual manner, but I rolled back the sleeves of my dress and showed him my arms, all black and blue from his beating, and I hissed at him, 'You will pay for this.'

Mr Warde's manner changed instantly. He sprang up from the table, but one of his coat-buttons was hooked up to the table-cloth, and he pulled everything on to the floor with a crash — teapot, plates, knives, cups and saucers. He rushed after me and knocked me out of the room. We careered from room to room, with Mr Warde trying to catch me, and me trying to escape from him. I was panting and sobbing and screaming at him to stop. My dress caught against countless objects of vertu and pieces of fragile furniture, knocking things all over the place and causing hundreds of pounds of damage. Mr Warde lurched into the glass panels of a mahogany bookcase and the fragments of glass flew everywhere. There was blood all over the table-cloth and a trail of my blood led from room to room right through the house, spoiling all the carpets. We had the most violent struggle. My best bonnet with the pink ribbons was torn all to pieces. My left ear was cut in two. One of my toes was broken. I owed my life only to my whalebone stays.

This time I could not walk at all.

Mr Warde just went calmly back to his breakfast, picked up the newspaper and carried on reading it. Miss Grey called Dr Pritchard for me, who came running up the stairs, I was so grievously injured. I heard him say he would be dead before his bill was paid, but I said to him, 'Dr Pritchard, I shall be dead before your bill is paid if things go on like this' and I said, 'I wish I was dead, for an eternity in Hell could not be worse than living here with Charles Warde.'

After that I made up my mind. I had to leave Mr Warde. I could not remain at Clopton House any longer, whether it meant abandoning my children or not. Even if it meant destitution and the Workhouse I had to get away while I was still alive.

I was battered and bruised all over. I was scarred for life and bandaged in every limb. As soon as I could put one foot in front of the other I walked out, cursing myself for a fool for ever leaving Brighton in the first place, and wondering why oh why I hadn't married poor Mr Cheeseman and stayed at home with my mother.

The day before I left him Mr Warde struck me in the face with a whole pineapple which he was carrying indoors from the glasshouses. I was sitting quietly in the little drawing-room writing letters. I was most grievously hurt, and the spines were deeply embedded in my chin and cheeks. I screamed and screamed. It was the last straw.

I took my youngest daughter with me, but I left behind my three eldest daughters at the mercy of their father, though he never did, as far as I know, turn his anger upon them.

I left everything else behind me: gold watches, portraits of me and the children by well-known Academicians, and all the jewels Mr Warde had bought for me over the years – including the diamonds from the necklace which he smashed in London.

I have not set eyes on a single one of the articles detained by Mr Warde. I should say the value of all the jewellery is £400. Mr Warde has since refused to give any of it up to me, and he has persistently refused to allow me to see or have anything to do with my children.

So now I have no money at all. I have not a penny in the world, but am dependent upon my kind friends, for since I left Clopton Mr Warde has given me nothing with which to support myself. I have not even the price of my next meal.

It is true that I did save the sum of £100 in the Stratford Bank for Savings, of which Mr Warde is a Trustee, for I thought that if I ever left Clopton or if Mr Warde ever sent me away, or if Mrs Warde should come back, I should then have something to fall back upon. But I stupidly decided to lend all my £100 to Mr Jevon Perry, who had been kind to me on a number of occasions, and who was locked up in Warwick Gaol for debt. He had put his last sovereign on one of Mr Warde's racehorses that was bound to win the Leamington Stakes but came in last.

Mr Warde objected to my generosity at first. He saw no reason why Mr Perry should not learn the folly of his ways and enjoy a bit more of Her Majesty's hospitality. He found the idea of Jevon Perry in gaol a huge joke and kept laughing about it. The tears ran down his face. But later he changed his mind and said that if I would give him my £100 he would give me a note for £200 in exchange for it. I agreed, and we went off together to buy Mr Perry out of prison and Mr Warde opened a bottle of champagne to celebrate.

I should have known better, for I afterwards discovered that the note for £200 was on a wrong stamp and therefore quite worthless. I was sure he had done it on purpose. I was no better off than when I arrived at Clopton. All my escape money was

*gone and Mr Warde refused to look at the note or take any
notice of it at all. Whenever I brought the matter up Mr Warde
just said 'Pooh, pooh' and walked away whistling.*

*It is also true that in 1849 Mr Warde did most generously
give me a small house at Brighton for my own use exclusively,
but since I left him I have been forced to sell that house in order
to keep body and soul together. I am now quite homeless. He
has given me not one shilling. Not one sixpence, and he has
thousands a year.*

*I don't believe Mr Warde ever did pay Dr Pritchard's bill for
attendances during the years 1857, 1858 and 1859. The bill was
exclusively for treating my injuries that resulted from Mr
Warde's violence. It amounted to more than £33.*

*I have not set foot in Stratford-upon-Avon now for twelve
months, and a good thing, but I understand that Mr Warde's
scullery-maid is now living with him as his wife, and that she
has given birth to Mr Warde's child.*

*I will swear that all my children are the children of Mr
Warde, and that the story that my youngest daughter is
Williams' child, and not the child of Mr Warde, is an idle story.
It is a lie.*

Lord Chief Justice Cockburn wanted to know who Williams
was, and why anyone should have even suspected that he
might be the father of Miss Hooper's child.

Miss Hooper explained that Williams was a footman at
Clopton House but she was reluctant to say any more.

Pressed to reply she said, 'Mr Warde complained of my
conduct on many occasions.'

Pressed to say what sort of conduct and explain what she
meant Miss Hooper said, 'On one occasion I was in the pantry
with Williams when Mr Warde came in.'

Under cross-examination she denied everything.

No, she was not in the habit of kissing Williams in the
pantry.

No, she did not exchange rings with Williams.

No, she did not give Williams her portrait.

No, she did not receive Williams' portrait in return.

No, she was not fond of Williams at all, and she never
suggested to Williams that he was the father of her child. It was

true, however, that she went with Williams to the Woolpack Hotel in Warwick. She did spend the night there with him. It was not because Williams was after her, it was because Mr Warde had beaten Williams with his stick and they went there to talk. There was no sleep for either of them that night. They had no sleep, no supper and no kissing. The hotel cost more than they had expected. Their money ran out. They could not afford any supper and they could not sleep for hunger. They only went back to Clopton because neither of them had any means of support at all. They were wholly dependent upon Mr Warde. They were both his prisoners.

Yes, Mr Warde knew of her going to the hotel with Williams. No, of course he was not worried – he knew they would come crawling back in a day or two.

The court buzzed with interest.

The Lord Chief Justice asked, 'What was it that gave rise to the threats of assault, and what was it that gave rise to the singular animosity between Williams and Mr Warde?'

Anna Hooper could not avoid the questions any longer. She decided to tell the whole story, the part of the story which she had thought the day before it would not be necessary to reveal, thinking that, surely, she would be granted substantial damages without having to expose the whole story to public scrutiny. It was a story she did not want to tell to anybody. But she thought again of the damages. She wondered again where her next meal was coming from, and she took a deep breath and started to speak again, in a voice that was hardly more than a whisper, so that Lord Cockburn had to keep asking her to speak up.

Williams was fourteen years of age when he came to Clopton House. He entered Mr Warde's service in order to look after a child's carriage for my eldest daughter, Maria Charlotte, who was then two or three years old.

It was the same carriage that Mr Warde's Aunt Purefoy gave to him, in which he so liked to pull his children round the gardens. But he would never pull my children round the gardens in it. He used to make excuses. He said he was getting too old for that sort of thing. And so it was Williams' job to take them out and watch that they didn't fall into the ponds or run into any kind of danger.

Unfortunately an improper intimacy took place between Williams and me. It was at Mr Warde's request. One day he brought Williams to the bed where I normally slept with him.

It was quite dark, and I had already gone to bed, so I suppose it must have been between six and twelve o'clock in the evening. The boy had on all his clothes but I did not then know who he was. I did not know anything about him. I could not see him because it was dark, and he did not say a word the whole time he was there.

I resisted the boy and pushed him off, but he remained with me for half an hour and Mr Warde was in the room all the while. Mr Warde didn't say anything either. He had said nothing to me previously on the subject. I didn't know what on earth was going on.

After the boy had gone I asked Mr Warde who on earth he was, and what he thought he was doing bringing him to me like that.

But Mr Warde said only, 'I will tell you in a few days,' only he didn't tell me anything.

The next morning I breakfasted with Mr Warde as usual and continued to live on as friendly terms with him as before. This was before all the violence began. Mr Warde behaved as if nothing had happened at all out of the ordinary.

Lord Chief Justice Cockburn addressed Miss Hooper very seriously: 'It must have seemed a very extraordinary circumstance for Mr Warde to have brought a strange boy into your bedroom.'

'Yes,' said Miss Hooper faintly, 'it did.'

'Miss Hooper, I beg you to remember what happened.'

'I cannot say when it took place, or on what day of the week, but it was not long after Williams entered Mr Warde's service. After that night Williams was brought to live in the house.'

'I presume you asked Mr Warde what he meant by it. What were his intentions and his motives, and so on?'

'I told Mr Warde I thought it was very strange conduct, but he said nothing.'

'Miss Hooper, I beg you to recollect. It must have been one of the most extraordinary events in your whole life.'

'Yes, it was.'

'Well, what was Mr Warde's explanation of this most unheard of occurrence?'

'I cannot say what he said, my Lord.'

'Upon the solemn oath which you have just taken, do you assert again that every word of this is true?'

'Yes, my Lord.'

'It is all true, you still persist in it, yet you cannot tell the court what Mr Warde said afterwards?'

'No, sir, I cannot.'

'Are you living with Williams now?'

'No, sir.'

'Are you married to him?'

'No, my Lord.'

The court held its breath. Miss Hooper's demeanour had changed from almost careless gaiety to that of an intensely nervous person. She became extremely pallid and had to be given a chair and a glass of water. She sat down on the chair with a bump and knocked back the glass of water in one go.

Thomas Williams was called, and appeared in his Sunday best. He was carefully shaved, with his face scrubbed and shining and his yellow hair slicked down with Electric Oil as usual.

'Tell us, Mr Williams,' said the Lord Chief Justice, 'as Miss Hooper cannot or will not tell us, what has been going on at Clopton House, if you would be so kind. You may take your time.'

Thomas Williams rolled his eyes a bit, scratched his head a bit, as if he was not sure where to begin, and in the end he began at the beginning.

> My father conducted a brickyard for Mr Warde, sir, and so I was born upon Mr Warde's estate, was bred by Mr Warde you might say, and belonged to him in a manner of speaking. I am now twenty-four years of age.
>
> When I was between the ages of fourteen and fifteen Mr Warde took me into his service as a boy in the garden, picking up leaves, rolling and cutting the lawns, raking the gravel paths and such like. I remember it was the year of the Great Exhibition, when I came to London for the first time, and that would have been the year 1851.

Well, one day I was just standing upon the lawn in front of Clopton House in my shirt-sleeves and peaked cap, minding my own business and surveying the work I had just done and the work I still had left to do, having a bit of a rest, in fact, for it was a hot summer's day, when Mr Warde walked up to me and said to me, 'Williams, should you mind going with a pretty girl?' I couldn't help grinning. I said, 'No, sir, I shouldn't mind at all, sir.' And Mr Warde told me to go round to the little drawing-room at half-past six or seven o'clock that evening.

I did as I was told – I always obeyed orders – though I didn't quite know or even guess what was going to happen, and when it did happen no one was more surprised than I, for I thought he meant going out in the carriage or suchlike.

When the time came I went in search of the little drawing-room, though I had never been properly inside the house before and I got lost and had to be shown the way by one of the housemaids.

When I found the little drawing-room it was in pitch darkness. The shutters was all closed. Mr Warde was lurking there just behind the door and he grabbed me by the hand and pulled me into the room. He guided me to an armchair or couch, I couldn't see which it was, and he told me to put my hand where he directed. I did as he told me.

I was pretty frightened, I can tell you. I didn't quite know what he expected me to do, not having done that kind of work before. I was just a servant. There was a woman lying there who I didn't know. Nothing like this had ever happened to me before in my lifetime. But nothing in fact did happen on that occasion because the woman, whoever she was, began to cry. Mr Warde just gave me a shilling and told me to go away and say nothing about it to no one.

A few days later I was none the wiser about what this was all about when Mr Warde came up to me a second time and asked me to go and live in the house and go out with the children in the carriage as a sort of page or footman. I was pleased by that. It was a better life than dragging about the gardens in all weathers. It was a step up in the world, though I had to wear a flunkey suit of green velvet with a red collar and a load of gold all over it wherever I went and I could have done without that, not to mention the white silk stockings. But I got more money and I didn't mind that.

It must have been four days afterwards that Mr Warde came to find me a third time and took me along to his library. It was four o'clock in the afternoon but all the shutters was closed and the room was quite in the dark. All I could see was a shine of gold off of the backs of Mr Warde's books. We was surrounded by gold books on all sides.

There was a woman in the room and Mr Warde took me to her and pushed me on top of her, but she pushed me off violently and I fell on to the floor. I wasn't expecting it and I hurt my back. I didn't know who the woman was, but she began to cry like the other woman did. I was frightened. I tried to find the door of the library in the dark, before Mr Warde dismissed me, but it was a hidden door disguised as bookshelves and I had to be shown the way. Then Mr Warde gave me another shilling and that was that. It was money for old rope. A piece of cake you might say.

Seven days later or thereabouts Mr Warde sent me up the back stairs to his dressing-room where there was a full-sized brass bedstead. It was during the afternoon but the curtains and shutters was closed again and it was so dark that I couldn't hardly see what I was doing.

Mr Warde ordered me to get undressed and get into the bed. I was a bit nervous about that. I didn't know what was going to happen. I'd never been told by the Squire to take my clothes off for him before, nor for no one else for that matter, but I did as I was told. I always did as I was told. I was paid to obey orders. I was determined to be a faithful servant. And so I took off my clothes and dropped them on the floor and climbed on to the bed. It was quite the softest feather bed I've ever climbed into before or since. I wondered again what it was that was going to take place, but Mr Warde wouldn't of told me even if I'd asked. He wasn't the kind of gentleman that told you nothing. But what he did next really made me shake in my boots, in a manner of speaking, for I wasn't wearing them, or anything else at all. For what he did next was to tie the counterpane tight over my eyes.

I couldn't hardly breathe because it was over my nose as well. I resisted a bit but he told me quite sharp not to remove it

179

and said I was to lie still. Then he went off out of the dressing-room and I was able to peek out of my blindfold. By this time my eyes was getting used to the dark. In about five minutes he came back with a woman.

Some words passed between them. They quarrelled a bit. I could not make out exactly what it was they said, but I could hear him shouting at her a bit. I couldn't hardly see because of the blindfold and I couldn't hardly hear because my ears was trapped inside it.

So I still didn't know who the woman was, or whether she was the same woman as the last time or not. I heard her try to get away out of the door of the dressing-room but Mr Warde went after her and slammed the door and brought her right back. He was very rough with her and then there was a great ripping noise and a tearing as he tore all the woman's clothes right off of her and put her by force into the bed with me.

Mr Warde, I could tell, was standing right by the side of the bed. I could hear him breathing. The woman's face was against my face. She was crying. I could feel her hot salt tears against my face. That upset me a bit, but I heard Mr Warde's voice close up to us, saying, 'Nonsense, nonsense, lie still.'

I remained there in the bed half an hour obeying Mr Warde's orders as he told me what to do and what not, and I just floated away until he said quite sharp, 'Right, time's up' and ordered me to get out of the bed and get my clothes on again.

I did as I was told, though it was difficult to get my clothes on with the blindfold still over my eyes and I didn't hardly know what I was doing. I couldn't see what clothes was what and I fell over, but Mr Warde still wouldn't let me take the blindfold off. The woman in the end helped me. She was giggling a bit and had cheered up a bit, like she'd enjoyed it, or like she'd had a drink or two.

Mr Warde then gave me a pair of boots and told me to say most particular to anyone I met on the stairs, 'Mr Warde called me up to take his boots down.' Then he took me out of the dressing-room, and it was only then that he took off the counterpane, so that I never did see who it was that I'd been with, and I set off, blinking with the light, to take the boots down.

I met four of my fellow servants on the stairs and I said to them I remember most particular, for I still could not make head nor tail of these strange goings on, 'Mr Warde give me the boots to take down and he give me a shilling for doing it.'

The same thing happened two or three times a week until I was quite accustomed to having my bit of exercise and my bit of fun in the afternoons, quite regular like, but it was not always with the same woman and I was still none the wiser about why it was all going on. It was a mystery. Mr Warde was a mystery. I just enjoyed myself and asked no questions. I knew I wouldn't get no answers. It was better than digging the garden.

It was not until five years of going on like this had gone by that I found out who the woman was, and that it was one and the same woman all the time.

One morning Mr Warde called me into his library in broad daylight. He was sitting at his desk with his feet up on the desk, and smoking the biggest cigar I'd ever seen, and blowing rings of smoke up to the golden ceiling. He asked me straight out, quite cool, 'Williams,' he said, 'would you like to marry Miss Hooper?'

I said nothing. I just stood there. I looked at all the books. It was a very splendid room and I'd never been there in daylight before. I didn't know what to say to him.

Then he said to me, quite sharp, 'Have you a tongue in your head, boy?'

I looked at him. I didn't say anything. I didn't know who Miss Hooper was.

Mr Warde told me to go to the dining-room with him. I did as I was told. I saw the mistress sitting in a chair with her nose in a book. Mr Warde said to me, 'Take hold of her and give her a kiss.'

The mistress said, rather sharp, 'You'd better not.'

But Mr Warde lifted her up in his arms like she was made out of nothing but feathers. He put her upon a sofa and pushed me on top of her. The mistress pushed me off and said she would not allow it, but she did, and I had to kiss her.

It was then that I found out that the mistress and the woman called Miss Hooper was one and the same person I'd been taken to so many times. She had the same soft skin. It was the *way she pushed me on to the floor. And she smelt the same. It was the perfume that made me realize in the end. She felt the same and smelt the same. I must have been taken to her twenty or thirty times before I was twenty years of age.*

On all those occasions I swear Mr Warde was present the whole time, though I couldn't say or see what he was doing. I was too busy to notice. I suppose I could say that he was watching in the dark.

Before I discovered who Miss Hooper was I behaved towards her as a servant should. I called her 'Madam' or 'Mistress', but when all was revealed I became much more familiar with her. She always said something about 'the proper relations between a mistress and her servants should be one of familiarity without conversation' and she would always laugh about it.

Mr Warde kept on asking me to marry Miss Hooper, but I never did get to marry her, and in the year 1858 I left Mr Warde's service altogether and went to work instead as butler to a Mr Butler Johnstone in Scotland. I left that employ also a year and a half ago, and have been out of work ever since, living with my friends. Sometimes I stay with my father in Staffordshire. Sometimes I stay at Stratford-upon-Avon.

For a while after she left Mr Warde Miss Hooper lived at Slough with a Mr O'Brien, who was a friend of Mr Warde's, but she left him too after a time and came to live with me at Mayfield Cottage, Dalston. We lived together as man and wife but I didn't have enough money to keep up the grand way of living Miss Hooper had been accustomed to, and we quarrelled about money. It didn't last. Neither the money nor living with Miss Hooper. It was all over between us in five weeks.

We have exchanged some letters since then, but I haven't set eyes on her until today. Most of the letters was to do with me being a witness in this case.

I loved Miss Hooper though. She was very kind to me. I still love her.

I have been alone with Miss Hooper dozens of times in the little drawing-room at Clopton House, but not for any improper purpose. She was giving me lessons in reading and writing, though I never was very much of a scholar.

On one occasion, though, Mr Warde found us in the pantry

182

among all the pheasants and venison and other meat that was
hanging up there. We did not hear Mr Warde come in. We was
too busy kissing. He just stood there behind us waiting for the
moment when we should realize he was there. Then there was
the most fearful row. His eyes blazed. He raged and screamed
and shouted. Fur and feathers flew everywhere. He smacked
me repeatedly round the face with a dead rabbit so that I was
covered in blood. Miss Hooper thought it was my blood and
she screamed the house down until Mr Warde stopped. It was
horrible, but I was not much injured and all the blood washed
off.

There was other occasions, of course, when there was
trouble and a rumpus on account of Mr Warde accusing me of
having Miss Hooper without his knowledge or consent. He
always liked to think he was in charge of it, in control, so to
speak, but after I found out who Miss Hooper was I got rather
bold. Generally I observed my oath. I went by Mr Warde's
orders in all that I did, but I was on very affectionate terms
with Miss Hooper. I used to go and kiss her without orders.
After all, Mr Warde always led me to believe that she should
one day be my wife. But towards the end of my time in his
service Mr Warde couldn't seem to make up his mind what I
was meant to be doing. He would discharge me from my post
one day and shout at me and tell me to pack my bags and clear
off, only to take me back the next morning just as I was setting
off down the Coach Road with my tail between my legs, as you
might say.

I never did understand Mr Warde, I never did understand it
all. I still don't understand. I can't sleep at nights for not
understanding it.

I did hear that Mr O'Brien wanted Miss Hooper to sue out a
Commission of Lunacy against Mr Warde and bring an action
for assault and I wrote to Mr Warde to put him on his guard
against illegal proceedings, thinking he would not much like all
the details of the goings-on at Clopton to be brought into the
public view for all to know about.

I thought Mr O'Brien was at the bottom of it all. Their
intentions was to put an end to Mr Warde's future happiness
by taking all his children by Miss Hooper away from him. I
could not let that happen. I could not sit by and watch traps

being set for Mr Warde, not after all those years. He was a good master to me and I was a faithful servant. Nearly always, that is. Sometimes I deserved what I got. That time he beat me with his walking-stick, for instance.

And there was the time I threatened to shoot him. He withdrew the charge against me on condition that I signed a paper promising not to send or cause to be sent to Miss Hooper any letters of any kind. I had to swear that I wouldn't have nothing more to do with her. That I would never try to see her again. Well, I did write some letters after that, of course, and I did see her again, but the magistrates didn't know nothing about that paper being signed when the court case was going on.

That's about all I have to say, sir.

The court buzzed again with curiosity as Mr Warde's name was called. He was still a powerful figure, who could not be overlooked or ignored, for he towered over everyone else. Asked to give his version of the story Mr Warde referred to two huge books of memoranda in order to refresh his memory, and drew some laughter from the court. He began to speak and in the still room his voice was the only sound, rich, purring, articulate, loud and clear and confident.

I am the defendant, Charles Thomas Warde, and I live at Clopton House, Stratford-upon-Avon. I am a magistrate and a Deputy-Lieutenant of the County of Warwick.

I first met the plaintiff, Anna Maria Cobden Hooper, at Brighton and I engaged her as my housekeeper. I had been annoyed by thriftless servants and thought she would be a useful person to spy over them.

As far as I was concerned Miss Hooper was a virtuous girl until the month of January 1849, but the way she went about at Brighton shaking hands with every able-bodied man she met made me wonder whether in fact she was a virtuous girl before I met her.

Latterly there were quarrels between us on account of Miss Hooper's levity of conduct. She would constantly invite the labourers from Stratford-upon-Avon up to Clopton House to visit her, and they would knock on the front door as bold as you please and ask for her, saying they had an appointment, or that they had some business to discuss with her.

They were the very lowest of the low: tradesmen and abandoned servants, Irish navvies, farm labourers and apprentices. She would absent herself overnight and would frequently go off into the plantations on my estate with these men. In consequence scenes of violence occurred between us during the last six years that she lived with me.

I remember one occasion in particular when I sent for the Police because Miss Hooper was fighting and quarrelling with me. The row arose from an argument over her children. In her sober moments she had expressed a wish to make over to me, as far as she could, all parental rights over her three daughters.

I told her I would not allow her out of the house until she signed a Deed about the matter, and she ran about the passages like a madwoman with a brace of my pistols, threatening to shoot me. I was not frightened by that but I was anxious to have the Deed signed, and I was anxious in case she fired off the pistols by accident and hurt herself.

I threatened to have her taken away by the Police although I would never have carried out such a threat. I loved her too well. I love her still.

On that occasion Miss Hooper was very drunk. She had been drinking all day and she reeked of alcohol. She was perpetually drunk and quarrelsome and would drink anything she could lay her hands on. She drank a pint of brandy a day for two months.

When she was inebriated, and often when she was not, Miss Hooper used to go about my house abusing me in the worst Billingsgate language. She abused my wife, my aunt, my children, my ancestors and everything that belonged to me. Such abuse provoked me.

On top of all that I was perpetually annoyed by her having men up to the house. They would appear at all hours of the day and night, and sometimes when I had guests to dinner one of her labourers would tap on the windows of the dining-room and off Miss Hooper would go in the middle of the meal to see him. They would ask if she was at home, and would loiter outside waiting for her, whistling or singing, or just waiting to catch a glimpse of her. Miss Hooper was a very attractive woman. She still is. But it was becoming common knowledge in Stratford what was going on, and I was anxious to avoid a scandal.

Unfortunately I suggested to Miss Hooper that instead of

bringing men up from Stratford and from all parts she should have a man upon the estate. It was on account of Miss Hooper being extremely amorous. She justified her levity of conduct on the grounds that I was old and used up. I am no longer a young man, my Lord. I am now forty-seven years of age.

Unfortunately she took me at my word. I never spoke a word to Thomas Williams upon the subject until his intimacy with Miss Hooper had existed for some time, but it was I that sanctioned it. I told Miss Hooper that she could do as she pleased. 'I don't mind what you do,' I said. 'Do what you like. This is Liberty Hall.'

At the time of our conversation upon the subject Miss Hooper went so far as to give me a memorandum, quite of her own free will. She wrote me a note which said: 'If you get me a nice little fellow to give me a kiss I solemnly swear I will never go out of the house again.'

I did not suggest the terms. It was a voluntary statement on the part of Miss Hooper. I will swear that I have never been present in a darkened room with Williams and the plaintiff and I will swear that I only knew of what occurred from what Miss Hooper told me afterwards.

I first heard of it soon after I had pointed out the lad Williams on the lawn and advised Miss Hooper to take him. He was a stalwart youth. He was just what she needed, a sturdy little fellow. I knew of her going out to Williams. I knew where she went to in the evenings and I slept with her the same night myself.

On one occasion Miss Hooper demanded that I should turn away an old nurse who had lived at Clopton since the year before I was born, but I was not going to be told what to do in my own house. Miss Hooper stormed into the housekeeper's room in a passion and slammed the door in my face. I put my foot against the door and kicked it open and Miss Hooper was hurt by the handle. Afterwards I heard her telling everyone that I had injured her.

On another occasion Miss Hooper fetched a double-barrelled shotgun and threatened to shoot Smith, the gardener, who had broken three of Miss Hooper's ribs for not knowing how to turn the horses round a corner and driving the carriage over his lawns and making two great ruts across them. It was *her way of getting her own back, but I took the gun away from her.*

Another time Eleanor Rose, one of the housemaids, came running to find me and said, 'Oh, do come down, Sir, or mistress will kill Sarah Carter.' When I arrived on the scene I thought it looked like an artificial quarrel. Miss Hooper was standing before the fire holding the poker and brandishing it at Carter in a most dangerous and threatening manner. I told Rose that if she knocked Miss Hooper down I would give her a handsome present. Miss Hooper advanced with the poker regardless and Rose knocked her down with a single blow. Afterwards I gave Rose two sovereigns. It was to teach Miss Hooper a lesson.

As for the cartwhip I kept it in the dining-room to drive out the cats. I only struck Miss Hooper with it because she hit me as hard as she could with a brass curtain-rod. She often used to throw all kinds of things at me. Candlesticks. Knives and forks. Salt-cellars. I was quite accustomed to it.

I deny, however, that I ever beat Miss Hooper with a billiard-cue and I deny that I ever threw gravy all over her, but I will admit that on one occasion I threw everything on the table at her: the cutlery, plates, candelabra, glasses, and all the food. Some of the things hit her. Some of them smashed against the wall behind her. She just sat there at the other end of the dining-table with cream dripping from her face, custard in her hair, with her knife and fork still in her hands. Thomas Williams, who was then the butler, witnessed that incident. He could not leave the dining-room until he was ordered to go. He had to stand there and pretend this sort of thing was quite a normal occurrence at Clopton House. Such things were not, in fact, uncommon. I was determined to enjoy myself in every way I could. Miss Hooper enjoyed it all, it was all a joke. Miss Hooper is no ordinary person. She did not flee from the room as Mrs Warde used to the moment something out of the ordinary happened. It was a sort of game we played.

As time went on Williams became impudent. He used to follow Miss Hooper about the house all day, kissing her in every room in front of everybody. I once found them in the pantry together. Once they were on the sofa in my library in broad daylight. They would go off to the haylofts, or into the

187

coppices and absent themselves for hours. Hence the quarrels between us.

I suppose I must have beaten her some twenty or thirty times before she left me. I was sorry she was injured but she had only herself to blame. I never did pay Dr Pritchard's bills for her treatment, but when Pritchard died there was a public subscription for his widow and I sent the sum of £200.

I broke Miss Hooper's jewels at Hatchett's Hotel because she abandoned me at my club in St James's Street and went off to visit her brother-in-law instead, without telling me where she was going.

I broke the jewels as a lesson to her, much as you might box a boy's ears. I really cannot say what she took away with her from Clopton when she left me, or exactly what was sent on to her in the way of jewellery, but I do know that some thirty large boxes and trunks full of clothes were sent, though there were still vast quantities of her belongings left behind. I always hoped she might come back to me. I still hope she will come back.

I have not set eyes on a single one of the jewels since she left. I have not the slightest idea where they are. I should think she took them with her.

I did not send her away. I would have given £10,000 rather than she should have gone away. I send away the mother of my children? I weep at the very thought of it. I said just now 'I love her still' and so I do. I wrote a letter to Miss Hooper's attorney in 1859 to say that I was ready to defend myself against any proceedings his drunken, dissolute client might choose to institute. The Chinese love the Devil. I love Miss Hooper and I wrote that letter.

Sarah Carter was called and appeared in striped dress, plaid shawl and lace-trimmed bonnet to tell a story of poisoning. Miss Hooper had laced Mr Warde's brandy and water with Emery's Beetle Poison and Mr Warde had drained the glass to the last drop before Miss Hooper told him what she had done. Mr Warde had raged and retched and choked.

'He got Miss Hooper by the throat,' said Sarah Carter, 'and said something like, "If I'm going to die you're coming with me" and he squeezed her neck and would have strangled her had I not told them about Emery's Beetle Poison being not poisonous at all, but read them the label "Free From Danger to Human Life", and then they was both roaring with laughter and couldn't hardly stop themselves.'

Miss Hooper had not bothered to read the label properly.

At other times, Carter said, Miss Hooper would go about swearing at the servants, shouting at them and making unreasonable demands:

'She would ring the bells in the middle of the night to be brought bacon and eggs, or a glass of water from the jug on the other side of her room. She liked to make the housemaids spend all day running up and down stairs on ridiculous errands till they were panting for breath, and then she would throw things at them and abuse them mercilessly. She was drunk from morning till night.'

William Horseley the coachman was called and told how he was sent for one night to fetch Miss Hooper home from Stratford Fair.

'It was very late,' he said, 'ten or eleven o'clock at night and when I got to the town I found Miss Hooper beastly drunk. She was dancing and singing in and out of the ox-roast and waxworks and fat boys and fortune-telling ponies. There was a great crowd round her, cheering her on and clapping. She did not want to come home at all and she fought me, biting and scratching and screaming at me, and she danced out of the way whenever I tried to catch her. Mr Warde was not with her. He was at home in bed, sound asleep. When he found out about it he wasn't very pleased.'

Henry Cross, Mr Warde's agent, admitted to the court that he had been at one time on very friendly terms with Miss Hooper.

'I received my orders from her,' he said, 'and although I have heard Miss Hooper say that she could swear she'd never kissed me and that I wasn't in the habit of kissing her, I have to tell the truth, which is this: that there was trouble and a quarrel on my account between Mr Warde and Miss Hooper. There was kissing between us, and more. I was very intimate with Miss Hooper. There was plenty of justification for that quarrel.'

*

Joseph James said that he was Inspector of Police at Stratford in 1857 and that Mr Warde had written many notes of complaint about Miss Hooper's conduct.

'I was often called out at all hours of the day and night to help control her,' he said. 'I often found her in a very excited state and very much the worse for liquor. Once I saw her throw a heavy silver candlestick at Mr Warde, but he caught the missile and was not injured by it.'

He told of the time he had found Miss Hooper brandishing a pair of pistols. 'She was as drunk as a boiled owl on that occasion,' he said, 'and directly the door was broken down she was very violent. Afterwards I went down to the drawing-room and found her with her arms round Mr Warde's neck, embracing him, and Mr Warde with his arms round her waist. They were very much in love in spite of all their quarrels. Miss Hooper denies that I was a pet of hers but unfortunately that is not the truth. The fact is that I too became very intimate with Miss Hooper myself during the latter part of her time at Clopton House. I am still in the Warwickshire Police Force but I was reduced from the rank of Inspector on account of my intimacy with Miss Hooper. Mr Warde got to hear of it and complained of me. I am now only a Constable.'

Mr Serjeant Pigott, summing up the case for Mr Warde, did not refrain from applying terms of approbation to Mr Warde, but commented with great severity on the lewd and debauched conduct of Miss Hooper.

One of her letters to Williams left no doubt about her feelings towards the boy. The letter spoke for itself:

'My darling pet, do not think I have forgotten what you are like in my dreams . . .'

'He is more jealous than ever . . .'

'I dare not move or look . . .'

'We shall one day be one . . .'

'Thousands of kisses . . .'

And Mr Serjeant Pigott recommended the jury in the strongest terms to kick the case of Hooper v. Warde out of court 'like a dog with a kettle to its tail' and give Miss Hooper only one farthing damages, for it appeared that she deserved all the ill-treatment she got from Mr Warde. She was after his money and she had brought all her misfortunes upon herself.

Mr Edwin James QC addressed the jury on behalf of Miss Hooper, saying, 'It is melancholy for the sake of English society that the veil should be torn aside and expose to view such gross immorality.'

He condemned Mr Warde for suggesting that Miss Hooper should take Williams to satisfy her lust, and he condemned Mr Warde for now turning round and complaining that she had done as he suggested.

He condemned Mr Warde for saying he loved Miss Hooper to distraction and at the same time reproaching her for her lewdness with other men.

He condemned Mr Warde for hinting that Miss Hooper was a prostitute before he met her, for this was not true.

He condemned Mr Warde for slandering the mother of his four children and he condemned him for exposing her to want and temptation since she had left him by not giving her money to support herself.

Mr James said, 'Gentlemen of the jury, you have heard of Mr Warde's cruelty to Miss Hooper – cruelty that makes the blood creep and shudder – cruelty so brutal as at last to drive her out of Clopton House. It will be melancholy for the sake of English justice if you do not award substantial damages for the wrongs which Miss Hooper has suffered at the hands of this monster of depravity who sits in court today smiling and smiling as if he does not know the meaning of what he has done.'

Lord Chief Justice Cockburn had no doubt that a long and aggravated series of vicious assaults had been committed at Clopton but he instructed the jury most carefully: they must not fail to distinguish between outrageous violence inflicted upon a meek, submissive, unoffending woman, and violence of which the victim had in some degree been the cause.

'Nothing can justify beating a woman with a cartwhip,' said Lord Cockburn, 'and nothing can justify beating a woman with a billiard-cue or an archery bow, but you will have to consider whether Miss Hooper's conduct did not in some degree excuse the conduct of Mr Warde.'

The Lord Chief Justice condemned Miss Hooper as a drunken, libidinous, passionate woman of most violent temper, who was unfaithful with a variety of men, and noted the vast amount of evidence that proved her habits to be habits of intemperance.

He condemned Mr Warde for leading Miss Hooper away from the paths of righteousness, to a miserable condition of mind from which drunkenness was her only escape, and he condemned Mr Warde for leading Miss Hooper to degradation such as had been rarely disclosed in an English Court of Justice.

He condemned Mr Warde for himself suggesting the immoral courses which Miss Hooper pursued. It was Mr Warde's own suggestion that she should have intercourse with other men. There was no possible way in which Mr Warde could claim that Miss Hooper's infidelity with other men was the excuse for his shocking violence to her.

'Yesterday,' said Lord Cockburn, 'the impression upon my mind was that this was one of the most extraordinary stories, not only within my personal experience, but in the whole of history. Today I see plainly why Miss Hooper hesitated so much when urged to give an explanation of what happened: she actually drew up a paper in which, on condition of Mr Warde finding someone for her, she undertook to stay at home. Mr Warde's mistress for a considerable time had, with his acquiescence, knowledge and sanction, an intimacy with Williams. It could not therefore be put forward as an excuse for his violence. Why then should Mr Warde complain after having allowed and permitted this liaison? The explanation was this: A child was born and it bore such a strong resemblance to Thomas Williams as to leave no doubt at all that it was Williams' child.'

'Mr Warde said himself: "I found I had committed a most unfortunate fault. I intended Miss Hooper's activities with Williams as a pastime, never expecting the result. Soon after the girl was born I sent Williams away, but Miss Hooper pleaded and begged so much that I changed my mind and allowed Williams to stay."'

'Mr Warde was so disgusted at having Williams' spurious issue put upon him that he tried to put a stop to the relationship that he had started, and of course that was an impossible thing to try to do, for the lady had come to prefer the younger lover to the older one, and then Mr Warde, finding that they persisted in spite of all his efforts, was led into the tumultuous quarrels and violence. The root of it all was jealousy – Mr Warde's jealousy of his own footman.'

At half-past five on 19 December 1860 the jury retired, and half an hour later the foreman announced that they found their verdict for Miss Hooper, and that they awarded damages of £100 for the jewellery and £500 for the suffering in body and mind which she had endured as a result of Mr Warde's assaults.

There was prolonged applause in court and it was some fifteen minutes before order was restored, for Mr Warde was jeered at and abused and shouted at, and on his exit into the street all the rotten tomatoes, bad eggs and mouldy vegetables which the women of Stratford had brought with them from Warwickshire were hurled at him, for the women had travelled up to London on the Great Western Railway at Miss Hooper's expense.

When Mr Warde returned to Clopton there was not a servant to be seen, and he found that all his windows had been smashed, and that all the manure from his capital stables and all the cow-dung from his spacious cow-sheds, and all the human excrement from his most modern cess-pit, had been carefully spread across the carpets in every room throughout Clopton House, and upon the seat of every gilded chair, and that the faces of the portraits of all his family had been carefully cut away and removed.

When he found the servants huddled in the bakehouse heatedly discussing what to do, there was a sudden silence.

'Get to work,' he shouted, 'clean the house.' And they scrubbed from attic to cellar all night, and the cook, governess, nursemaids, butler and footmen had to help as well.

When Mr Warde retired for the night he found that his handsome and substantial bedstead too had been carefully filled from head to foot with stinking dung, carefully concealed between the sheets so that he did not find it until he was well and truly in.

Mr Warde spent the whole night walking his estate in the dark, raging and shouting and cursing and swearing at the stars, so that the deer stampeded down the Coach Road into Stratford-upon-Avon and he lost his voice altogether.

After Christmas the Lord Chancellor sent a letter to Mr Warde which said:

> *I feel it to be my duty to order your name to be struck out from the Commission of the Peace for the County of Warwick. . . .In your evidence given in the trial of Hooper v. Warde you showed a recklessness of conduct and an unconsciousness of the distinction between right and wrong which proves you to be a person wholly unfit to be entrusted with the power of taking part in the administration of the Criminal Law.*

Shortly afterwards, in the New Year of 1861, *The London Gazette* announced that Her Majesty Queen Victoria had been graciously pleased to accept the resignation of the commission held by Mr Charles Thomas Warde of Clopton House, Stratford-upon-Avon, as a Deputy-Lieutenant for the County of Warwick.

Mr Warde did not grin or smirk any longer. His face was wooden, his jaw was set, and he sat motionless at the breakfast table in his newly-disinfected dining-room with *The Morning Herald* in front of him, for a substantial space had been devoted to the aftermath of the case of Hooper *v.* Warde. Mr Warde's fists clenched, gripping the paper like a vice as his eye ran down the columns.

> . . . *Nobody could derive good by becoming acquainted with these unworthy secrets* . . .
>
> . . . *If Mr Warde was not morally mad, then no man ever was so* . . .
>
> . . . *It was doubtless thought his intellect was not sufficiently impaired to make him out insane* . . .
>
> . . . *Continually occurs in Mr Warde's career evidence of imbecility and weakness only to be set down to a damaged intellect* . . .
>
> . . . *A man of wealth and power, he could at once have discarded his mistress when he discovered the extreme irregularity of her conduct, and her drunken, libidinous habits* . . .

. . . He himself was corrupted with the same vices . . .

. . . both were demented . . .

. . . both went on from year to year wallowing in crimes and vices of the most revolting nature . . .

. . . filthy and pestilential disclosures . . .

Mr Warde sat on at his breakfast table, quite alone and quite still. A skin formed across the surface of his coffee. After some time he stood up and strode purposefully across the still stinking carpet and into the vast kitchens full of copper pans and priceless china, scattering the servants who had not yet walked out but were preparing to leave, and helping themselves to whatever was immediately portable and whatever was of the most value.

They fled at his coming, and crouched outside, beneath the window-sill, peering over, watching to see what Mr Warde would do next, and they were rewarded by the sight of Mr Warde systematically smashing his way through every piece of china in the house, so that the stone floor of the kitchen was completely covered with the debris of Minton and Spode and Wedgwood, and the most expensive crockery that money could buy.

It was Caroline Sutton, who had not left Clopton, and had no intention of leaving, but was determined to stay, who sent for the Doctor and bandaged Mr Warde's cut and bleeding hands.

NINE

Caroline Sutton, subsisting on the sum of £10 a year, had almost nothing to lose. The day after Anna Hooper left Clopton Mr Warde's eye had lit upon Sutton, not for the first time, but with a new gleam in it, and Sutton was easily persuaded to turn her back on her fish kettles, hair sieves, dripping tins and all the greasy pans in her steaming scullery, in order to begin the ascent from below stairs to above stairs, ignoring for the time being that a climb up would surely involve before long a climb down again, all the way back to where she started.

'Meanwhile,' thought Sutton, 'I will be a lady.'

She made a bee-line for Anna Hooper's still laden dressing-table and plastered bottle after bottle of miracle-working cream over her face and hands. She discovered, amongst other things, a bottle of Auricomus Fluid, which produced the rich golden flaxen colour so much admired in ladies' hair, and which had been left behind by Mrs Warde.

Sutton made liberal use of Piesse & Lubin's New Scents – Stolen Kisses, its sequel Box-His-Ears and Kiss-Me-Quick – until Mr Warde announced that he preferred her to smell of starch and dripping and kitchen soap, and she sadly gave up using scent altogether.

She spent most of her waking hours, and many of her dreams, up to her elbows in Fluide d'Hiver, which was guaranteed to impart delicacy to the complexion and beauty to the skin and to render every chapped hand soft, beautiful and white, and remove every mark of hard usage, be its condition ever so unpromising, until Mr Warde said, 'I prefer your hands to be red and rough and hard,' and Sutton gave up trying to give them a gentle touch.

She abandoned her servant's bedroom and moved lock, stock and barrel into Miss Hooper's old apartments where everything was very grand, and made of silk or satin or cloth of gold. Her fingers strayed across the bullet-holes that peppered the walls, and she picked up from the bedside table a well-thumbed copy of *French in a Fortnight Without a Master*, but when she turned the pages the letters danced like gnats on a summer evening before her eyes.

She pretended to read her way through *The Ladies' Pocket Book of Etiquette* until Mr Warde said, 'You don't want to be bothering with books' and the pages remained uncut beyond the words 'ladies do not wear gloves during dinner' which was as far as Anna Hooper had managed to get.

Sutton stepped into Mrs Warde's old boots as far as she could and squeezed herself (until her pregnancy was far advanced) into Mrs Warde's old dresses, and pretended to be Mrs Warde and Miss Hooper rolled into one. She spoke very carefully and practised all Anna Hooper's mannerisms and imitated all the genteel vowels which she had been rehearsing for months, and her voluminous dresses, some of them containing upwards of 500 yards of the most costly silk, swished and rustled as she glided genteelly through the rambling house on silent feet.

Until the day when Mr Warde asked her to put her scullery maid's dress back on, so that he could chase her through the house and rip it off, and so that they could wrestle together on the bare boards of empty attic rooms, or stand together up against the wall in the pantry, or roll together in the middle of the cornfields, where their laughing and giggling made the farm labourers pause in the middle of their bread and cheese and wonder what was going on, and raise their eyebrows when the pair emerged dishevelled with straw in their hair.

One day Mr Warde stopped himself in the middle of calling Sutton 'Caroline' and asked whether he might not go back to using her surname, as he had always done, for he always thought of her as Sutton. And Sutton could do nothing but agree to his request and put up with the indignity. And he said, 'You might stop using that new voice as well, and stop trying to sound like a lady, for I much prefer your Coventry voice' and Sutton nodded and did as she was told.

And one afternoon Mr Warde suggested that Sutton should give up her magnificent apartments with the handsome and substantial half-tester bedstead upholstered in green damask, and together they climbed up the narrow twisting staircase to the attics, carrying Sutton's belongings between them, and they both squeezed into a narrow box of a room with nothing in it but a narrow iron bed and a prickly horsehair mattress, and Mr

200

Warde would grin and leer and put his head round the door, and wrestle with Sutton and rip her clothes to pieces, and Sutton only pretended to resist and only pretended to scream, and only pretended to be outraged, but put up with everything. And they squashed into Meller's narrow iron bed and slept there instead, night after night.

Gradually Sutton got used to her new situation, which lay somewhere in between servant and lady, neither one thing nor the other, for she was required to wear her servant's clothes in the mornings and perform the most menial tasks: lighting Mr Warde's fire, delivering his hot water, sweeping the floors and milking the cows, and she would wear silk in the afternoons and sit on a *chaise longue* while Mr Warde talked away to her about his past and about his business affairs, and in the evenings Sutton would put on her diamonds and Mr Warde would hang necklace after necklace round her neck, so that in the end she would be wearing the whole contents of his enormous safe, and they would dine alone, one at each end of the twenty-six foot dining-table, waited on by a dozen servants.

A nurse took care of Charles Aprilius, Sutton's thumping baby. The servants called her 'Madam' or 'Mistress', and a new housekeeper, a new cook, a new butler and five new house-maids, who knew little of Sutton's history and nothing of Mr Warde's, treated the new lady of the manor as Mrs Warde in all but name.

Mr Warde's hair gradually turned grey and the lines of middle age crept deeper into his face. He grew a full beard, a great bees' nest of a beard, which tickled Sutton and Charles Aprilius when they tried to kiss him goodnight.

Stratford, however, saw less and less of Mr Warde, for in the winter months he would take mistress and child abroad, to Paris or Geneva or Florence, and in the spring they sometimes did not return home at all, but stayed on for longer and longer periods, lingering in the sun, and keeping away from lawsuit after lawsuit, and trying to forget the past.

When Mr Warde was at home Clopton House was often quite empty. The old streams of visitors had quite dried up and whole wings of the house were disused and locked up, with dust-sheets over the furniture. Often there was no sound but the diligent clipping of thirty gardeners in the distance, the click of billiard-balls as Mr Warde played billiards against himself, and the chiming of all the clocks, all out of time with each other.

Callers were rare, but one spring afternoon Thomas Williams appeared at the door in search of Anna Hooper's address.

With tears in his eyes he told Mr Warde, 'Miss Hooper has left me again.'

Mr Warde said, 'She was the only woman I ever loved, and I love her still,' and he begged Williams to find her and persuade her to come back to him.

'You can hardly expect her to return here as long as you are keeping Miss Sutton in the house,' said Williams, but he went off to deliver the message all the same, still obeying orders.

In due course Miss Hooper sent her reply, which said she would be quite willing to return to Clopton, in spite of all she had suffered, for she still loved Mr Warde. Her only condition was that he should turn off the woman that was living with him.

But Mr Warde wrote back to say that he loved Miss Sutton too, and though he saw no reason why the two mistresses should not peacefully co-exist under the same roof, keeping to their separate apartments, he could not turn Sutton away, for she was the mother of his delightful little son.

And so the attempt at a reconciliation came to nothing.

One afternoon in the summer Thomas Williams came back, driving his own carriage and pair up the Coach Road rather faster than gentility allowed, with Anna Hooper inside. Williams was very smartly turned out, in top hat and frock-coat, as if he had learned a lesson or two from Mr Warde's valet over the years. Miss Hooper was arrayed in yards and yards of brand new scarlet silk supported on a vast steel frame, that took some minutes to extricate from the carriage. She emerged glowing, radiant, smiling, smiling her old seductive smile, looking forward to see Mr Warde again in spite of the past.

Mr Warde came to the door expecting to see some wealthy neighbour, some Justice of the Peace, some Director of Railway Companies, someone come to rebuild broken bridges or invite him to play his part as pillar of the community again.

When he saw Anna Hooper he snapped, 'What the devil do you want here?'

Anna Hooper's smile vanished at once. 'I have come to see my children,' she said, and she could not stop herself from adding, 'supposing you have not sold them for dog's-meat or sent them to work in the mines.'

'Well, you've come on a wild-goose chase,' growled Mr Warde, 'for they're not here. They are not at home. They're away at school.'

Anna Hooper's daughters waved at her from an attic window, vainly trying to attract her attention.

'And what the devil are you doing here, Williams?' demanded Mr Warde, and without warning his fists flew up and he struck Williams a very severe blow on the chest. There was a hollow sound and Williams was felled to the ground before he could answer the question.

'If that is not enough I will lay my stick across your back as well,' said Mr Warde, 'now get off my land.' And he strode inside the house and slammed the door so hard that all the glass panels fell out and shattered on the marble floor of the entrance hall.

Miss Hooper did not manage to see her daughters at all, though they were still signalling from their window. Instead she had to drag the dead weight of Thomas Williams' body into the carriage single-handed and see him home without delay.

She climbed on to the box with her scarlet dress spread all around her and drove the horses herself as Smith had taught her, whipping them into a gallop and careering too fast down the Coach Road, apparently out of control, still unable to turn the horses round a corner, and disappeared in a cloud of dust.

Thomas Williams coughed and groaned in the carriage with his eyes closed, clutching his chest, his face deathly pale. The Doctor prescribed opium and embrocation and said that Williams' health would be permanently damaged.

In the case of Williams *v.* Warde which was brought in due course in the Court of Common Pleas, Thomas Williams was described as a landed proprietor resident in the County of Gloucester, and appeared handsomely dressed in black clothes and a Eureka Shirt, with his hair slicked down, but he looked older, tired and worn out, with the lines beginning to appear on his face.

Mr Warde pleaded Not Guilty to the charge of assault and said that Williams was trespassing on his property.

'I was not trespassing,' said Williams, 'I was accompanying Miss Hooper on a visit to see her children. The violence used by Mr Warde was in any case far in excess of what was necessary to remove me from his premises.'

A Dr Blank, who examined Thomas Williams at Guildhall, said that his nervous system had undoubtedly suffered a shock, but the stethoscope showed no signs.

The jury found their verdict for Thomas Williams and awarded him forty shillings damages.

Williams continued to take the opium but in spite of the fine clothes bought with the proceeds of Anna Hooper's damages, and the carriage and the modest country estate, he spent more money than was wise, and ended up turning to drink and larger and larger doses of opium. Nothing matched up to the powerful experiences of his youth and he descended the slippery slope, unable to wipe out his past and unable to get back into it. He faded like a spirit, began to hear voices and lost his reason. Eros grew old. Cupid lost his psyche.

Mr Warde went abroad again, with Caroline Sutton travelling everywhere as Mrs Warde. Anna Hooper's daughters, having reached the age where good or bad government might seriously affect their future welfare, were packed off to the most expensive ladies' boarding-school Mr Warde could find, where they could not remind him of their mother, and where their raven locks and perfect skin could haunt him no longer.

When he returned home Mr Warde found that Stratford-upon-Avon had spawned a new monster in the form of the Grand Pavilion, an eyesore made out of 20,000 cubic feet of timber, twelve tons of wrought iron and four tons of nails, which protruded above the trees in the form of a duodecagon some 74 feet high and 152 feet in diameter, and spoiled the view from Clopton House.

It had slipped Mr Warde's mind that the year 1864 was the Tercentenary of Shakespeare's Birth and that the occasion would be the excuse for unrestrained rejoicing in the town. Mr Warde complained but he complained too late and in vain, for the arrangements were all made, and the Grand Pavilion, with a stage and an orchestra-pit with room for 500 musicians, and an auditorium lit by a giant gaselier with a thousand and one lights, was ready for use.

By 23 April Shakespeare's image was in every shop window and his name, or the name of Hamlet, or Romeo, or Juliet, or Mistress Quickly, was on every hotel and boarding-house, and there was no escape from the Immortal Bard without leaving Stratford altogether.

Mr Warde wanted to know why no one had consulted him about the Festival, and he complained about the Grand Pavilion again, but in spite of Mr Warde quickly presenting a very generous sum of money to the Festival Fund, no one took any notice of him at all.

On the Anniversary itself the Earl of Carlisle, the Archbishop of Dublin and the Lord-Lieutenant of Warwickshire arrived in state at Stratford Town Hall drawn in an elegant landau by four handsome grey horses and attended by postilions in elegant livery, and were received by the Mayor and Corporation and a cheering crowd.

The bells of the parish church pealed without stopping all day long and Mr Warde complained about that too, and was completely ignored, and the Shakespeare Tercentenary Festival began.

That evening 750 eaters overate themselves at a very grand Shakespearean Banquet in the Grand Pavilion, and were watched from galleries by 300 spectators who could afford only to watch.

Everybody who was anybody was present: all the Justices of the Peace, all the Aldermen and Councillors, all the clergy and all the solicitors and bankers in Warwickshire, all tucking into turkey, roast fowls, capons, ducks, boar's head, York hams, tongues, roast beef ('What say you to a piece of roast beef?' – *Taming of the Shrew*), potted meats, aspics of eels, soles, salmon, dinner rolls and dressed potatoes ('Let the sky rain potatoes' – *Merry Wives of Windsor*), jellies, creams, meringues, beehives and fruit, all washed down with gallons of bitter ale and champagne and hock and port and sherry.

There were speeches and toasts to the Queen (Cheers), and toasts to the Prince and Princess of Wales (Applause), and to The Memory of Shakespeare (Great cheering, then repeated rounds of cheering), and the choir sang Arne's 'Thou Soft Flowing Avon' and 'Ye Warwickshire Lads and Ye Lasses', all of which was heard, rising and falling, by a gentleman who stood outside the Grand Pavilion in the drizzle, who had been unable to lay his hands upon a ticket at any price, either as an eater or as a spectator, but had been refused entry under any circumstances, and had that day been moved to curse the name of Shakespeare and all his works.

Mr Warde stood in the darkness by the river, listening to the champing of the 750 jaws, the muffled laughter and the muted applause, all of which floated to him through the wooden walls.

Later Mr Darby the Pyrotechnist sent up his first Shakespearean rocket as the grand wind-up to the First Day, and the sky echoed with explosions for more than an hour. Two illuminated fire balloons rose over the heads of the 5,000 spectators but the *pièce de résistance*, an illuminated portrait of the Bard himself, intended to be the Grand Climax, was sadly obscured by the density of the smoke. But compared with the display overhead put on by nature herself Mr Darby's handiwork was poor indeed, for, as an observer wrote afterwards, 'Cynthia had risen in her full majesty; the chaste stars were revealed in the dark blue canopy; the nightingale charmed the listener's ear, whilst the soft Avon flowed on, paying its tribute to the Severn and the sea.'

Long after the crowds had gone home Mr Warde remained standing by the river, looking into the water.

On the following Sunday the parish church was thronged to inconvenience by hundreds of Stratfordians in their Sunday best who were anxious not to miss a three-hour sermon in honour of Shakespeare preached by the Archbishop of Dublin.

Mr and Mrs Joseph Callaway and their daughters, arriving late, found every seat taken and to their alarm were put into the Clopton Pew, which was the inviolable preserve of the Squire of Clopton and his family. The Callaways were as reluctant to sit there as Mr Warde, but reflected that he would hardly show his face on such a grand occasion.

But they were wrong, for no sooner had the Callaways sat down than Mr Warde himself loomed up, spotless and shining, with the scullery-maid radiant and unrecognizable on his arm, sleek, meek, reeking of Olympian Dew, with her rough hands hidden away in the finest gloves Paris could supply; with Anna Hooper's three newly refined daughters straight from school and oozing gentility, all dressed alike in milk-white silk, and Charles Aprilius, in whose mouth butter would never melt, an angel in a sailor suit.

Every Stratfordian head craned to look and every Stratfordian mouth opened to whisper, for Stratford had never known such scandal.

The Callaways, ousted by Mr Warde's icy smile, crept out of the Clopton Pew, and found what had earlier that day been their Sunday best curiously outshone by the Warde family's perfect attire.

The Callaways fought their way into a side aisle, but found their exit blocked by extra chairs and outsize bonnets, so that they were forced to make their way out against the processional tide of choir, clergy, bishop and archbishop as the service began, and so that by the time they reached the church door not an eyebrow was unraised and the Callaways' humiliation was complete.

On subsequent days the crowds flocked to performances of *As You Like It, Romeo and Juliet* and Handel's rather un-Shakespearean *Messiah*. There were convivial boat trips down the Avon. There were shows in the Market Place from Punch and Judy to the dancing elephants from Wombwell's Menagerie. There was morris dancing, maypole dancing and Scottish country dancing, and the tall distinguished gentleman in the top hat, and his handsome wife dressed in the very height of fashion seemed to be everywhere, and everywhere they went people asked, 'What are they doing here?' and everyone ignored them.

At the end of a week of Shakespearean festivities 400 dancers in costumes of all the colours of the rainbow thronged to the Grand Fancy Ball, representing (amongst others): Lady Capulet, Ophelia, Shylock, Herne the Hunter, Charles I, Britannia, Agamemnon, The Fat Woman of Brainford, Ceres, Desdemona, Cleopatra, Touchstone, Garibaldi, A Spanish Matador, A Turkish Pasha, A Scotch Girl, A Water Nymph, Banquo's Ghost, and several William Shakespeares, all jumbled up in splendid and riotous confusion, as if someone had knocked the lid off a box marked History and they had all rushed out, to the tune of Messrs Coote and Tinney's Quadrille Band.

And they danced and waltzed and galloped and quadrilled and jigged up and down without stopping from ten o'clock in the evening until five o'clock the next morning, when the Shakespearean Festival proper came to an end, and the whole cast of historical, mythological, Shakespearean and miscellaneous characters surged out of the Grand Pavilion on to the grass and walked along the banks of the Avon in the rising mist. They appeared not to have the use of their legs, but floated forward like ghosts, laughing and calling, as if all Shakespeare's characters had materialized for this rendezvous in his honour, a sight which almost startled Stratford's workmen, going early to work, out of their wits.

At the rear of the party trailed a smiling figure dressed as Hercules, who wore what appeared to be a handsome lion-skin hearthrug, and carried an enormous cudgel, and who had danced with as much indefatigable vigour as anyone all night. He was masked, like many of the dancers, but presented a powerful figure, upwards of six feet tall, with greying hair and a grizzled beard. On his arm was a slighter figure, on whose handsome costume no expense had been spared, and who wore a fortune round her neck in diamonds. She too was masked, but both Hercules and his lady, whom most people assumed to be Deianeira in spite of the fact that her dress was more Elizabethan than anything else, were unidentified by the other dancers, who pretended not to know who they were, but noted none the less and with some curiosity, the elegance of the lady's carriage, and the delight and abandon she displayed in every dance, as if she had never danced before, but displaying all the accomplishments that a dancing-master could instil into a willing pupil.

The scullery-maid danced recklessly, as if the future mattered not at all, but only the present; as if tomorrow could bring disaster; as if it did not matter if she never danced again.

Sutton and Mr Warde might have been ghosts as far as Stratford was concerned, for Stratford treated them as if they did not exist; as if they were invisible, furiously ignoring them for all they were worth.

*

Dancing the night away took its toll, however, and although Mr Warde kept up his charitable donations, paying at Christmas 1864 for 1,000 pounds of beef to be distributed to 300 needy families, the Fancy Ball was the last Stratford saw of him, for by the end of the year Mr Warde's bedside was attended not only by the woman who had come to be known to many as The Whore of Clopton, but also by Nurse Hoare, plain Harriet Hoare the carter's daughter, who came in by day, and later by night as well, from Clopton Lodge, in order to bathe the Squire's roasting forehead and to help Sutton to change his sweat-drenched sheets.

For Mr Warde, who had hardly known a day's illness in his life, was being eaten away by disease. The vultures began to circle round the handsome and substantial bed: the solicitor, the trusted servant and the faithful retainer began to help themselves to anything portable that came in the way of their fingers. At first it was the odd cigar, then a box of cigars; at first a gold watch, then a handsome gilt bracket-clock; at first things that could be easily concealed beneath an overcoat, things not easily missed, but then the objects gradually increased in size, and tables that had once been crowded with objects of vertu and memorabilia of Pompeii or Herculaneum began to look bare, and then the table itself would be gone.

Mr Warde was not in a position to notice such goings-on. Sutton was not in a position to care, for her whole time was taken up with carrying bowls of hot water upstairs and bowls of blood downstairs.

The servants took what they could while they could, not knowing what would happen once he was dead; knowing only that there would be no one to pay their wages.

The last of the witnesses signed their names to the seventh codicil to Mr Warde's inordinately long and inordinately complex Will. The servants that hung on expectantly began to count the Doctor's visits, and when the Doctor gave Mr Warde three weeks to live they began to count the days.

But just as Mr Warde had been a long time being born, he lingered on week after week, reluctant to die, and had enough time and enough presence of mind to make an eighth codicil to his Will, cutting his old mistress out, putting the new mistress in, paying off old debts and old scores.

On 5 May 1865 the silver-haired Vicar of Snitterfield, the Reverend Donald Cameron, who had once borne witness to the shining character of his wealthiest parishioner, called unannounced at Clopton, dressed in his cassock, with Prayer Book in hand, and asked to see the patient, thinking he might extract a deathbed confession and a handsome legacy for his Church Restoration Fund. But Mr Cameron waited in vain, and coughed and cleared his throat and said his prayers by the bedside to no effect, for Mr Warde did not give vent to any remorse or any repentance, but lay with his eyes closed pretending to be asleep, and did not acknowledge the Vicar's existence any more than he acknowledged the existence of the Vicar's employer.

Mr Warde had already entered a different world, a world of his own, with his past floating before his eyes, in which heaven and hell played no part.

He saw a series of pictures, magic moments in the bosom of his family; dancing with his children, carrying them upon his back, pulling them along in their carriage, as much a child as any of them.

> *Ye Warwickshire lads and ye lasses*
> *See what at our Jubilee passes;*
> *Come revel away, rejoice and be glad,*
> *For the lad of all lads was a Warwickshire lad . . .*

He saw the family gather round his bed: the tearful wife and dutiful children. He saw all the Justices of the Peace for Warwickshire grinning down at him, rubbing their hands and shaking their heads.

> *Be proud of the charms of your County*
> *Where nature has lavish'd her bounty . . .*

The discarded mistress gloated over her lover's misfortunes, displaying a hundred cuts and bruises, her face running with tears and gravy and custard, her hands clutching her broken diamonds. The pouting footman with the rolling eyes was at her side, aping the gentry on Mr Warde's money, come to have the last laugh, smiling away.

> *Each shire has its different pleasures*
> *Each shire has its different treasures;*

> *But to rare Warwickshire all must submit,*
> *For the wit of all wits was a Warwickshire wit . . .*

Caroline Sutton in her black silk dress, mourning already that her rise to glory had been so short-lived, stood with the women of Stratford, priestesses of the sacred grove, who piled through the bedroom door for a last look at the fallen hero in his nightshirt. Each one in her Sunday clothes, each one with illegitimate babe in arms, each come to claim one last sovereign, and to scrabble on the floor for it as Mr Warde flung out his last armful of gold from the bed.

They came and went before his eyes. To gawp and wonder. To accuse him of squandering and wasting the countless thousands of pounds he had inherited and which he could have given to them.

> *There never was seen such a creature*
> *Of all he was worth he robb'd nature;*
> *He took all her smiles and he took all her grief,*
> *For the thief of all thiefs was a Warwickshire thief . . .*

And as life passed away from him, far from Mrs Warde's accusations, far from all thought of Anna Hooper, Mr Warde was far out and way back in the sea of his past, striking out for the horizon, his mind back in his youth in the green Warwickshire lanes, in the back of his father's trap, with all the green world slipping away from him as it did now, with everything – trees, houses, fields, people – getting smaller and smaller.

Everything flowed past him faster and faster: the children at his knee, Meller with her hot water, the business of the Eureka Shirt, the charred ruin that was Luton Hoo, the children's pale faces peering out of the carriage window, taken away from him for ever; the table in the dining-room groaning with food at Christmas and no one to eat it, and his smashing everything on to the floor.

Mr Warde was perfectly lucid, sitting up in bed asking for his mother. His mother who would never come when he wanted her to, but always sent a servant smelling of kitchen soap and starch and flour, more comfortable, more consoling in fact than his mother, who kept herself as dry as dust and as distant as she could, at arm's length, as if she wished she had never had him in the first place.

211

He saw all green Warwickshire spread out before him: his own acres spread out for his final inspection, and on the footpaths, strung out, picking up sticks, pausing in their labours to look up, he saw again all his handsome young women: Harriet Cox, Ann Davis, Mary Jane Moore, Mary Cooper, Isabella Grimes, Elizabeth Southam, Ann Thorns, Thorns of the beautiful skin, all of them waving.

A carriage procession snailed through Clopton Park, his own funeral. A giant hearse with nodding horses and black plumes and hired mutes in black crêpe and weepers. He saw the cortège wind onwards, pelted with filth by the women, and he saw the coffin overturned. He heard once again the shouted abuse, the screams and insults, the women's squeals just like the Shrewsbury boys hunting their boar so many years back, only now he, Charles Thomas Warde had become their quarry, tomorrow's bacon. How they would have liked to have had his flesh all these years!

But he was suddenly very tired of fleeing his assailants, tired of holding on, tired of watching. The world caught him up in the end. The screaming women tucked up their skirts to run all the faster, out for his final destruction. He gave himself up to them, the maidens and the sacred wood, and thinking of Hercules he gathered them up, and made for the plantation of his dreams, and let the world slip.

TEN

Nettles grew where ornamental flower beds had been. Cow parsley stood six feet tall on every lawn. Brambles grew across gravel paths that were once swept daily by an army of gardeners. For the army of outdoor servants had long since retreated. Clopton's windows were mostly shuttered. The park gates were padlocked and had been for months, for there were no visitors. The whole place had an air of neglect and decay, as it had before Mr Warde moved in. There was no sound but the buzzing of flies and the cawing of the crows in the trees.

Sutton sat behind closed doors, unable to eat even if there had been food. At night her anguished screams echoed through the house and she wandered through rooms full of priceless gilded furniture covered with ghostly white sheets. Mr Warde's portrait, newly restored, winked and leered at her on the staircase. His image grinned at her from every gilded pier-glass. She heard the click of billiard-balls though she knew there was no one there to play. She heard the faint tread of ghostly footprints and saw shadowy presences disappear down dark corridors. Finally she returned exhausted to her chair, afraid to consider tomorrow, and clung to yesterday. She sat on with her memories, unable to shift the giant body, not knowing what to do with it, not having been touched by Death before.

She sat waiting, hoping that Nurse Hoare's message would get through to Mr Warde's solicitors, to Captain Walhouse, to Mrs Warde and her family. Sutton sat doing nothing, looking at her once callused hands, listening to the ticking of the clocks.

Five-year-old Charles Aprilius, quite forgotten, played with his Noah's Ark, lead soldiers and whip and top in a nursery still hung round with portraits of pale children he had never known, whose shades alone prevented him from falling out of the window or wrapping ropes round his neck, and dying before his time.

Charles Aprilius was quite alone. When hunger came he went in search of food. He could not find his mother. In his

215

father's bedroom he tugged at a white sheet covering something that was not his father for it would not talk, or laugh, or give him a ride on its shoulders.

Charles Aprilius found the kitchens deserted and the larder locked up, abandoned long since by the skeleton staff, who had not waited to be paid but made their way down the long road to Stratford to the bright lights, to normal life, to the land of the living.

Sutton waited, knowing that eventually someone would come and read her the Will and tell her whether she was to stay or whether she was to go. She took off the silk dress that did not belong to her in order to spare herself the indignity of being told by the executors to remove it, and hung it up out of habit in the giant wardrobe with row upon row of Mrs Warde's and Miss Hooper's clothes, and with some of her own: a bright history of Mr Warde's private life hanging there in the dark.

Sutton put on her old servant's dress and looked and remembered until she could bear it no longer. Then, without thinking what she was doing, she pulled armful after armful of dresses off the rails and threw them out of the window, where the wind took them up and floated them out over the lawns: reds and greens, blues and blacks, whites and yellows, the plain and the patterned, the striped and the spotted. And Sutton let her tears flow.

The women who came to Clopton to pick up sticks and dream of Mr Warde noticed the splashes of colour on the lawns in the distance and came closer to look. They found not only the hundreds of dresses but also a small boy in a sailor suit, his face purple with blackcurrants and strawberries and tears, playing happily with an archery bow that was bigger than he was.

And thus it was that visitors to Stratford in the 1870s and 1880s were often heard to exclaim how very well-dressed the ordinary working women were, and to comment favourably upon the vivid colours of their dresses.

Sutton and Charles Aprilius were at last led away before the curious gaze of farm labourers in their shirt-sleeves, making hay while the sun shone, and who paused in a long row, scythes in hand, and touched their hats to the temporary lady of the manor with a shade more deference than usual.

Sutton carried no luggage, had brought nothing with her to

Clopton and carried nothing away, except a faded daguerreo-type of the young Charles Warde in a gold frame with a red velvet inlay. She was weighed down only by experience. She was twenty-three years of age, a broken woman, a fallen woman, with all the vast desert of her life before her: an eternity of mourning. Her lady days were over.

As she walked to the solicitor's carriage, clutching Charles Aprilius by the hand, she raged inwardly: not at the £800 which would cushion her fall; not at the £2,000 which Charles Aprilius would inherit if he was fortunate enough to survive to the age of twenty-five; not at the thought of Charles Aprilius in his handsome and substantial residence, Number Six, Curzon Street, Mayfair, refusing to have anything to do with his aged and destitute mother. Sutton raged at the thought that Mr Warde could even dream of leaving her the two cottages in Clopton Terrace for life. That he could have imagined her sitting there for the rest of her days in the shadow of Clopton, on his doorstep, to be gossiped about, and whispered about, and pointed out wherever she went as the Clopton Whore, and spat upon in the market and snubbed and shunned by the whole population of Stratford-upon-Avon.

There were still people down in Stratford who would have been delighted to bring out their rotten vegetables and bad eggs one last time in order to pelt Mr Warde's coffin as it passed through the town, but they were not given the opportunity, for the Vicar of Stratford flatly refused to have Mr Warde buried anywhere near the bones of Shakespeare or to have Stratford's black sheep inside his church again.

And so it was that the hearse was trundled slowly up the steep lanes that were overgrown with giant cow parsley to Snitterfield, where the Reverend Donald Cameron read the burial-service too fast, still smarting over his lost legacy and the fact that the deceased sinner had gone unrepentant to his grave.

There were no mourners except Mr Warde's solicitor, who planned to add a fee for his attendance to his outstanding bill. And a slight woman in a plain black dress, who looked over the churchyard wall from a distance, and only approached the grave with her flowers when everyone else had gone, and remained there weeping for some time, while the child that was with her wandered about hitting at the dusty nettles with a stout stick.

It was 13 May 1865.

After a decent interval a plain tablet was erected on the north wall inside Snitterfield Church *In memory of Charles Thomas Warde*. Rumour said that Mrs Warde had paid for it.

Stratford raised its eyebrows upon learning that its monster had left only the sum of £80,000, and it raised its eyebrows again upon hearing that £20,000 of it had been left to Miss Hooper's three eldest daughters. Rumour said that Miss Hooper lost no time getting her hands on the money herself.

In due course Clopton House was let and no Squire Warde ever set foot in it again, for there were, in a few years' time, no male Wardes left, for Mr Warde's much-vaunted dynasty fizzled out like a damp firework and came to nothing at all.

In 1859, at the age of twelve, Henry Charles Lloyd Warde had been sent to school at Eton, where his contemporaries enjoyed reading of his father's exploits in all the newspapers.

Shortly after his father's death Henry Warde went up to Cambridge, where it was rumoured that herculean quantities of champagne were consumed, and he led the wild life that was expected of his father's son.

Henry Warde passed the Civil Service examination, was employed for some months in the Foreign Office in London, and in 1868 was appointed to an Attachéship.

In February 1869 he was posted to the British Legation at Copenhagen, where he purchased a scarlet parrot and began to teach it to swear in Danish.

In April 1869 he was transferred, after a minor incident with a female domestic servant, to St Petersburg, as 3rd Secretary to Her Britannic Majesty's Embassy.

The scarlet parrot went with him and he began to teach it to swear in Russian.

In August 1870 a cholera epidemic broke out in St Petersburg, for which the Persian merchants at the Nijni Novgorod Fair received the blame.

Henry Warde took elaborate precautions, made liberal use of Burnett's Disinfecting Fluid as recommended (and supplied, in large crates) by his mother, and began to drink whisky instead of water. And lest the parrot contracted cholera he gave the parrot whisky too.

For fifteen minutes while shaving each morning Henry Warde would patiently swear at the parrot, as his father had taught him. But the scarlet bird kept up a stubborn silence.

For fifteen minutes while dressing for dinner each evening Henry Warde would swear tirelessly at the parrot, saying 'Repeat after me . . .'

But the parrot kept quiet. In fact it had never once uttered a single word in any language in its owner's hearing.

Henry Warde was not discouraged. He put his face to the parrot's gilded cage one morning in January 1871 and swore religiously at the bird over and over again for several hours. But the bird had nothing to say to Henry Warde. It just fixed him with a bead-like eye, fluffed out its magnificent scarlet feathers and bit him on the lower lip.

Henry Warde swore again and his lip poured blood until his pocket handkerchief was the same colour as the parrot and he was obliged to summon the assistance of a Russian doctor who lived nearby. But the doctor spoke so fast that Henry Warde could not understand what the doctor required him to do. Then the bleeding stopped and Henry Warde did nothing for several days, thinking that the wound was not so serious after all and that it would clear up in its own good time, and he almost forgot about it.

But by the end of January he was languishing in bed with a high temperature and every assistance the St Petersburg doctors could offer, and every comfort that his brimming bank balance could buy.

But it was too late. Early in February Mrs Warde received a black-edged letter informing her that unfortunately her son had died of a malignant abscess, that the funeral had already taken place, and that Her Majesty's Ambassador at St Petersburg sent his deepest sympathy.

Henry Warde was twenty-four years of age.

Among the effects sent back to England to the distraught Mrs Warde was the scarlet parrot in its gilded cage, which no one at the Embassy had quite liked to sell or dispose of without her permission.

When the parrot arrived in her sitting-room at Rothamsted Mrs Warde said, 'What on earth do I want with that?'

But five minutes later the bird swore at Mrs Warde in her husband's voice. Her tears dried up on the spot and she spun round with a gasp, thinking that Charles was in the room.

'But how silly,' she said, 'how could he be?'

Mrs Warde sat on quietly at Rothamsted for another twenty years, wearing the same black dress. Sometimes Sir John Bennet Lawes, who had sold his business for the manufacture of mineral superphosphates for manure for the sum of £300,000 and been created a baronet by Queen Victoria, kept her company. Sometimes her married daughters kept her company and smoked the occasional cigar, but more often than not Mrs Warde was alone, with only the aged Meller – now bearded, blind and bent almost double – for a companion.

Often there was no sound in the house at all except the chiming of the clocks and the sound of the scarlet parrot swearing in Mr Warde's voice, and on very hot days it would swear without a break for six or seven hours.